INTRODUCTION AND DEDICATION

Dear readers of the *"Chronicles of Belleadaire,"* I hope you enjoy this first volume. It really explains how Belleadaire was created and how the characters you will come to love in the future volumes evolved. *"Seeding the Stars"* will lead you through the last years of earth and the amazing discoveries that were made to allow the human race to be sent forth to the stars to begin anew.

It is truly amazing what people can do when they are challenged with extinction and given an unlimited budget. It also shows what people can do when they come together for a common goal. Nothing is impossible when we all pull together. The human spirit is like no other we know of. Likewise, it is human nature to be doubtful and somewhat skeptical of what can really be accomplished when we put our minds to work and push them to the brink. The element of risk is ever present when we are under pressure and sometimes the bigger the risk the larger the rewards.

You will understand the risks and rewards as you begin reading this book. Sometimes the rewards do really outweigh the risks.

I have been challenged in this volume to lead you to a place, a planet were the human race can start anew. Even though we will only be looking at what happened and evolved from just one Ark of Life, you will find out that there were supposed to be twelve of them launched. Other arks did reach their destinations and maybe in the future we may have to look in on them to see how they survived and if they flourished on their new home worlds.

This planet will yield discoveries that have yet to be explored. Maybe the new monarchs of Belleadaire will someday explore the rest of their home world and share their experiences with us as well. Who knows?

In the meantime take the opportunity to sit in your easy chair and start reading how it all came to pass.

My passion for writing and the love of my life continues to encourage me to share my tales with all of you. Without my Queen Marjorie I would be just another storyteller and probably not write at all.

I still have my very good friend and technical companion David that helps me with some details when I go too far astray from the believable. Sometimes I have to convince him that what I write could be believable but more often than not he keeps me on the straight and narrow.

Remember there are three more volumes to that tell the total story of Belleadaire. This is just the first installment. Be sure to look on line or at your favorite bookstore for:

"Earthtime Chronicles of Belleadaire-Volume 2 - The New King"

"Earthtime Chronicles of Belleadaire –Volume 3 - The New Discovery"

"Earthtime Chronicles of Belleadaire –Volume 4- The Heirs"

Thank you all again for supporting my efforts to rid my brain of this book worm twisting and winding its way through my noggin until it spilled out on the pages of these books.

I hope we all meet again in another wonderful adventure.

Sincerely,

G. W. Born

TABLE OF CONTENTS

INTRODUCTION AND DEDICATION 0

TABLE 0F CONTENTS 4

PROLOGUE 7

Chapter 1 – Designing the Arks of Life...............13

Chapter 2 - Preliminary Designs 20

Chapter 3 – The Concepts 28

Chapter 4 – Review of the Plan with the World Governing Council...58

Chapter 5 – Anti-Gravity.....................................67

Chapter 6 - Interstellar Light Slipstream Drive 91

Chapter 7 - Third Year of the Arks of Life Design 119

Chapter 8 - Dr. Harold Boranum 136

Chapter 9 - Building the Arc Ships 143

Chapter 10 - 2132 The Year Crew Training Started 150

Chapter 11 - 2135 Launch of ARK SHIP #1......168

Chapter 12 - Ark Ship Destinations 183

Chapter 13 - Planet 1 of the Fennel Galaxy 192

Chapter 14 - Discovery Mission One.................201

Chapter 15 - The Meteor...................................213

Chapter 16 - THE Bengarie (First Race - Second Nation)..228

Chapter 17 – Transport of the Ark Crew 231

Chapter 18 - Dr. David M. Martin and the Woggles 259

Chapter 19 - The ARK of Civilization.................277

Chapter 20 - The Lady of the Green 284

Chapter 21 - The Lady of the Green Meets Mergrom the Magnificent....................................310

Chapter 22 - Training the Lady of the Green.....328

Chapter 23 - Mergrom Becomes Mergrom the Great 339

Chapter 24 - Uglias the First 343

Chapter 25 - Mergrom Growing Older and Wiser 347

Chapter 26 - Educating young Prince Gerald....352

Chapter 27 - Prince Gerald's Forest Training....363

Chapter 28 - Learning to Fly..............................380

Chapter 29 - The Cave of the Birds...................401

Chapter 30 - Woodsprites 418

Chapter 31 - Mirth the Invisible 460

Chapter 32 - The Fight with William the Woodsprite 476

Chapter 33 - The Teachings of Mergrom 482

Chapter 34 - Phillip Grimley Learns to Fly........497

Chapter 35 - Living with Mergrom 523

Chapter 36 - New Creatures and Magic Training 553

EPILOGUE 571

PROLOGUE

Year 2020 - Energy resources are dwindling and prices for oil, natural gas, and coal have reached an all-time high. Gasoline for private transportation has reached $20.00/liter. Coal seems to be the largest fuel source for power generation. The once thought one-hundred year natural-gas-reserve is now down to thirty.

Year 2030 - Greenhouse gasses are warming the earth at an alarming rate. The polar ice caps are sixty percent melted and the sea levels are rising threatening the coastlines on all continents. Coastal populations start to move inland.

Year 2040 – Carbon dioxide and carbon monoxide are now the major atmospheric polluters and the ozone layer is now depleting over the northern and southern continents.

Year 2050 – Energy rationing starts in all countries. Gasoline for private transportation is now only affordable to the very rich. Oil reserves are reassigned to the military only. Worldwide rebellion against the energy rationing ensues.

Fracking the oil shale for natural gas is accelerated in earnest throughout the world.

Year 2060 – The polar ice caps are completely melted along with all glaciers. The sea has risen seventy feet above current levels. All coastal towns, cities, seaports, and homes are under fifty feet or more of water.

Year 2070 – The ozone layer surrounding the earth is now depleted and the earth is being bombarded by hazardous amounts of solar radiation. The surface temperature of the earth has now risen to twenty degrees above current normal temperatures. Iceland and Greenland are now choice vacation spots for the rich and famous. Florida is only a very small island. Most of its population fled toward the north. Cancer is now the number one killer of humans and animals.

Year 2080 – The fracking of oil shale for natural gas has now contaminated ninety percent of the earth's water aquifers and water rationing throughout the planet has started. Fracking for natural gas is outlawed on the entire planet.

Year 2090 – World population is moving to locations where water can be boiled and

8

consumed. The four hundred trillion people now share what land is left after the oceans have consumed more and more of the continents. Food shortages and food rationing is the norm in most populated areas. Hotter temperatures and less rainfall have reduced food supplies to a minimum. Livestock herds are dwindling to the point of extinction. Zero population growth has become a reality.

Year 2100 – A world panel is convened to centralize relief and recovery efforts throughout the planet. A world president is appointed along with a cabinet of thirty made up of the world leaders from all countries.

Year 2105 – Riots break out throughout the planet over food and water shortages and rationing. Martial law is declared planet-wide to control the looting and riots. Thousands die at the hands of the military while trying to bring the starving masses under control.

Year 2115 – World leaders have decided that in order for the human race to survive other planets will have to be discovered and our human seed must be spread to them. A program is initiated to have twelve interstellar explorer ships built and outfitted with the latest tested and some untested technologies to send crews of humans to distant galaxies to start afresh. DNA samples are gathered from every race on the planet as well as every animal left on the planet. These samples are divided equally between the ships. Each ship will not only carry the technologies of our race but also the arts, sciences and craftsmanship's that our race is noted for.

Year 2125 – Utilizing all the remaining resources left on the planet three awards are granted to build the "Arks of Life." Airbus will build ships one through four. Lockheed-Bowing-Grumman will build ships five through eight. Bell Laboratories will build ships nine through twelve. An ISLSD (interstellar light slipstream drive) is discovered by Lawrence Livermore National Laboratories which will shorten the flight time to all planets. This new discovery is shared with all the ark builders.

Year 2130 – The surface temperature of the earth is now forty degrees above normal. The average daytime temperature in all climate zones hovers around one hundred twenty to one hundred thirty degrees Fahrenheit. The oceans are now starting to evaporate. The world's brightest and best scientists, geneticists, chemists, botanists, biologists, mathematicians, physicists, roboticist, sculptors, painters, carpenters, stonemason's mechanics and electricians are assigned to the explorer ships as crew. Their training begins. A global lottery is introduced and held to fill out the remainder of the crews that will staff the explorer ships. A selected few are pressed into service and start their training to run, maintain, and support the technical staff.

Year 2135 – Training of the crews is finished as well as ships one through four. Due to the new ISLSD system on each ship the planet suffers magnetic anomalies each time a ship is launched. Time is needed for the planet to heal between launches. Only one ship can be launched per year. Construction on underground bunkers are started to house millions of inhabitants from the deadly radiation on the planet's surface.

Year 2147 – Explorer ship number twelve launches with the remaining crew and professionals. The launches have caused a shift in the earth's magnetic poles and the rotation of the earth starts to wobble on its axis.

Year 2150 – Bunkers are finished and the remaining earths masses move underground to help salvage what is left of the earth's population. Food and water shortages plague the underground dwellers and humans start to die of starvation. Disease from the dying now spreads through the remaining population. Radiation sickness becomes the number one killer of humans most all animal life is extinct.

Year 2155 – Communications between underground facilities is lost along with remaining power for resources. The only hope now for the human race to survive is the explorer ships.

Chapter 1 – Designing the Arks of Life

Dr. Phillip Bradman and two hundred project members are given the task of designing and outfitting the Ark ships. Bradman has PHD's in physics, chemistry, and aeronautical engineering His work at NASA's Aeronautical Engineering Laboratory as well as his designs for the Mars Probe, Mars Lander, Saturn Probe and Lander more than qualified him to design a ship that would explorer the galaxies. The World President has handpicked him from almost two hundred potential candidates. The other thirty world advisors have filled in the rest of the project team with their best and brightest engineers and physicists. Their task was overwhelming at first especially with the time line available to engineer such a craft. These ships are not expected to return to earth. They are to spread the human race across the universe.

They were given only five years to come up with a design and build package that the world government could put out for bids. Dr. Bradman knew that this was almost an impossible task and knew that he would not be a member of any of the Ark ships. It would be unlikely that any of his project team would be part of the crew on any of the ships. The task they took on was a task of dead men and women. Their real task of the project team was the survival of the human race. Personnel were flown in from all over the planet to NASA's abandoned space center in Houston, Texas. NASA had been disbanded about forty years earlier and the center had not been used since. The center was opened and a cleaning crew hired and within three days it was ready to accept the two hundred plus project team members. They had all been informed that they would be living and working in the same location. The military provided security. A completely stocked five star restaurant was situated on the ground floor. Living quarters were located on floors two through five and floors six through twenty-five housed laboratories, CAD stations, support facilities, and offices, meeting rooms and conference rooms. On the ground floor sharing the space with the luxurious dining facility and wine bar was an assembly hall that could easily accommodate three hundred plus people.

So it was on July 10, 2115 that Dr. Phillip Bradman walked to the podium in front of the assembled team in the hall. He stared out over the multi-colored, multi-national team of professionals. He approached the microphone and said, "Ladies and gentlemen welcome to project Ark. "My name is Dr. Phillip Bradman and I will be your project leader throughout your stay here. For the next five years you will design an interstellar ship that will save the human race by spreading our genes throughout the universe. We must assure that the ship we design will last many life times and travel to planets that are just numbers on a map of the universe at this point in time. Our goal is to have the design of the Ark Explorer ships ready for bidding in less than five years. Ten years from now the first ship will leave this planet and go in search of a new home where humans can once again populate a habitable planet and try not to repeat what our race did to this world. Some of you may be picked as crewmembers for the Arks of Life. Most of us will not. Our main objective is to see that those aboard our newly designed ship will stay alive and will have the resources available at their final destination to begin life anew. I am going to divide you into three main groups. Each main group will be then sub-divided into three sub groups. I have chosen the three project leaders and have assigned you to the three main groups based on each of your background and experience. The three main group leaders will assign their own sub project leaders. The three main groups are:

Ship Design and Propulsion systems

Life support and habitat

Resource allocation and storage for genetics, agriculture, terraforming and robotics

Your assignments are being posted on the bulletin boards outside this auditorium as we speak. The workdays will be long. Our accommodations will be sparse but functional. Our main goal is to save what is left of the human race and give it one more chance to survive. Conceptual designs are due on my desk for review one week from today. I suggest that you all find your assignments and report to your designated locations. We will meet here in this room once every two weeks for a project update. Your presence for the updates is mandatory, no exceptions. All of us are in this together to the end. We will succeed and the human race will survive. The new human race will be stronger, smarter and hopefully have a strong sense of stewardship to their new homes and environment. We will give them the tools to meet any challenge that confronts them. Now I would like to introduce you to the three main project leaders of the Arks of Life.

Head of ship design and propulsion systems will be Dr. Fredrick Von Huffman. Dr. Huffman is best noted for his designs of explorer ships to Uranus, Mercury and the five moons of Jupiter.

Head of life support and habitat is Dr. Leslie Cunningham. You all know her from her design of the Mars Life Pod and her design of the Neptune Habitat that is still functional and in full operation after ten years of habitation.

Head of Resource allocation and storage for genetics, agriculture, and terraforming is Dr. Harold Boranum. His breakthrough in gene manipulations in human and animal species and his hybridization of plants and living tissue well suits him to lead this part of the Arks of Life project.

You all have your assignments and you all know the project goal. Let's not waste another minute talking about it. Let us all start saving mankind."

Chapter 2 - Preliminary Designs

All of the scientists and technician started filing out of the auditorium and gathered around the bulletin boards to see what their assignments were and who they would be reporting to. As people found their names they started dispersing to their respective assigned areas and reporting to their new leaders. In less than an hour everyone had found who and where they were to work. Office, lab, and technical support were set up for each of the three groups. As expected each group was then subdivided into individual work groups and each were given specific assignments for conceptual designs.

Group 1 - Ship design and propulsion systems

Dr. Fredrick Von Huffman wasted no time in making his assignments and splitting his group of fifty engineers and designers into three groups. Group A would design and specify the outside or hull of the ship. Group B would design and specify the propulsion system. Group C would design and specify all the support equipment and backup systems that would sustain the ship for its long and unknown journey through the vacuum of space. These three groups had to interface with the other main groups in order to build a ship sufficiently large enough to house everything needed for a journey that could take two or three generations or even longer. Their task was daunting indeed and all the engineers and technicians worked as a cohesive team to be able to put a conceptual design in Dr. Hoffman's hand in seven days. Not only did they offer one concept, they offered three. Ultimately only one design would survive, but since they had no budget constraints and the entire human race was at risk, their creative juices flowed in abundance.

The ship design and propulsion system area took up the least amount of the space in the building. Floors six through ten were designated as ship and propulsion design and engineering spaces.

Group 2 - Life Support and Habitat

Dr. Leslie Cunningham organized her group a little differently than most project leaders. She let her team members pick the category they wanted to go into but held the last decision of personnel placement if she thought that she had too many people in one category. Her people could choose from one of three categories, Cryogenics, Creature Comforts and Habitats and finally Exercise/Nutrition. Each of these fields was assigned a leader by Dr. Cunningham and they were assigned the tasks of conceptual designs by weekend. Floors eleven through seventeen were designated life support and habitat.

Group 3 - Resource Allocation, Genetic and Agricultural storage, terraforming and robotics

Dr. Harold Boranum was known as a micro manager. He would plan things down to the finest detail. He was always looking over the shoulders of his team members no matter what project he was working on. This project was no exception. He had already dissected the backgrounds and experience of his entire team of ninety-one people. Each of them was being assigned to the fields that he thought to be their strengths. His appointed project leaders were men and women he had worked with before and knew he could manipulate them if he needed to. Because he had the responsibility of storing and ultimately spreading the human genome throughout the universe he was going to be exacting in his analysis of any concept as well as any delivery system.

If he had one technical weakness it was in terraforming. His knowledge of it was as a neophyte at best. He would have to rely on one of the world's most renowned terra-formers and physicist Dr. Miranda Hurly. She was the designer of the terraforming that took place on the moon, Mars and Neptune. She single handedly designed and built the robots that worked in non-breathable and corrosive atmospheres. He had handpicked her to head up that division of his responsibility. She was the only person he had not worked with before, but felt if he needed to he could manipulate her.

His areas of responsibility cover gene storage, seed and plant storage, resources needed to establish human seeding of new planets. If the planet being discovered does not have a breathable atmosphere, then terraforming will have to convert it into a planet for air breathers. The other alternative is to develop a genetically altered race that could live on the planet. Doing the latter would change the human race as we now know it to something else. The latter is not part of the World Presidential directive to repopulate the universe with human beings as we know them to be.

The top floors eighteen through twenty-five of the now defunct NASA Space Center were assigned to resource allocation, storage for genetic material, agriculture, and terraforming equipment including robotics.

Dr. Boranum's directive to his team was to have their preliminary concepts on his desk no later than five days hence. He personally would develop the concept for gene storage and dispersal. His own personal team of scientists and technicians would work around the clock to justify his concepts and techniques.

The first week of the Arks of Life project went swiftly with everyone working in unity to develop a concept that would become the driving force for the next five years. Once the concept is adopted it then is refined for an additional month. At the end of that month the concept is either approved or scrapped. If approved then the detailing of everything starts and the endless detail meetings between departments and the endless changes due to this or that start between each team and between the three departments. Over the course of the next four years a bid package of exact specifications and drawings and details will be assembled so that the bidders and makers of these Ark ships will successfully complete them and send the human race to the stars.

If the concept is scrapped then the process starts all over again. That is why each department is supplying multiple concepts in the beginning. This usually causes one to be selected and then the refinements can start right away as well as some preliminary detailing.

As promised on the morning of July 18th the three group leaders walked into the office of Phillip Bradman promptly at 8:00 AM with bundles of paper, computers, tablets and each carrying a very large cup of coffee. They all knew that this concept meeting would go on for hours, sometimes days until a concept was decided upon that would send the rest of the team into a veritable frenzy of work for the next four and a half years.

Chapter 3 – The Concepts

Dr. Bradman's office was one of the largest in the building. It housed not only his desk, computer and furniture it also touted a computer screen wall, a conference room with one wall overlooking the city. His office also housed a full kitchen and bathrooms for both sexes. His sleeping quarters were also attached to his office so that he would always be available twenty-four hours each day every-day. The conference room was electronically connected to the world president's office complex and the world military complex. The conference table alone could sit at least thirty people with chairs lining the walls of the room for at least double that amount.

When Doctors Huffman, Cunningham, and Boranum entered the office they found Dr. Bradman sitting at the head of the conference table sipping coffee and eating a Danish pastry. He stood as they entered and said, "Welcome ladies and gentlemen to what will become the concept room. From here will spill forth the ideas that will save mankind. From here we will send our race to the stars. From here we will perpetuate the human race. With your concepts and your dedication we will embark on one of the largest ventures ever conceived by and built by the human race. It has only one purpose and that is to survive. In this room there will be no boundaries, no egos, and no theories that are too radical and last but not least we will have not bickering between project groups. We will all work together as a well-oiled machine, or by god I will build a new machine with new parts. Is that understood by all of you?" They all nodded their heads in the affirmative and then sat down.

Dr. Bradman said, "Good, let's get started. First I want to hear from the ship and propulsion group followed by the life support and habitat and then the resource and allocation group. Since we are all highly educated people in this room with several degrees behind our names and titles let us forgo the use of doctor this and doctor that. You will all use your first names and refer to each other by their first names. Since we are to be here in this building for another five years together there is no time like the present to start being civil and friendly with each other. You're first up Fredrick, let's see what you have to present to us."

Ship Concept #1

Fredrick Von Huffman stood and plugged his laptop into one of the ports in the center of the conference table. He spent several seconds on the keyboard and then a giant, colored, 3D model of a star ship appeared on the computer screen wall. The ship was huge in comparison to anything anyone had seen before. The nose of the ship was made up of four command shuttle modules that could be used as explorer ships once the main ship orbits a potential planet. From these four command ships the body tapers outward into a delta formation. Once the body reaches its outer apex it stays at that width for about four hundred feet. At this point in tapers back into a grid work of rails and cylinders that house cargo, laboratories, supplies, storage, fuel and spare parts. Behind that cluster of cylinders is another ring of cylinders that represent engines and fuel. All in all the entire ship is almost two thousand feet long. Fredrick said, "I know what you are thinking, you think this ship will never get off the ground. You would be correct in this assumption. This ship will be built in space and will be assembled in pieces. Once it is built, the fuel to drive this ship to the stars will be derived from space itself. The ship will be equipped with eight enormous vacuum accelerators. The concept works like this. In the vacuum of space there is always dust, fine particles of dust just floating around in the vacuum. These particles are from meteors, comets, exploding starts, suns, and planets. Some of the dust has been there since space began. One thing we have learned about this space dust is that it is magnetic. No matter how fine or coarse it is magnetic. This ship will be equipped with eight particle chargers and eight particle accelerators that run the full length of the ship. Particles are scooped in just under the four command modules and the particles are magnetically charged. The particles are then accelerated using their magnetically induced field to propel them through the particle accelerators. Such force will be created that the ship can obtain faster than light speed. To slow down, the process is reversed and the particle instead of being accelerated is decelerated by using reversing magnetic fields around the accelerator tubes. To simplify it for you think of two magnets.

One has a north pole the other a south pole. What happens, they attract each other. Two north poles repel and two south poles repel. Instead of charging the particles coming in the intake as north poles, we will charge them as south poles and the accelerator magnets will also be south poles and the ship will slow down because the dust is no longer being accelerated. Since we have an unlimited supply of dust in space this ship could conceivably travel through space forever. The command module engines are chemical engines. This fuel can be made on board the ship as needed to supply the command shuttles. The engine concept is why this ship must be built and launched in space. Power for the particle accelerators are gathered from solar collector panels that line the top and bottom of the delta portion of the ship. These panels will charge capacitors banks located in the winged portion of the ship and create enormous amounts of discharge energy to supply the engines, life

33

support, navigation, laboratories, cryogenics, and all other ancillary sections of the ship. The ship can cover the solar panels if all the energy is not needed. This way a reserve of power is always available if the need arises. If the capacitors were to fail during the trip, the solar collector panels are more than sufficient to power the ship and all other systems on board. In fact, if fifty percent of the solar panels were destroyed there would be no system on the ship that would not function.

The system of rails and cylinders you see toward the rear of the ship will be cargo holds, laboratories, medical bays, cryogenic storage for human plant and animal genetic matter. Crew's quarters, fitness and eating areas are housed in the delta-winged section of the craft.

This conceptual design is to have the sections of the craft built here on earth and the pieces delivered to and assembled in space. Once the ship is assembled it will start up in space and leave the orbit of the earth and head to the starts. Questions anyone?"

You could have heard a pin drop in the room. No one said a word for an entire minute. Then Phillip Bradman stood up and approached the model of the ship seemingly to float in the vastness of space on his wall of one hundred inch colored plasma monitors. Stroking his chin he walked up and down the room never taking his eyes off the concept ship. Then he said, "It's too bad we don't have a system of lifting this ship into the air after building in on the ground. That would make it quicker to build and easier to assemble and not to mention that the cost of such an endeavor would be monumental. I like the concept very much. What is your next approach?" No one else said a word at that point.

Ship Concept #2

Fredrick turned back to his lap top computer and punched in some additional commands and the image on the massive audio-visual wall disappeared and was replaced with a sleeker and shorter ship design. This ship looked like a train in space. The nose of the ship was developed with two command shuttles belly to belly. From the rear of these command shuttles a series of tube and cylinders grew away at odd angles and were attached together by a series of air locks and hallways. The outside of the ship was almost entirely made up of tubing, struts, and structural support members. All of the periphery structure surrounded hundreds of cylinders and rectangles. At the rear of all of these housings was a gigantic solar sail that was three times as large as the ship. The sail was split into two large triangular shaped sails supported by a structure of grids and girders. The sail was a golden color and was reinforced with what looked like walkways at intervals from top to bottom of both sails.

Suddenly thc three D picture started to move and the sail started to fold up and store itself along the outside of the ship. Once it was stored another sail like the spinnaker sail on the front of a sailboat unfurled and inflated at the rear of the ship to slow the vessel down. This sail was also made of the same gold colored material as the first sail but lacked the grids and supported runways that held the sail in place. This sail was held by fine tungsten cables that attached to the rear of the ship. Fully inflated the sale measured almost two miles across. Once the ship had slowed to maneuvering speed the drag sail was pulled back in by a series of wenches and neatly stored in a single canister at the rear of the ship. Once stored maneuvering engines and jets were used to put the ship into an orbit around a planet and one of the two-shuttle type command modules could be sent down to investigate the planet surface. All types of systems aboard the main ship could test the planet for atmosphere, life forms, vegetation, and whatnot. But the actual surface exploration would have to be done the old fashion way by people. Fredrick went on with his explanation of where the laboratories and storage compartments were located along with living quarters, navigation, cryogenics, and support facilities. When he had finished his explanation both concepts appeared on the video wall side by side.

Phillip Bradman stood and walked to the video wall and just stared at the two concepts. After moments of contemplation he turned to Fredrick and said, "Again you present a ship that must be built in the upper atmosphere or in orbit. The concept of building twelve such ships in the time allotted to build them is a task that is almost impossible. The resources needed to accomplish this task would be the largest endeavor that the entire planet has ever undertaken."

Fredrick cleared his throat and said, "It is the combined opinion of my entire team that no ship that can be launched from the planet surface will be large enough and strong enough to accomplish maybe generations of travel through space and then re-colonize a new planet once it arrives. These concepts present the type of ships that will be needed and also contain the resources for setting up civilization at the other end. These types of ships can be disassembled and transported to the surface of a new planet to set up habitats, laboratories, factories, offices, and whatever is needed to start anew. While it will be costly and it will be a monumental project unlike any that has ever been accomplished before, my team believes it is our only hope for the human race to survive."

Phillip nodded his head and said, "Do you realize that if these are the types of designs we are going to recommend, that your team will also have to design and specify the construction

39

methods as well. Are you staffed well enough to complete all of these tasks in the allotted time?"

Fredrick replied, "My staff has calculated the manpower requirements need to produce the added specifications and construction standards needed to build these ships. They estimate an additional thirty engineers and technicians will be needed immediately to finish on time. They have prepared a listing of the skill sets needed for the new additional team members."

Fredrick handed Phillip a piece of paper outlining what they needed and in most cases even the person needed to fill out the team. Phillip looked at the list and nodded his head eying several of the names that he had omitted for his original team list.

He nodded his head in agreement and looked at Fredrick and said, "I will have the new members here by Friday. I expected that our numbers would grow and we can fit about seventy more people into this building before it becomes crowded. You have taken almost half of my expected team member growth. Manage them wisely because that is all you are going to have till we are done here. Leslie you're up next. Let's see what you have to offer." Fredrick unplugged is computer and Leslie stood up and plugged her computer into the video wall.

Life Pod Concept #1

Leslie typed at her keyboard and a 3D image of an acrylic life pod appeared on the screen. Unlike previous pods used on deep space exploration and the ones used for the Mars expedition this one was molded in the shape of a human and slightly larger in all aspects. Several tubes and cables were attached to the outer skin and it appeared to be totally transparent in all respects.

She began her presentation by saying, "A considerable portion of this design was developed because of the breakthrough of Dr. Boranum on the preservation of the gene structure after prolonged freezing in cryogenic stasis. Harold developed a liquid that could be filtered into the blood stream that combines with the blood cells and is disseminated throughout the body and combines with every type of cell structure in the body to preserve the genetic strands without freezing them. While his discovery has not been tested over generations it has been tested for prolonged periods without any adverse side effects. We are proposing that the crew of the explorer ships be put into stasis at the start of their journey and awakened only when needed to run or maintain the ships. It takes approximately ten minutes to completely filter the blood and the body to awaken form deep sleep. The remaining liquid will stay in the body attached to the other cells while the crewmember is awake. If we want to permanently remove all the liquid form the body that process takes about thirty minutes on a removal dialysis machine that Dr. Boranum also invented. A crewmember can function perfectly well without the full dialysis removal of the liquid with one exception. The will not be able to propagate the species without the full removal of the liquid. This stasis module is molded to each of the crewmembers dimensions and is twenty percent larger than the person. The inside is lined with a transparent gel to act as a cushion during weightlessness. The life pods will be stored in an area of the ship that does not have artificial gravity. They can be used in any position and can be spaced very close together. They will be monitored by the ships computer systems and the crewmembers that are awake and tending to the ship and its systems. Crewmembers will be revived on three-month intervals to run and maintain the ship and its systems. Repair parts and spare generic modules will be available in the ships storage bays. If a module should malfunction the person inside the module will not be harmed because the genetic liquid is in their system. Even if it is not circulated the person will not die. It is conceivable that a human body could live forever with genetic preservation liquid attached to all the body cells. This has not been proven, but there are subjects on test that have now been in stasis for more than fifty years and they show no signs of deterioration. Because of the prolonged journey for these ships there will have to be procreation taking place between crewmembers. This will encompass full awake times with removal of all the preservation liquid from the bodies. Births will have to be while the person is fully awake and no preservation liquids. With babies being born they must be educated. The computer will be their teachers and professors. The will have to grow to adulthood and complete their training prior to going into stasis. Because of the genetic materials being taken on these ships women who do not prefer to mate can be artificially inseminated with some of the best genetic strains available. It is conceivable that we could genetically engineer new crewmembers that will be better than the people we started with. But that is Harold's area of expertise and I will let him discuss that topic.

Life support and sustenance will be provided by hydroponics and standard oxygenated air generated by the O^2 generators aboard the ship. Carbon dioxide and carbon monoxide will be removed from the ship by the use of scrubbers which will regenerate every seventy-two hours. There is enough regenerative material on board to last longer than ten-thousand years. This new material discovery is organic and is grown as a byproduct of the ships waste systems.

Crew's quarters are in the artificial gravity section of the ship along with a fitness center and eating areas. Gaming and sporting areas will be provided in this area as well. A considerable portion of the ship will include live foliage and plant life. Atmosphere in certain sections of the ship will mimic the once diverse climate zones on earth.

Medically the ship will be provided with a state of the art medical laboratory with all the provisions to do major computer surgery no matter what the operation. Surgery manipulator arms controlled by the on board medical computer can provide any surgery that was ever performed on a human being. A full staff of nursing robots will be provided along with two full time staff human nurses. Again these nurses will have to be replaced during the lifecycle of the expedition. It is conceivable that new medicines will be discovered during the trip along with new technology based on the new students that will be born, raised, taught, and matured during the flight. There are four redundant systems for each main system.

The likelihood of them all failing is one in ten million.

What we are showing is very new technology, cutting edge you might say. Some of it is tested some of it is not. Evaluation of my team indicates a 99.99999% success rate. We feel this is the best chance for the human race to survive. This is our top recommendation and the one we would like to adopt. Are there any questions about this concept?" She sat down and waited.

Dr. Harold Boranum spoke up first and said, "You flatter me with your praise over the genetic preservation liquid and I thank you. This method of prolonged space travel and sleep has never been tested and may not be the end all for continued life. I would recommend that we wake up all crewmembers every fifty years or so and remove all the liquid from their systems. Let them live and stay awake for several months and the

47

put them back into stasis. I would feel better about their chances of survival and this would also give them time to procreate."

Leslie nodded her head in agreement and then Phillip stood and walked to the screen and looked at the transparent stasis module.

He turned to Leslie and said, "I suppose your next concept would use suspended animation by freezing and thawing the crewmembers?" "Yes," she replied. "The cryogenic chambers would look somewhat differently and would take up more space and there would be more cycles of freezing and thawing of crewmembers. The big drawback to cryogenic suspension is one of destroying body cells with each freeze. The crewmembers awake time between freezing cycles would have to be longer so the body can regenerate the destroyed cells. We would also have to use some genetic repair in order to keep the crew alive for longer space travel. This would

48

use up some of the genetic samples being stored for future use. My group believes that concept number one is the best chance for the human race to survive to live another time and place. "I agree with you and your group. We will proceed with your first concept. Ok Harold you are up," said Phillip.

Leslie sat down and unplugged her computer and Harold took her place. He plugged in his laptop and the screen came alive with the inside of a laboratory.

Genetics Concept #1

"What you see here is one of eight state of the art genetics laboratories. The growing tubes you see in this laboratory number twenty. We are proposing to grow human embryos from the genetic material from the crewmembers alleviating the need for crewmembers to breed to produce the offspring to man the ship through the universe.

By using the crew material we eliminate the need to dip into the cargo of DNA that we carry to populate the stars. We will be able to reproduce absolutely the same person over and over again. We will clone the crewmembers again and again with one exception. When you clone another being from a clone some of the genetic strands are broken. If we were to repeat cloning a dozen times we would probably end up with clones that could not learn or perform simple tasks. To counteract this destruction of the DNA strands we will keep DNA from the original crewmembers and inject the clones with the original strands which will easily combine with the clone because in all actuality it is the original. Using original genetic material we will fill in the broken strands with new original ones making the new clone an original copy of the first crewmember. This may be able to eliminate the need for the stasis chambers that Leslie described. We would simply duplicate the crewmembers over and over again until we arrived at our final destination. This as we all know may take several generations. Growing clones is the best way to preserve the knowledge of each crewmember. We all know that a clone will have the same memories as the host and will eliminate the need for primary and secondary education. We can even hook the clones up the computer and teach them advanced education properties that were learned by the previous crew. Each crew would become smarter and smarter and more efficient than the last. I know this is a radical concept and that the world governing powers takes a dim view of cloning human beings. They have begun to loosen their thinking when it comes to cloning food animals, fish, and fowl. Being able to clone the original crewmembers will also cut down on the size of the ship. Stasis chambers will not be needed. Food supplies will have to be increased and exercise and recreation will be important to prevent the boredom of prolonged space travel. We as a team feel this concept is

51

the best way for the human race to survive. Who knows what wonders these clones will discover on their journey. I just wish I were going along to see what it would be like by the time we reached the other end.

The roboticist's and the geneticists have combined both genetic material and mechanics to create mechanical human hybrids that can basically perform most of the ships repairs and act as nurses, doctors and engineers along the way. They would be an invaluable resource to the crewmembers. Since the development of the mechanical human hybrid is still in the research stage my team did not feel right in turning the ship over to the HRmans during their voyage through the stars. Some human interface will be necessary for the HRmans to function.

Phillip interrupted and said, "Please explain the term HRman. What is it and when can we see one?" A HRman is a cross between a robot and a human. The skeletal system of a HRman is pure mechanical. The muscle, fiber, skin, nerves, and skin are composed of almost human tissue. What I mean by almost human tissue is that the liquid that flows through its circulatory system is not blood, but a white liquid developed by my company to preserve human tissue and develop a growth system to repair damaged or mal-nourished muscle tissue and organs. The HRmans have no organs to speak of and they do not have to eat. They will periodically need to be serviced and repaired. Their brains are comprised of redundant biometric computer systems that use some living tissue for faster synapse response. We have developed three of these HRmen and they can be seen now if you would like. They are waiting just outside."

Harold pushed a button on his computer and three HRmans came into the room two resembled males and one resembled a female.

They were dressed in street clothes and lab coats. The fell in line in front of the video wall and just stood there. All present except for Harold had an astounded look on their faces. Leslie, Fredrick, and Phillip stood and walked over to the HRmans. Harold said, "Go ahead and engage them in any conversation you would like. They are well versed in all of the sciences and they each can speak twelve languages fluently. Everyone was amazed at how life like they looked and sounded when they were asked a question. Their voices seemed as real as any in the room.

Harold said to Leslie, "Take Martha's pulse." Leslie reached out and grabbed the female's right wrist. The skin was cool to the touch and she could not feel a heartbeat, but could feel pressure pulsation in the veins like a pump pushing liquid through a garden hose. Martha just looked at Leslie and then said, "My core temperature is 88.9°F. My internal pressure is 2.3

pounds per square inch. All of my systems are functioning within their designed parameters." She smiled and then winked at Leslie. Leslie was stunned.

Harold spoke up then and said pointing toward the three HRmans, "Would you three please wait in the hall for me to return. All three HRmans turned and filed out in single file and closed the door behind them. After they were gone, no one said a thing. They all took their seats and just stared at Harold.

Harold continued his presentation by showing the cryogenic storage facilities as well as the genetic storage facilities and finally the robot and HRman building and growing labs. When he finished, he said, "Any Questions?"

Again no one said a word. Finally Phillip spoke up and said, "You don't have a plan B or option #2 do you Harold?" "No," said Harold. I think what I have presented here is the only way for the human race to survive. I don't know of a better or an alternate way that would present the same prospects of success as the one I just described. I am always open to suggestions but honestly my team and I think this is the only way."

Phillip stood and said, "Please forward copies of your presentations electronically to me by the end of the day. You all have presented wonderful and astounding proposals to save mankind. We have spent almost twelve hours listening to your proposals. Now I think it is time for you to relax and have a meal and a bottle of wine and let me review your data. By noon tomorrow I will have made my decision on what options to proceed with and may have some recommendations of my own. Please reconvene back here tomorrow at 1:00 PM. Thank you and your teams for all the hard work over the last wcck. I bcliovo wo truly have a plan to save the human race from extinction."

With that he left the room and went to his quarters to freshen up, order his dinner, and contact the World President and his council. This type of meeting was expected and planned. For some of the radical ideas he would put forth to them he would need their approval to proceed. He had discussed some of the options with the President when he was picked to head this project. Some of the ideas he would offer tonight were going to be so radical that approval of all of them was doubtful. He took a quick shower and put on some fresh clothes and then made the secured satellite call.

Chapter 4 – Review of the Plan with the World Governing Council

On the second ring the Presidents operator answered and said, "Good evening Dr. Bradman. He is expecting your call. I will put you right through. Please stay on the line until all of the council has been contacted and is linked in."

Bradman has never gotten used to the operator knowing him when he calls. There must be some system that tells her who is calling in on the secure encrypted line.

The president's office is now located in Brussels, Belgium. It would be about six to seven hours later there and no way of telling what time it was where all thirty advisers were located. In less than a minute President Mathew Farber answered the telephone and said, "Good evening Dr. Bradman, I was expecting your call and all world advisors are linked in on this line. Each one has a video feed as well as audio and translation services attached. Please proceed with your presentation."

"Mr. President and World Council, what I am about to tell you is extremely wonderful and will probably go against some of the moral conventions of society in ways that you cannot imagine. I will supply video with my explanations and will answer questions at the end of my presentations. I will only try and give you a summary of what we would like to design and specify for the saving of the human race. If you need more detail I will supply that at the end of the presentation as well. I have several programs to present. The first I will present is the ship and propulsion system which will scatter us among the stars."

Phillip entered a code on his keyboard and the ship he believes humanities best hope was immediately flashed upon his monitor as well as each monitor attached to this line. He presented the concept of what type of ship the propulsion system and how all of the ships would have to be built in space in an orbit around the earth rather than made on the ground and launched. This presentation took him about an hour and when finished he said, "Are there any questions?"

The president came on the line and said, "Can we manage a project of this scale and magnitude in the vacuum of space? This could surround the earth with a network of ships in the process of being built and not allow any of our satellites direct access to the surface below."

Phillip responded by saying, "To reduce this effect, a ship will be built over the twelve continents of earth. This will allow space between each ship construction and give the satellites unfettered access to the areas in between the construction zones."

There was some mumbling on the other end of the telephone and the president came back on line and said, "No that will not do. Instead of being built over the continents we want them built over the oceans and seas of the earth and you can use the north and south poles as well. Our satellites must have a clear view of the continents in lieu of the upheaval that these constructions will undoubtedly cause. We must be able to see what is happening on the ground at all times."

"Very well, Mr. President, that is acceptable," said Dr. Bradman. "Are there any more questions on this topic of discussion," Phillip continued? "If you have no further questions about the ships and their propulsion systems then I would like to cover the life support systems and habitats."

Dr. Bradman touched his keypad again and life support pods came on the screen. He talked tirelessly into the night until he felt he had sufficiently covered all of the structure of the life support and its subsequent sub systems. He paused for a minute and then said, "Are there any questions or more details required about life support?"

When he heard no reply he then said, "The next topic will cover genetics, robotics, gene storage and will be the most controversial of the groups presented thus far."

Once again the typed a few codes into his keyboard and the screen came alive with the three HRmans. He presented the facts about these human-robot hybrids and what their function would be aboard the Ark's.

Phillip cleared his throat and then went into the explanation of cloning the crew of the Ark ships to allow the same crewmembers to land the ship as the ones that launched it. This entire presentation had taken about three hours and Phillip was feeling the strain of the day and this evening.

The president came on the line and said, "Phillip, please hold the line for a few minutes while we discuss these issues amongst ourselves." Phillip took off his headset and put the telephone on speaker and leaned back in his chair and rubbed his temples and ears. He brushed his silver white hair back over his head and stretched his shoulders to relax him a little.

Fifteen minutes later the president came back on line and said, "We can all agree the HRmans being part of the crew and an invaluable aid to the crew members. But as a total group we stand behind the laws of no cloning. We adamantly refuse to have the crewmembers cloned. We will not allow this on any of the Ark ships. Do I make myself perfectly clear on this issue?" Phillip thought before he spoke and then said, "Yes, Mr. President, I totally understand your stance and policy on this issue."

The President spoke again, "The council and I approve your plans to move forward and create a bid package so that we can get these ships built. Please forward the details of your presentation to me and each member of the council. When do you think you will have a preliminary budget for this program? We will need to go before every governing continent and state to procure the money, labor, and materials to build these ships. Please proceed post-haste to complete your designs and bid document. I know I speak for all of us when I say that what you have accomplished in just seven days would have taken months or even years at any other time in our history. We all applaud your efforts as well as your team. Please pass on to them our gratitude and thanks for a memorable start."

Phillip swelled with pride and said, "Thank you, Mr. President and World council, we will continue our efforts and will meet and all of our goals on time and within our budget once we have decided what it will cost. Until then we will progress down the path we have chosen here tonight. Thank you all for your patience and understanding along with your approvals. He placed the telephone receiver in the hook and leaned back into his chair. He would send the presentation details tomorrow morning to the president and world council. All he wanted to do

65

right now was to curl up and go to sleep. He looked at his watch and it was four AM. He yawned and walked to his sleeping quarters and fell fast asleep. He was awakened sharply at 8:00 AM the next morning by a restaurant steward delivering his breakfast. He stumbled out of bed and answered the door. The steward pushed in his tray and left. The food smelled so good, he thought. He sat down and ate then showered and began putting together his presentation to his team. Today would be the day that not all of his team would like what he had to say, but the governing powers had decided on a plan and that was how it would be for the next five years.

Chapter 5 – Anti-Gravity

Far away from Houston, Texas, in
Petaluma, California, a seasoned physicist by the
name of Dr. Gerry Pardu had just completed his
first experiment developing an anti-gravity
platform. Gerry worked for Bell Laboratories and
had been with them for almost twenty-two years.
He had worked on a sundry of projects during his
employment but none that excited him as much as
Project AG1009. This was the Bell designation for

what he was developing. The crux of the project had been developed in theory by himself and Dr. Abby Pinkerton. They had studied together at UCLA and then USC for their postgraduate work. Both had graduated with honors and received their doctorates in Quantum Physics. Soon after graduation they both were offered research positions at the Petaluma research facility. They were both involved with other significant others and had never developed a personal relationship toward each other. They had studied together and worked side by side together for so long that each of them could complete the other's sentences or thoughts when the need arose. Their entire lives had been centered around physics, physics, and more physics. An easy day for them was fourteen hours. Often they would stay at the lab and would sleep in makeshift sleeping quarters and then jump right back to where they left off the next morning. They ate their meals in the lab offices and kept their experiments to the lab. This had become a golden rule shared between them. Their offices would often contain partially eaten pizza, burger wrappers, french fry trays, chinese cuisine, and their always favorite fried chicken. They had promised each other to go home at least twice a week and spend time away from the lab and each other, but in the last seven months they had broken that promise time and time again. Today was one of those days.

Last night they had experimented with a small hover board and they got it to lift two feet in the air by using their anti-gravity generator. The board weighed three pounds but it had floated in the air all by itself. Gerry who weighed in at one hundred and ninety pounds stood on the hover board and energized their generator again. This time it rose about three inches off the floor. Next Abby stood on the hover board and again the generator was started. She was much lighter than Gerry. She only tipped the scales at one hundred and twenty-two pounds. The board rose one foot above the floor and could be directed left- right, forward and back by just leaning in that direction. The hover board was tethered to the generator by a one hundred foot connector cable. With Abby on the board she moved it around the laboratory and even up and down a flight of three or four steps. They were ecstatic that they had finally perfected anti-gravity propulsion. They had celebrated with a bottle of wine and a bucket of fried chicken. They had crashed for the night in Gerry's office with Abby taking the couch and Gerry falling asleep in a recliner.

It was now 9:00AM and the banging at their laboratory door told them that they were late for the daily staff meeting. They both rushed to the door to find Belinda Manning the executive assistant for Donald Harbaugh, the managing director for Bell Laboratories in Petaluma, California.

She was staring back at them with that jaundiced eye that she could affix on you and expects you to do exactly what you were told. "The boss is waiting for you both in the tower conference room. You are both late and it looks like you slept in your clothes again, am I right? Straighten yourselves up and get upstairs pronto or there will be hell to pay!" She was known for her flamboyant speeches. Gerry and Abby looked at each other and started to laugh. "Why are you laughing, Belinda roared? You guys are in for it this time."

They continued to laugh and started running down the hallway toward the tower elevators. Belinda fell in right behind them and they all entered the express elevator to the tower conference room. Upon exiting the elevator they could see the meeting was breaking up. From the look on the of face Mr. Harbaugh was in a very foul mood this morning. He could be heard

71

shouting at several of the scientists as they were leaving the conference room. He was threatening to curtail their funding and decrease the size of their laboratories and such if they didn't show progress by the end of next week. He had just about peaked out his anger when he saw Gerry and Abby saunter into the conference room by the rear door and took seats at the far end of the table.

Donald moved down the length of the table until he was standing very close to both of them. Carrying a small leather bound notebook under his arm he stopped in front of Abby and said, "Do either of you realize how many of these meetings you have been late for or do you just miss them to press my anger button? Have you seen your budget to progress ratios over the last month? Have you a desire to continue your work here, or would you be more comfortable at say a place like Berkley."

Gerry and Abby thought they would let him go on shouting but just couldn't restrain their excitement any longer. In mid-sentence Abby broke in and said, "We have done it! Gerry then spoke up and said, "Yes, sir. Donald we have accomplished what no other human has been able to. We can fly. Yes you hear me correctly, we can fly and we can control it."

Donald dropped his notebook on the floor and said, "Say that again. Did you say you can fly? Have you discovered anti-gravity?"

"Yes, we have", Gerry and Abby said simultaneously. Now they had Donald excited.

"I have a thousand questions," said Donald. "Rather than ask your questions, why don't we just show you," said Gerry with Abby nodding her head. "Come with us down to the lab, we will show you, heck, we will even let you try it out" said Abby. They practically ran to their lab in sub level

3. When they arrived they were still talking about how they had made some adjustment to the anti-gravity generator based on the latest readings of the earth's magnetic fields measured the world governments research satellite. Once the flux field was tuned to the exact earth's core coordinates the generator had worked perfectly. They had been working from data collected by the Bell satellites but evidently they were not as accurate as the governments newly launched magnetic explorer one.

Donald said, "How did you get access to the new explorer satellite?"

Abby spoke up and said, "We sort of hacked our way into their data stream and we sort of siphoned off what we needed. We bounced our signal off several servers around the world before be found the right data stream. There is no way they can trace our siphon back to here, no way."

Donald rolled his eyes and said, "I've warned you both before about hacking information from other sources especially the government or military data streams. What if they do trace it back to us, then there will be hell to pay. You two have to stop breaking the rules and start following them. Do I make myself clear on this issue? No more hacking of any body's networks or data streams."

Both Gerry and Abby nodded their heads in agreement but could hardly keep their excitement under check. They both slid their access cards and had their bio-scans read and finally their retinas scanned then there was the ominous click of their lab door and it opened. All three stepped inside.

The hover board was sitting in the middle of the lab where they had left it. The cable was still attached and Abby mounted the hover board and motioned for Gerry to turn on the generator. Gerry fussed with the controls and flipped the switch that turned on the generator. The hover board rose into the air carrying Abby with it. She tilted it left and then right. She then tilted it forward and back and slowly hovered around the room. As she hovered she felt a tingling sensation in her feet that she hadn't remembered from last night. She just passed it off as not noticing it due to the excitement of the board working for a change. Many times over the past month the generator had been turned on and nothing had happened. They had several small fires and one time every metal tool in the lab sailed toward the hover board like it was a giant magnet. But with this new data input to the computer generator the board had worked perfectly.

Donald stood in the lab with his mouth hanging open not saying anything. He was watching Abby fly around the lab on the hover board. Abby hovered over to him and said. Would you like to try it once? It is very easy and stable. Donald weighed about one hundred seventy pounds and was wearing a three-piece business suit and Italian loafers. He looked every bit the quintessential director of a company or laboratory. Donald was the type of person who does not get in the trenches but one who looks down into the trenches. Gerry lowered the flux field of the generator and the hover board slowly came to rest on the floor of the lab. Abby jumped off and Donald stepped on. Gerry increased the flux field until Donald was hovering about ten inches off the floor. Abby was explaining to him about the balancing process and not to overdue any leaning. It was almost like the board knew what you wanted to do by detecting slight minute changes in your posture. Abby was holding onto Donald and he was trying out the leaning process. Several times Abby had to hold onto him to keep him upright. After about ten minutes of training Donald was navigating the lab with ease. He had even gone up and down the three steps. He

77

hovered to the center of the lab and motioned to Gerry to cut the power. Gerry did and the board slowly came to rest on the floor. Donald stepped off and grabbed Abby and Gerry in a group hug.

He turned to them and said, "I think you two are on your way to a Nobel Prize. Another one for the lab would be great. It has been a while since the last one. Now, what do you need to perfect, enlarge, maximize, and make this portable. This has so many useful and military implications, the list is endless. When do you think you will have your reports and research to a point that we can take it before the review board for additional funding?"

Both Gerry and Abby looked at each other and said in unison, "We can be prepared in two weeks. We will be able to give the board a demonstration in the boardroom. They will not have to come to the lab to witness the first anti-gravity machine." Donald said, "My feet are

78

tingling, are yours?" Abby spoke up and said, "That's probably a residual left from the intense magnetic field the board generates. It should go away in a few minutes. Mine were tingling when I first got off of it, but they are fine now." Donald smiled from ear to ear and shook their hands and slapped them on the back then turned and practically ran out of the lab. Gerry and Abby just looked at each other and started to laugh. They both knew that Donald was on his way to tell the board of directors about this new discovery.

For the next two weeks neither of them left the confines of the laboratory. Donald made sure that there were enough clerks, typists, and technicians to make the two week deadline a success.

Gerry continued to refine the generator and started making a smaller more portable unit that could be carried on the back or on the craft they were lifting. It would be equipped with a GPS tracking device that would continually tell the generator where it was in reference to the earth's magnetic core and flux generated fields. With its portability, smaller size, higher output and GPS tracking it was conceivable that the device could go anywhere and work perfectly.

With his new supplied technicians he built the unit he was thinking of. In a matter of five days the new magnetic generator was complete and it would fit into a small computer case. The new generator ran on capacitance-inductance and could be fully charged in under ten minutes. It could keep the hover board afloat for almost twelve hours on one charge. With its increased strength it would raise a two hundred pound weight two hundred feet into the air on the hover board. It would hover just like before and would almost anticipate the command of the rider.

Gerry had tested it in the field and its top speed with a rider was one hundred and twenty

two miles per hour. Without a rider the speed
approached four hundred. Gerry unveiled the new
generator to Abby the night before the board of
directors meeting. She was amazed at its small
size yet powerful output. Gerry was the brains
behind the generator and Abby was the brains
behind the hover board. Together they could
tackle just about anything. They both knew that
they were at least three to five years away from
full-scale models of the board and generator.
There would be various refinements to their
original and then there would be an endless
amount of prototypes and so on and so on. They
had decided among themselves that the new
generator and the original board were to be shown
to the board. Abby mounted the hover board one
last time and Gerry attached the generator to the
board via a short cable and then put the generator
on Abby's back and turned it on. Abby's entire
body started to tingle. She said as much to him
and he just replied, "It's probably the field building

up around the generator. Remember, you just felt it in your feet the last time. Now that you are wearing the generator it stands to reason that you might feel it all over your body. I don't think there is anything to worry about, but just too be safe I think we will need to make a magnetic shield suit for the operator to wear during operations." He placed the generators remote control in her right hand. Gerry continued, "Red is off, green is on and yellow is standby. There is a small thumb wheel built into the side of the unit. That small thumb wheel governs how much power output the generator will produce. Full open and the board will rise to about two hundred feet. When you lower the output you will descend lower to the ground. Standby is only used if you want to hover in one place for a long period of time. It saves the battery/capacitors. Abby touched the green button and instantly the board rose into the air. It continued to rise until her head bumped the ceiling. She instantly decreased the power and the board slowly sank toward the floor. Once she had the knack on how to use the remote, she buzzed around the lab at various heights and speeds. In the past two weeks she had made some modifications to the hover board as well. She had attached a pair of ski bindings to the board and could now easily lean without fear of falling off the board. They would eventually have to be replaced with some sort of binding that would fit anybody's foot, but for the trials and presentation today, they would work fine.

Everything looked in order, the documentation was complete, the capacitor batteries were charged, and a spare pack was ready in case of any failures. The hover board was painted in a brilliant lime green and Abby had applied a small pinstripe to each side.

They showered, put on fresh clothes and by 9:30 AM they were ready to be called to the Boardroom. The call came from Belinda Manning shortly after 9:45AM to let them know they were to be in the Boardroom by 10:00AM. Their presentation material had already been delivered to the Boardroom so all that was left was the equipment. As they were leaving the lab Gerry grabbed Abby around the waist and kissed her gently on the lips. She looked startled and then smiled. Gerry said, "Now don't go all goo-goo on me. That was just a kiss for luck." Of course it wasn't and both of them knew it.

They had already decided what the demonstration was to be like and Gerry would do the document presentation. Just outside the boardroom door Abby slipped her feet into the bindings on the hover board, put on the backpack and slipped the power control into her hand. At precisely 10:00AM they opened the boardroom door and in flew Abby. She made a complete circle of the room and then elevated to the point that she hovered down the middle of the

84

boardroom table where she hovered just above the tabletop. You could have heard a pin drop in the room. Not one board member said a word. Then all at once questions came from everybody.

Gerry moved forward and said in a calm but firm voice, "Now, now all of you just calm down and we will answer all your questions in due time." He had never seen such excitement in a room full of executives, ever. While Abby just hovered above the table, Gerry commenced his presentation with facts, figures, videos, and finally wrapping up with this statement. "It is conceivable that we can make this type of device move just about anything we want it too. It is just a matter of field strength and generator power.

We would like to invite your outside to show you the real power of the antigravity hover board." Abby took the power control out of standby and hovered herself to the door and out into the hallway. She flew down the stairs and out the front entrance of the building.

After all the members were assembled in the front lawn, Abby put on a show of speed, height, and agility. She raised high into the air and even flew upside down over the group just to show off her new ski bindings. When she was finished she landed gently on the lawn and unclipped the board from her feet and turned off the generator. Donald Harbaugh led the board members back into the conference room to conclude his portion of the project presentation.

He took his place at the head of the table and said, "As you can see this is the biggest advancement in physics since the atomic bomb. We have actually created anti-gravity. This project will need additional funding to bring it to fruition. We estimate about two billion dollars will be needed over the next three years. At that time it should be commercially available to the market as well as to the World Defense Network. It is my firm belief that we are looking at the next Nobel Prize in Physics." All of the board members stood and applauded Donald, Gerry, and Abby.

Gerry and Abby were embarrassed and shortly after the standing ovation they excused themselves and went back to their lab. Once inside their lab they both breathed a sigh of relief and gave each other a high five. Gerry grabbed her again and gave her a big kiss and hug. Abby looked up at him, smiled, and gave him a kiss that was a lot more passionate than the one she had just received from him. What had seemed very strange at first now seemed very natural and he kissed her back with the same passion. When they broke their embrace there was a long silent pause as they just stood there and looked at each other wondering what to do next.

Their silence was interrupted by a knock on the laboratory door. They both turned and saw

Donald Harbaugh standing in the doorway looking very father-like at the two of them.

He stepped into the lab and said, "The board has granted additional funding for your project and you are moving your laboratory to wing-D. The largest and most well equipped laboratory is being put at your disposal along with twenty technicians and six clerks and assistants. Your funding over the next two years will be two billion dollars. Your goal is to make three types of hover boards or crafts.

The first one will be:

> Personal hover board - for national defense use. It will be for manned and unmanned use by the World Defense Council.

The second one will be:

> Commercial hover board - for moving cargo around the world. Maximum weight for each hover board will be four tons. These

88

devices will be sold commercially throughout the world.

The third and biggest challenge will be:

Maximum payload hover craft - used for ferrying objects into the vacuum of space and returning to earth. The maximum weight load for this craft will be two hundred tons. It will be able to be used many times on a charge and will carry a crew of two or three.

For the third and final craft you have been granted additional funding of four billion dollars. This third craft must have been tested and ready to use in five years."

Gerry and Abby were stunned. They just stood there in shock. Donald could see that this was an overload condition to their brains so he continued, "I have taken the liberty of hiring you a team of specialists that will work out all the details of the three projects once you supply them with the technical data. The team will start one week from today, so I suggest you get packed up and ready to move to laboratory D-13. The movers will be here tomorrow morning to start moving your equipment. Welcome to the big leagues you two. Your life will never be the same from this day on so make the best of it while you can. Your names will go into the history books. You will be known worldwide. Television and movie studios will be after you for interviews and scripts. Children will be taught about you and about your lives. Relish the next few days of anonymity because after that the entire world will be clamoring to meet and talk with you."

Before they had a chance to say anything, Donald turned and walked out of the lab. They turned to each other and Gerry said, "I'm hungry, how about we go out and find us a big juicy steak." "Maybe some Champaign," chimed Abby. "Of course," said Gerry. So hand in hand they left the lab. Moving would have to wait until tomorrow.

Chapter 6 - Interstellar Light Slipstream Drive

South of Berkley, California, at the Lawrence Livermore National Laboratory another struggling pair of physicists and mathematicians were trying to develop a new method of propulsion for space travel. Dr. Penelope Redman and Dr. Henry Pendergast were hard at work in their tiny lab filled with all types of machinery, tanks, computers, monitors, gauges, tubing and electrical apparatus. They both thought they were very close to finally developing and containing a very small blue matter quantum singularity.

Unlike its big brother the black hole the blue matter singularity was very different. Instead of the unparalleled pressures within the core of a black hole, the blue singularity would spin in the opposite direction making the center almost weightless. The blue singularity accelerated objects inserted in its core. The black hole crushed them. During their experiments Penelope and Henry noticed that right in the center of their blue singularity was a tiny white dot. Neither of them knew what it was. All they knew is that every time they had created a blue hole the white dot appeared. They had tried to take pictures of the white dot but the interference from the blue hole distorted the pictures and rendered them unreadable. The same thing occurred with any televised or video pictures. They had not been able make a larger blue hole so they could see the white dot more clearly. They both were absolutely convinced that the white dot held the key to the blue singularity. They had presented their findings and shortcomings to Dr. Helen Foss the Managing Director of Research, but had not been able to persuade her to let them have larger equipment and lab spaces to create a larger blue hole so they could study the white dot in the center.

They remembered Helen's argument. "What makes you think that a bigger blue hole will have a larger white dot? What are the benefits of creating a blue hole? What can it do for space travel?" She went on and on with her questions. Ultimately she had said no to their requests for more equipment and a larger laboratory. She had said, "You will have to do with what you have. Times are hard what with the world being in the condition it is. I just can't give you more equipment and funding on a whim. Bring me some solid evidence that a blue quantum singularity can power a craft through space and I will gladly open up the purse strings and give you additional funding and space. Until that time comes, don't come crying to me for anything. You two were at the top of your classes and graduated Magna Cum Laude from the most prestigious universities that money could buy. You teamed up and did create a blue hole. But so far you haven't told me what good it is."

Now back in their laboratory Henry said, "If she won't give us the funding we will just have to requisition what we need. You know, Penny, how long it takes for a requisition to be passed around the site from office to office before it gets to Helen. We can get what we need and build our device before she even gets the first requisition."

"I don't know," said Penny. "If she gets wind of what we are doing she will sack us both."

"By the time she gets wind of what we are doing we will have something she can sell and everything will be alright," said Henry. He continued, "What have we got to lose, our jobs? You and I both know we can walk out of here and right into job at a top paying research lab. Let her fire us. We will go somewhere else and continue."

"Well, there is our dilemma Henry," said Penelope. "You know we can't do that. We both signed contracts with LLNL and we just can't go anywhere else and do what we are doing here. The government will not allow us to continue this work for some private company."

Henry looked at her then smiled and said, "Well then our course is clear. If we want to make a larger singularity then we will have to build a bigger containment field and a larger generator. The only way we can do that is by requisitioning the parts here. When we make the breakthrough that you know we will, Helen will be shaking our hands and patting us on the back. You know she will." Penny just looked at him and grimaced. They began filling out requisition forms for power supplies, containment towers, liquid nitrogen to keep the containment module at super cooled conditions and any other equipment they needed to scale up their experiments. In less than ten days they had built an entirely new lab and had returned the smaller versions of their equipment to the complex's stores and requisition building. If you walked into their lab now you would have thought it had always been that way. Their containment towers were now situated in a diamond shape around the portal generator which could accommodate a singularity about six feet in diameter. Henry and Penny had spent the last two days running cables, making connections and trying out each of their new pieces of equipment prior to hooking it up into the system to generate the blue singularity. Since their generator required a considerable amount of power they decided they would develop their first hole around midnight when most of the other labs had shut down for the day. This way the sudden surge on the power grid would not be as noticeable. At precisely the stroke of midnight Henry flipped the switch and things started to happen. They donned their protective goggles because when the singularity formed there was always a bright flash of light and a steady rush of air toward the forming hole.

The containment field lit up like a Christmas tree and formed a barrier around the singularity platform. Then the blue hole started forming. It was small at first and then started expanding until it hit the edge of the containment field. In front of them was a five feet diameter blue hole. In the center of the hole there was a white ring that was about one foot in diameter on the outside and eleven inches in diameter on the inside. The middle of the circle was deep black with faint white dots in a random pattern. The edges of the singularity seemed to fold back in on itself with wisps of the blue outside edges being pulled back into the white ring. Penny and Henry just stood there marveling at what they had accomplished in ten days with the right equipment. Because of the size of this blue hole, there was a constant draw of wind into the black center of the hole.

Carefully Penny picked up a piece of copy paper and watched as the paper drew itself toward the singularity. Henry said, "Be careful Penny don't touch the containment field. It is perfectly balanced to contain the hole." Just then the piece of paper slipped out of Penny's hand and was sucked into the blue hole. When the paper hit the containment field there was a large crack and the paper burst into flames and immediately was sucked into the center of the hole and disappeared. Penny was on the front side of the singularity and Henry was on the opposite side. Five video cameras were recording everything that was happening in real time. The paper disappeared into the hole, but it or ashes or what remained of it didn't come out the other side. Henry said, "Where did the piece of paper go? Did it come back out your side, Penny?"

Penny said, "No, did it come out your side?"
Henry just shook his head negatively. "Where did
it go," said Penny?" " I don't know," replied
Henry. "Maybe it burned up."

The blue singularity was almost opaque
except for the center hole. It looked transparent
but when you looked into it all you could see was
blackness with faint white dots. Henry leaned
down from his side and peered into the center.
Penny was doing the same but they couldn't see
each other.

They had installed six video cameras with
magnetic shielding to record all of their
experiments. They could analyze the entire
process later. Henry shut down the platform and
the containment shield after about twenty minutes.
Both of the just stood there in amazement
because everything had gone so smoothly. Henry
said, "Let's look at the video and see if we can see
where the sheet of paper went." They turned on

the video feed from the recorders and hit the playback button. This time they got very high definition video from the six cameras all fed into one monitor. They viewed the recordings for all angles but could not see where the paper went. The cameras showed it going into the hole and then it just vanished. Then they methodically went about checking all of the equipment and data collected during the experiment. There was a slight spike in the energy level output of the blue hole when the paper entered the black center but that was all. Then everything went back to the readings before.

Henry said, "For the next experiment let's place a metal disc with a hole in it and attach it to a roll of wire. We can set it up inside the containment field and release the disk with the wire attached and trace where it goes. Let's put about ten feet of wire on a spool and attach one end to the disc and the other to a pole we will mount inside the containment field." Penny nodded her agreement. It took about thirty minutes to rig the experiment.

When they were ready, Henry turned on the containment field and then switched on the platform generator. Again a huge flash of light and the blue hole started to form. As before it expanded to the limits of the containment field and stopped. When all power outputs registered as before, Henry motioned for Penny to release the disc. They had been watching it as the blue hole formed. It was made of non-magnetic stainless steel and was about six inches in diameter. They painted it with international orange paint so it would be visible in the black center of the singularity. Penny pushed a button and the clamps holding the disc released it. It immediately shot toward the center of the blue hole and disappeared. The cable attached to the disc went taught and stayed that way. It started to pull tighter and tighter until the bar it was attached to started to bend.

Penny pulled her hand across her throat and Henry shut down the power. Nothing happened. The containment field and the singularity did not change. Henry checked the switches to make sure he had turned them off. Both the switches were in the off position but the singularity was still emitting energy this time at a much higher output than before. The pole attached to the cable continued to bend until the bolts holding it to the platform broke and the pole was sucked into the black center of the hole. As soon as the pole entered the hole it disappeared, everything shut down. They both ran to the video recorder playback and ran the images over and over again trying to determine what happened. They shook their heads in disbelief. The disc, the cable, and the pole simply vanished into the singularity. Once they were gone, the energy

102

levels dropped and everything shut down. The energy output levels during the time the items were in the mouth of the singularity were three hundred times what they were when it was empty. It was now close to 6:00 am and they both thought that they should not turn it on again. All the other labs would be starting up again soon and they wanted to stay anonymous on their power usage for a few more days.

They did, however, set about designing their next experiment. This time they would enlarge the containment field so they could affix a steel pole into the concrete floor and epoxy it in place. The steel cable was being replaced by a one-half inch stainless stranded aircraft cable and the disc was now a one-half inch thick titanium plate with the cable braided through two holes and welded to the plate.

They were both exhausted by midnight but all the work was complete and ready of the next experiment. A last minute addition by Henry was to attach a strain gauge to the cable and post to record the pull strength of the singularity. At the stroke of midnight Henry flipped the switches. The containment field fired up and stabilized. The singularity flashed into existence with such ferocity that Henry and Penny could feel the heat from its initiation. The singularity was now about eight feet in diameter and the black center was now about two feet across. The white random dots throughout the black field seemed brighter and more well defined this time, but still could not be recognized as to what they were. Henry was monitoring the readings and noted that the power to generate the singularity was exactly the same as last night. It was generating the same amount of power output as last night even though it had almost doubled in size. Once all the readings were confirmed and the video cameras were on line and recording Henry told Penny to release the disc.

Again she pushed the release button and the disc flew into the center of the hole. The cable went "Thwang" as it reached its limit. It was stretched about as tight as it could be. Henry noticed the strain gauge reading sixty thousand pounds per square inch. At the same time the peak power output registered two thousand times the input power. Then the cable broke and the strain gauge was sucked into the hole along with the cable and disc. The power levels dropped back to normal and Henry shut it down.

"Wow, did you see that," Penny said. Henry said, "I think we should go home and get a good night's sleep and come in tomorrow and determine what we have here. We need to find out what is happening in the middle of that singularity." Penny shook her head in agreement and they shut down everything and put biometric security locks on the lab door as they left.

The next morning both were fresh and had their thinking caps on and began to dig into all of the data they had collected over the last two days. After spending the morning going over chart after chart of readings Penny spoke up and said, "Duh, why have we not remembered the most important thing about this blue singularity." Henry looked at her quizzically and said, "What are you talking about?"

Penny said, "Black holes have their roots in the universe, why can't blue holes do the same? What we do know about the blue holes is that the gravitational forces in the center of the hole are not crushing like its black sister. What we really don't know is what is on the other side of the blue hole? If we can find that out, then we may have a way to go to the stars without being crushed. Suppose those white dots we see in the middle of the blue hole are actually stars. What if the center of the blue hole is actually a gateway to the universe? We know that what goes in doesn't come out the other side here in the lab but suppose it comes out somewhere in the universe?

"That's a lot of speculation," Henry said. "I know it is," said Penny. "But bear with me for a moment. Play back the camera from your side of the singularity and play back mine side by side." Henry put the two images up on the monitor side by side. The pattern of white dots on her side did not match the pattern of white dots on Henry's. They were the exact opposite. They were a mirror image of the other. Now Penny said, blow up the image of your side as I release the disc from my side. Expand it as large as you can." " What are you looking for," asked Henry? "Just do it and watch the screen," she said.

Henry did as she asked and enlarged the image on his side until it pixilated. At the exact time she released the disc he could see a change in the image. It was blurred beyond recognition

107

but there was definitely something there. When the cable snapped the blur moved out of the picture and disappeared. Together they watched it over and over and over. Finally they both slapped each other on the back and danced around the lab. Henry said, "We have to tell Helen about this. This is the breakthrough we have been waiting on." Penny bit her lip and said, "Are you sure, she was pretty upset the last time we spoke to her. What is she going to say about all of this equipment?"

"Look Penny here is what we will do," said Henry. "We will set up the last experiment only this time we will use a larger disc. Maybe that way it will be clearer on the video. We will also use a larger cable and strain gauge. That way we can also show her that the hole generates its own power until whatever caught in its center is all the way through. Let's get it all set up and then you call her."

"Why me," said Penny. Henry replied, "Well that way she can blame me for requisitioning the machinery and she will be happy with you and us for making such a big discovery." They scurried about setting up the next experiment and using a much larger cable and this time a disc almost two feet in diameter with a one and one-quarter inch stranded mooring line from a ship. This was all attached to the ten-inch steel pole that was epoxied into the concrete floor. The mooring line was coiled up on the floor attached to the largest strain gauge the procurement department could find. This was shackled around the post and to the mooring line. This gauge was supposed to be able to measure over two million pounds per square inch. When all was ready Penny made the call. When Helen answered Penny told her they would like to show her a breakthrough in creating wormholes. Helen said, "I'll be right down, because there are some very strange requisitions hitting my desk for equipment I didn't authorize. We will get to the bottom of this immediately."

Henry saw Penny's face and knew exactly what was wrong. "I guess the requisitions hit her desk sooner than I thought, huh?" "Oh yeah," said Penny. "Boy did she sound mad." Henry replied, "She'll calm down once we show her what we have accomplished." No sooner had the words left his lips when there was a loud knocking at the lab door. Henry handed Penny an additional pair of darkened lab glasses and then motioned for her to open the door.

Helen flew through the door in a rage holding a fist full of equipment requisition forms. She stopped suddenly in the middle of the lab and started looking around and then going through the papers in her hand as if she was doing a mental inventory of everything. Penny sheepishly handed her the pair of safety glasses and asked her to turn toward the containment area. Before Helen had a chance to say anything Penny explained what they were about to witness and told Helen that afterward if she wanted to discipline them for the equipment they would both understand. Helen slipped on the glasses and Henry threw the switches. The containment field energized and lit up like the fourth of July. This was immediately followed by the snap and glow of the initiation of the blue singularity. Henry yelled, "Cameras are rolling." Penny pushed the button and released the new 250-pound disc. It immediately shot into the blue hole followed by the mooring cable. "THAWNG," sang the mooring cable and the strain gauge started sending readings to the recorder. The indicator on the strain gauge passed one million pounds per square inch and was continuing to increase. Then they all noticed the steel pole in the floor starting to bend. Concreted started cracking and the pole continued to bend. Henry turned off the power but forgot that while the eye of the singularity was occupied it was running itself. The pole continued to bend and the large shackle holding the strain gauge started slipping up the bent pole. Finally the large shackle slipped off the top of the pole and was sucked through the hole. Instantly the hole shut down and the dim lights in the lab brightened. Helen just stood there with a blank stare on her face. She was trying to fathom all that she had seen and her mind couldn't process it fast enough. Finally coming to her senses she said, "What the hell did I just see? And you better explain it in terms that I can comprehend or both of you are out of a job."

It took Penny and Henry the better part of an hour to explain everything they had witnessed. Henry summed up their findings with this statement. Now just imagine this device attached to the hull of a star ship. If we can devise a way for a rod to extend and be extracted from the center of the singularity it could propel the ship at untold speeds. If we want to go forward we insert one rod into this side, if we want to go into reverse or slow down we would withdraw this rod and insert a similar rod into the opposite side. We have a new star ship engine that generates its own power as long as the center of the hole is occupied. Imagine an engine without fuel. The other application is if we can build a singularity large enough to travel through the center to where ever it leads we could shave years off of space travel."

"Now, now," said Helen. "Let's not get ahead of ourselves here. I agree with you both that you have made and astounding discovery but we just don't know all the implications of it yet. Hell we almost destroyed the lab in one experiment which brings me to why I came down here. How did you get all of this equipment?" Henry explained and Helen listened very intently. Helen then looked at them both and said, "Ok, you are authorized for whatever you want to make the next step. But if you don't keep me informed every step of the way I will shut you down and bring in other scientists to finish what you have started and you will vanish into obscurity. Do I make myself clear?"

They both shook their heads in a positive manner and Helen turned and left the lab. Henry and Penny turned to each other and hugged each other and started dancing around the lab.

In a few short months several experiments had been completed to see just how big they could generate a blue hole. After several attempts the largest they could stabilize was twenty feet. But the center never increased larger than six feet. The center was not big enough for a ship to travel through, but maybe a person.

The last and final experiment on earth was to build a movable platform that could develop a singularity that metal rods could be inserted into either side to test the theory of propulsion. LLNL had several rail tracks on the property used for various testing of rocket-powered sleds, new engines, and whatnot. Henry and Penny had designed and equipped a rail car with the equipment needed to generate a singularity about two feet in diameter. Inside the containment field they had designed two devices that would allow them to enter and withdraw a rod into the center. These devices were attached to the rail cars frame. The only drawback was having enough power to start the singularity. To overcome this problem they laid three more electrical conductive rails between the tracks the wheels ran on. They put copper wheels under the rail car that rode on these three tracks. At one end of the rail spur they attached the power grid to these three rails thus giving them the power to start and sustain the singularity if it actually moved the car.

Everything was designed, built, checked, and double-checked. The big day had arrived. Henry, Penny, and Helen along with two other directors were in the control lab next to the rail car. Henry explained that they would insert the forward rod one inch into the singularity and see what happened and then pull it back and then do the opposite one to see if the car reversed its direction. Cameras were mounted in the rail car so that everyone could see what was going on inside the car. Henry turned on the power switches and a singularity was created in a matter of seconds. It was about two feet in diameter with about a one-inch center core. Henry slowly eased the forward rod into position and just barely entered the white core. The rail car slowly moved forward. Henry quickly withdrew the rod and slowly inserted the reverse rod. The rail car stopped and started to move in reverse. Henry quickly withdrew the reverse rod. Henry looked at the read outs and saw that he had only inserted

116

the rod one-sixteenth of an inch into the singularity for it to move a ten thousand pound rail car. He and Penny were beaming from ear to ear.

Henry said, "Here goes to one-eighth of an inch." He moved the joy stick forward and the rail car lurched and flew down the track and was picking up speed when he moved his joy stick to withdraw the rod it was too late. The car had reached the end of the track and exploded through the stop bumper and buried itself into a hill surrounding the rail spur. A resulting explosion occurred and then a strange thing happened. All of the debris from the explosion was being drawn through the confinement field and into the center of the singularity. As it drew larger pieces the singularity grew in size as it consumed the smaller pieces it grew smaller. When it had consumed the entire rail car and equipment, it just shut down and disappeared.

Everyone just stood in silence for about ten seconds or more and then Helen said, "We are going to have to do some more work on making that thing shut down when we want it too, but other than that, I think this was a success even though there is nothing left of the car. Please tell me you got all of this on video?" Penny and Henry shook their heads yes and then Penny said, "We need to build a star ship with a blue singularity drive unit."

Chapter 7 - Third Year of the Arks of Life Design

Three years have passed and the designs of the ark ships were moving along at a rapid pace. During that time a discovery of an anti-gravity sled had been developed and it would be used in lifting the pieces of the ark ships into space for assembly. Word of a new interstellar drive unit had filtered out of the Lawrence Livermore National Laboratories but it was only rumor and nothing more. Work was still proceeding on the ion accelerator drive unit as planned.

Dr. Huffman was ahead of schedule as was Dr. Cunningham. Dr. Boranum, on the other hand, had not been satisfied with the decision not to clone the crewmembers so he had been putting all his efforts into the development of the HRmans. What his team had accomplished in three years was amazing, but he had neglected the part of the project of genetic material storage, terraforming and agriculture. In those areas he was behind schedule. His HRmans were absolutely fantastic. They were stronger than humans, they didn't have to breathe air, and they didn't eat. What they did need was constant maintenance. Mechanically they had problems with breakdowns. Also the genetic material used in the brain to simulate brain synaptic functions was not as reliable as he once thought. After a period of about six months the tissue started to corrode some of the circuit boards and the HRman just stopped functioning. His designers were busy designing electronics that would withstand the connection of human material without malfunctioning.

Dr. Phillip Bradman had scheduled a meeting with Harold Boranum to discuss the issue of schedule on the other aspects of his responsibility. The meeting was set up for today at 9:00 AM. At precisely that time Dr. Boranum arrived at Phillips office and entered without knocking. Dr. Bradman was seated behind his desk with Dr. Boranum's latest schedule reports unfolded in front of him.

Phillip rose and said, "Harold please take a seat. There are some schedule delays I need to talk to you about."

Harold seated himself in front of Phillip and said, "Yes, Yes I know all about the delays. They are not as important as finishing the latest HRman.

121

We will find room to store the genetic materials. I have a special team working out the details as we speak. I should be back on schedule within two weeks. I will have the plans for genetic materials storage, agricultural material storage and the terra forming team will be ready to list their requirements to change any atmosphere we run into. There will also be some new added requirements for some genetic laboratories with growth and operating rooms. I know that the other two leaders feel they will complete their projects earlier than expected. I will do the same."

Harold got up to leave and Phillip said, "Please sit back down. I am worried about all the time and expense you are spending on these HRmans. The President believes that robot assistants may be just as good as these HRmans." Harold stood and with rage in his voice he said, "You can tell the President he can run the

world, but leave creating a new life-form to me."
With that he turned and stormed out of the room.

Phillip just starred after him in disbelief. He
knew now that Harold's ego was in the way of him
being able to direct the project to its completion.

That night during his tele-meeting with the
President, Phillip told him that he had decided to
replace Harold Boranum as project leader but
would let him continue running the HRman project
as part of the scientific team. In his place he
would like to bring in Dr. David M. Martin. Dr.
Martin was the world-renowned authority on
Marine Genetics. Like Dr. Boranum David had
mapped all the genetic codes of all known aquatic
creatures. He had even created three new
species to take care of some of the ocean and sea
pollution taking place throughout the world. Other
than Dr. Harold Boranum there was no one on the
planet that was more qualified to take over the
genetic portion of the project.

The President was a little skeptical as to how the two of them would get along after Dr. Boranum would be relieved of this position. Dr. Bradman assured him that Dr. Martin had a demeanor that would allow him to take charge of the project and yet allow Dr. Boranum the latitude needed to complete the HRman portion of the project. If need be Dr. Martin would close down the HRman project in lieu of not making the deadline on the rest of the genetic portion of the project.

The President said he wouldn't interfere with Phillips decision and to proceed with all undo haste.

Phillip picked up the telephone and called Dr. Martin. He picked up on the second ring. Phillip introduced himself and filled Dr. Martin in on his plans and expectation and asked David to join him in Houston where he would detail what he had in mind. Dr. Martin was ecstatic with being asked

124

to help on the Arc project. He assured Phillip that he would be in Houston the very next morning.

Phillip had asked Dr. Boranum to join him in his office at 9:00 AM. At precisely nine on the dot the door opened and Harold entered Phillips office. There he was met by Phillip and another man that looked somewhat familiar but could not place his face with a name.

Phillip said, "Dr. Boranum, I would like you to meet Dr. David M. Martin. Dr. Martin will be replacing you as head of the genetics portion of the project allowing you to work on the HRman project full time. I would like this to be an amicable turnover of your team and materials to David in order to bring him up to speed as quickly as possible." Harold looked at the two men and then without saying a word he turned and left the office.

David spoke up and said, "I think that went well. What do you think?" Phillip was somewhat embarrassed by Dr. Boranum's attitude and just blushed a little.

He cleared his throat and said, "Why don't I walk you up to the Genetic floors and I can brief you along the way and we can stop in and see the HRman project." They took the elevator to the twenty-fifth floor and as the doors opened they could hear Harold Boranum screaming orders to his people as well as acting in an unprofessional manner by cursing, slamming things around, and just generally being in a real shit. When he saw Phillip and David he screamed at the top of his lungs, "I WILL NEVER BE APART OF THIS PROJECT. I WILL GO SOMEWHERE I AM APPRECIATED FOR MY KNOWLEDGE AND HARD WORK. YOU CAN ALL DIE ON THIS DEAD PLANET FOR ALL I CARE."

With that being said, he finished throwing his personal belongings in several boxes he had on a cart and pushed it through the door passing Phillip and David. He shoved the cart in the elevator, turned toward them, and made a hand gesture that said it all.

Phillip said, "Well I never!" Flustered as he was he gained his composure quickly then turned to David and said, "The project is officially yours. Now let me show you the HRman project and explain its purpose to you." They went down two floors to the HRman laboratories. David was amazed at the phase three two prototypes that had been completed and were in the process of being programmed. The engineers in the lab bristled with excitement at showing off their new creations.

David said, "These are the most sophisticated robots I have ever seen." One of the engineers spoke up and said, "They are not robots

127

doctor. They are mechanical human hybrids. That is why they are designated "HRman" Human-Robot-Man." " They are certainly remarkable," said David. "What would be their purpose on the Ark voyage," he continued? The engineering staff was more than willing to tell him all of the functions they would perform so the humans could cryo-sleep without being disturbed. They also alluded to the fact that if the voyage was as long as predicted in some instances then the HRman would have time to develop themselves further beyond anything dreamed of now. Eventually they would start replacing themselves with newer and newer models until what you have here would not be recognizable in the future. They have been programmed to constantly improve themselves and become more advanced HRman's. David rubbed his chin and pondered that thought for a moment and then turned and took Phillip by the arm and walked back to the elevator.

He told Phillip on the way to the elevator that he would probably close down this part of the project based on what he had just heard. "If these HRman beings are going to constantly improve themselves on a maybe four or five hundred year voyage, then who's to say they will not decide that the human race is no longer needed. What if they decide to terminate the crew because the HRman are more advanced than their creators? I think these HRman might be more of a hazard than a help on this trip. Let me do some more thinking on it before I come to you with my final decision." Phillip nodded his head in approval and said he would like to meet with him in two days to see how he would proceed to catch up with the rest of the project teams. David said he would have a plan formulated by then and would see him in two days at noon.

When Phillip returned to his office his presidential telephone was ringing. Phillip picked it up right away and said, "Yes, Mr. President, how may I help you"? "It is I who will help you, Phillip," said the President. "There has been a major breakthrough in interstellar propulsion at the Lawrence Livermore Laboratory. Two young scientists have discovered a drive that would shorten the time to other solar systems by half, maybe even more. I have arranged for a plane to pick up select members of your propulsion and ship design team and transport them to California to visit with these two engineers and see firsthand an experiment showing how this drive works and it works on very little power when it is working. Once the drive is engaged, it generates its own power to continue to operate. I don't understand it all, but your people will. Just have them ready for a 0600 flight leaving from George Bush International tomorrow morning. They will be gone for three days and then return. I can't tell you any more than that right now. It sounds exciting and may change the entire way we travel in space."

The line went dead and Phillip just stood there looking at the telephone. He then called Dr. Huffman and relayed the Presidents message and told him to have his party selected and at the airport tomorrow morning by 6:00 AM. Phillip said that Fredrick could fill him in on his return.

Two days later Dr. David Martin arrived at Phillips office at precisely at noon. Phillip was sitting at a table in his office just opening his lunch. He said, "Come in, David, I have taken the liberty of having lunch prepared for you so we can talk while we eat."

David nodded his appreciation and said, "I have been up for two days going over every page of data from my project team. I would like to make some changes in their assignments and yes, I will shut down the HRman project. The engineers from that project will work on advanced robots to help maintain the ship and administer to the crew. They will be nothing more than interfaces between

131

crew and ship. In doing this and also changing the genetic material storage scheme we will be caught up with the other teams in less than four weeks."

Phillip said, "How and why will you change the genetic material storage scheme?"

David continued, "Looking at how the genetic materials were to be stored has caused me some trepidation. Harold was going to cryo-freeze a lot of the genetic material. Periodically he was going to thaw it out and let it repair itself. I think this is dangerous. It will be dangerous to thaw and dangerous to refreeze. My aquatic research has shown that all genomes do not heal themselves after thawing without injecting new compatible material into the gene clusters to repair the broken ends. My research had found that keeping the genetic material in an environment of just above freezing you can keep the material in like-new condition indefinitely. With the temperature issue solved, now comes the matter of radiation. As you know the ship will constantly be bombarded with solar radiation. Each star it passes will spit out some type and magnitude of radiation. We also know that radiation no matter what kind will destroy genetic tissue. To protect the genetic material, human, animal and agricultural, I suggest we build a triple walled aquatic pressure chamber to store the materials in. The center chamber will contain the genetic material. Surrounding the inner chamber will be a chamber containing heavy water. Heavy water is called Tritium and is a great insulator against fast neutrons and gamma radiation. This chamber will also be pressurized to four atmospheres. The storage chamber will be at five atmospheres of pressure or approximately 75 ft. below sea level. The heavy water filled second chamber will be three times the diameter as the storage chamber. The third and final chamber will be one foot larger in diameter than the second chamber and will be charged with nitrogen to three atmospheres. If anything leaks, it will leak away from the genetic material not into it. Also the containers will be perfect spheres. Each sphere will be made of 99.99% pure manganese-molybdenum steel. The outer chamber will be protected on the outside with a one-inch thick layer of high molecular weight polyethylene and outside that skin will be a one-half in thick coating of lead. This shielding should stop any known radiation from entering the genetic material. Also the genetic storage bays will be filled with circulated seawater with a salinity of about 35%. The storage bays if penetrated by meteors or stray particles will be absorbed in the water and never reach a storage chamber.

The terraforming teams are progressing very nicely on their own. I see no need to change their goals at this time."

When David had finished he noticed that he hadn't touched his lunch and suddenly was very hungry. Phillip sat back and thought about the changes and finally said, "You are adding a lot of weight to the ship, Dr. Martin." "Yes, I am," he said. He continued, "If what I hear about this new drive, that has been discovered, is true, then weight will not matter in space travel." Phillip raised one eyebrow and wondered how the word of the new drive spread so quickly.

Phillip sighed and said, "It sounds like your approach to storage is sound and will protect your cargo for years to come. It looks like you have taken every precaution known and then speculated on the unknowns. Please proceed with your plans and meet with the other sections to bring them up to date for I know they will have changes to make in their designs based on your changes.

Chapter 8 - Dr. Harold Boranum

After leaving the Ark project it took several months for Dr. Boranum to land on his feet and decide what he was going to do. He knew that the earth would not survive and to his core he felt the only way for the species called human beings to survive was to evolve into another type of being. His HRman project was human DNA combined with mechanics and electronics to develop an

136

evolved species. Part of the species would be a human being, but only part of it. In his mind he was still saving the human race. His HRman would be the best of both machine and man. To this end he solicited investors and quickly founded a new bioengineering development company called Ark Enterprises.

His investors were told that his approach to the human race problem was that humans could simply not cope with the environmental changes that they themselves had inflected. He would develop a mechanical human hybrid that would take a person's DNA along with a collective download of all of their brain memories, personality, and persona and transfer it into a bioengineered body of mechanics, tissue, and a brain of tissue and electronics. Conceivably this body could last forever with just a little maintenance and upkeep. It would also adjust to the changes in the earth climate and resources. It

137

would be devoid of illness, frailty and the aging process. Since it would need no food as humans need, dwindling resources of food and water would not matter. The HRman's only fuel was solar radiation. Could it be injured? Yes it could. But the healing process would be accelerated because it was pure tissue with no viruses or germs to infect a wound. The electrical engineered nerve tissue along with no blood, but a liquid of bioengineered cells that would heal and replace any damaged tissue within minutes.

To the doctor's rich investors the prospect of living forever was exhilarating. They poured money into his organization like it was a rebirth of the fountain of youth. The good doctor had promised them an HRman prototype in less than one year.

Since Harold was first and foremost a scientist he knew that he could not run a company and develop the HRman. His first job was to find a

138

person with excellent managerial skills an attitude that would exude success and a face that would be the cornerstone of Ark Enterprises. He hired an executive placement service to find such a person. Within four weeks this service had found four possibilities. They sent Harold four dossiers for him to review and set up four interviews with the possible candidates. After reading the information on the four possible directors of his company he was especially intrigued with a talented woman named Miranda Fitzgerald. Her background was nothing but success, her personality profile showed a wide variety of skills and technical expertise. She had negotiated her way to the top on several contract issues and had averaged a twenty-two percent margin of profit on every job she had undertaken. Her personal photo was breathtaking. She was not young, not old, not fair, and not beautiful. She was just right for the face of Ark Enterprises. After Harold's interview with her he had hired her on the spot and she had taken control of the reigns of his company. Their relationship grew into more than just business comrades; they eventually fell in love and were married.

As promised one year from the date of incorporation, the first HRman prototype was walked out of the laboratory and into a press conference. The female HRman named Melissa was introduced to the news media and journalists like she was just another human being. This was far from the truth, she was much more. Her strength was three times that of any human. Her mental acuity was the culmination of every volume housed within the library of congress, the national archives and every book ever written that had been digitized. She spoke seven languages fluently. Those languages that she could not speak she could recognize through speech recognition and within a matter of minutes after hearing it could speak it. Harold and Miranda were beside themselves with excitement and pride. They told the reporters that they were going to adopt Melissa as their daughter and bring her into their family. Dr. Harold Boranum had accomplished his lifetime goal. He had created a new life form.

Investors flocked to Ark Enterprises and the money flowed in like water. At the end of the second year Gerald Boranum was introduced to the public as Melissa's brother and he too was to become part of the Boranum family.

Behind the scenes Harold and Miranda had secretly been working on their own replacement HRman's. By the end of the third year their replacements were completed but not introduced to the public. Instead they introduced an HRman that could be purchased and engineered to down load a person's entire lifetime into its brain. A tissue sample from the purchaser would be genetically inserted into the HRman being and synthetically a new person was born without cloning. When the human person died off from whatever ailment humans succumbed to, the HRman replacement would continue to live on and take their place. There was no reproduction involved, try as he might; Dr. Harold Boranum never mastered that aspect of what he called human frailty.

Because of his success with the HRman introduction Harold, Miranda, Melissa, and Gerald were granted berths on the Ark ships that were being built above the earth. The world powers felt with his knowledge of genetics and robotics that he and his family would be the most valued persons aboard one of the ships.

Chapter 9 - Building the Arc Ships

Dr. Phillip Bradman and his crew of designers and technicians completed their task of design and as promised four years and six months from the day they started Dr. Bradman handed all of the specifications, designs, and schedules over the President Farber. This was a worldwide effort and the largest project ever undertaken. Dr.

Bradman recommended that they build twelve Ark Ships.

The President wasted no time in having the information put into bid packages and sent out to all of the major air and spacecraft builders on the planet.

He also started the daunting task of selecting the crews to man the twelve explorer ships. He convened a meeting of his advisors and enlisted their help in forming lists of crewmembers that would carry on the human race. Once that list was made and voted on by his council then the lists would be published and the potential crews would start their education in flying and maintaining the Ark Ships.

It took almost an entire year to sift through all of the bids and questions the ship-makers had about the construction of the Arks of Life. Phillip Bradman and his crew had been pressed into service to answer all questions and to come up with whom would build the ARK Ships. After careful deliberation the Bradman team came up with three winning bidders. The European continent was awarded ships one through four. The award was given to Airbus headquartered in Toulouse, France. The second award went to a group of companies that teamed together to form the Ark Ship Company they were formally known as Lockheed, Bowing, and Northrop-Grumman. They were awarded ships five through eight. The final bidder was none other than Bell Laboratories. Special consideration was given to them for the anti-gravity sleds that would make the construction of these ships a lot easier than it would have been trying to fly all the supplies and people into space for assembly.

Once the announcements were made construction started at a fever pitch. The majority of the components would be made and assembled on earth and simply transported to the vacuum of space where they would be assembled. Crews of space assemblers had to be trained and transported to makeshift quarters in space to make ready for the first shipment of parts. Factories started turning out modules, framework, hull plating, and endless miles of wire harnesses to string from one end of the ship to the other through which all signals, messages and control functions would be eventually passed.

Meanwhile President Farber had convened his advisors and together they hammered out the seemingly insurmountable task of picking the crews for each of the twelve ships. The list of would be candidates was the cream of the crop of all technologies here on earth. Each ship would carry a crew of one hundred of the best technologies earth had to offer. A support crew of one hundred would be made up of all trades people to accompany each ship as well. All in all, there were twenty four hundred human beings that would leave earth and their one goal was to create new human life throughout the universe. All other earthbound persons would be left to the fate of this once vibrant but now dying planet. With each ship carrying individual DNA from every person on earth that had donated samples as well as DNA from every animal, fish, fowl, insect, beast, their chances of success were better than seventy five percent. Even if just one ship made it to a planet in another galaxy that would support human life the race would survive as well as any other creatures that walked, flew, crawled, burrowed, or swam on earth. With seeds, spores, bulbs and other reproductive matter from all plant species the new earth would have some resemblance of the old. The time for the crew list publication was approaching and an international lottery had been established to pick the support crewmembers.

Each ship would have an equal complement of technological people as well as an equal compliment of trade's people. No ship would have more technology than any other. They would be equal in the sciences, philosophy, arts, religions, and trades.

There would be one exception to that rule and that was Dr. Harold Boranum his wife Miranda and their children Melissa and Gerald. When all was said and done they would be together on one of the ships. No one on earth had accomplished what he had so there was no equal to his talents. Whatever ship he ended up on was going to have an edge were genetics was concerned.

Lawrence Livermore National Laboratories was given the task of building and delivering thirty-six Interstellar light slipstream drives. Each ship would be equipped with two drives each. One drive would be their primary drive ant the other two would be a redundant backups. All the systems

148

on each ship had built in redundancy for each system installed. If one system failed a backup was ready to take its place.

Bell Laboratories not only had to supply the anti-gravity sleds to lift pieces of the ships into place for the other ship builders they also had to equip and build four ships of their own. In the entire history of the human race, nothing of this magnitude had ever been executed. They had to succeed, because the alternative was extinction.

The list of technical crewmembers was published around the globe. It also was sent out on every airwave possible. President Farber held a news conference and one by one read the names of the twelve hundred technical crews. There were also two hundred alternates picked that would take the training as the picked crew. This was done to compensate for deaths, disease, and anyone who absolutely refused to go.

The results of the global lottery were just as fruitful as if they had been handpicked by the World Government. People turned out in droves to sign up for the ARK Lottery as it was called. Each person had to prove the skills set forth in their application. In the end Phillip Bradman's group had been pressed into service to weed through all the paper work and pick the support staff from almost four billion applicants. After that list was posted all was ready for the next phase.

Chapter 10 - 2132 The Year Crew Training Started

Training to pilot, maintain, and maneuver the Ark Ships fell to the teams that had designed the ship to start with.

Dr. Phillip Bradman and a group of 300 of the engineers that had designed and specified the Ark Ships were once again assembled. This time they were to teach twenty-four hundred human beings how to survive the ordeal that they were about to undertake.

Again Phillip divided his team into two main divisions and then divided them again into sub divisions. Division one would teach the technical people and division two would teach the trades people.

Dr. Fredrick Von Huffman headed the groups to teach the ship and its functions.

Dr. Leslie Cunningham headed the groups to teach the life support and habitat systems of the ships.

151

Dr. David M. Martin headed the groups to teach the care and manipulation of the genetic materials as well as terraforming and robotics.

All instructors were university level professors and engineers. All systems had simulators built to teach in real time and real life environments. The sheer number of people to be taught would overwhelm most teaching centers so it was decided by the World Government that the University of Texas at Austin would close their doors for three years and allow their facility to be taken over to train the ship crews. The logistics were all in place, for housing, food, classrooms, and facilities. Simulators were moved on campus and the registered students were transferred to other colleges and universities around the state.

By the time the campus was ready and the crewmembers started arriving only three months had passed since their names had been announced.

Security was very tight on campus because of death threats against those chosen to go. Each crewmember was tattooed with a bar code on the right wrist and on the back of their neck. An infrared coded sensor was inserted in the left thigh of each member and alternate. Each crewmember was monitored twenty-four hours per day seven days a week. A team of security specialists kept track of each crewmember constantly. Strict guidelines were given and enforced. Members that broke the rules more than five times were ejected from the training programs and an alternate took their place. During the first year of training thirty-three original members were released and alternates filled their billets.

Training was hard and arduous. Simulator time was fun for the most part. Here students would learn what happened if they did not do as instructed for a particular scenario. In the simulator if a disaster occurred no one would be injured or die. The instructors always told the students. "Here you live, out there you die!" as they pointed toward the sky.

Both crews and sub crews mingled with each other and they all became vast and very close friends. No one knew what ship they would be assigned to until their last two months of schooling. At that time they would be assigned to a specific vessel and be taught by the makers of their particular craft. They ate together, played together, slept in the same dormitories together, and went to class together. They became over a period of time a very close-knit group. There was no time off for summer vacations or holidays. The Ark ships were large and the technology was cutting edge. Each ship had to learn about and maintain the blue hole drives. This technology alone was the most advanced of its kind. The two inventors of the drive had been busy around the clock for almost two years just refining and building the thirty-six scale models for the Ark ships. Henry and Penny spent their time in California and in Austin Texas. As the training wore on a larger and larger security area around the college had to be maintained. More and more people wanted to be part of the crew. By the end of the third year of training there were only twenty-alternates left. Everyone wore the standard blue and white jump suits of students. When they were finally assigned to a ship they would be outfitted with the ships colored uniforms. Each ship was to have its own uniforms. There was also a distinction between technical and trade crewmembers when it came to their uniforms. The trade crew wore a standard sky blue uniform with the ships colors splashing across the upper left quadrant of their jumper. The technical crew member's uniforms had the ships colors attached vertically to each leg of their kaki jump suits with

155

their name and specialty above their left breast pocket.

Training continued at a fever pitch five days per week. If you asked any of the crew what portion of the training they enjoyed the most they would all say genetic storage and maintenance.

Dr. Martin's laboratories, simulators, and classrooms were a perfect simulation of an Ark ship. He had constructed ten containment chambers that he called bubbles. His classrooms were under water and his entire complex outside of the bubbles and classrooms was painted black to represent the darkness of space. David Martin was one of the most well liked professors and trainers. He had pioneered the use of the Bioengineered Autonomous Genetically Enhanced Skin Suit better known as B.A.G.S., or the bag suit. Each student would enter his classroom through a pressure chamber which could hold twenty students. He always kept his laboratory and classrooms at two atmospheres. The entry pressure chamber also was flooded with infra-red and ultra violet rays to kill any contamination on any student. Once inside the pressurized laboratory each student would go to their assigned lockers and undress down to their undergarments. Inside each locker was a rubber skullcap that they then put over the top of their head and tucked in their hair. They would then proceed to the BAG chambers.

Standing in the individual BAG chamber the student would stand with their back to the entrance and put their hands in a small depression on the back wall. They would open their eyes and stare at two small red dots on the back chamber wall just about eye level. They would move closer to these red dots still keeping their eyes open. A mist of liquid would spray directly into their eyes and then the student would close them. A

157

transparent door would close behind them and the BAG process would begin.

The chamber would fill with a mixture of helium and oxygen and then a series of valves would open and the outer skin of the student would begin to turn black. Within a matter of seconds they would be covered from head to toe with a black outer skin that could by osmosis absorb oxygen and nitrogen but filter out all other unneeded gasses. The skin suit as it was called was now genetically connected to the student's outer skin. Instantly oxygen absorption begins and the respiratory system of the student begins to shut down. There was several seconds of panic the first time in a BAG suit because the brain tells us to inhale. Our brain says breathe or die. The Bag suit lets the outer skin of the wearer absorb oxygen throughout the entire surface of the body. There is no need to breathe in or exhale. Carbon monoxide and carbon dioxide is now genetically

158

withdrawn from the skin through the suit and into the water or air. Oxygen in the water or air is transferred through the suit and into the body. No tanks, no breathing apparatus and no mixture of gasses is needed while in the BAG suit. Inside the chamber a small beeper sounds to let the student know when the transformation is complete and they can open their eyes. If the student had not closed their eyes a thin translucent membrane was generated over the eyeball. The mist sprayed into the eye before the application of the skin suit along with the liquid tears which lubricate the eye are genetically made up of material other than the skin cell material and so the skin suit will not adhere to the eye.

Once the chamber door is opened the student can proceed to the bubble chambers. Air locks allow access to a series of bubble chambers. Inside the air lock are weight belts, foot fins, and eye masks that the student will need entering the bubble chambers. Since Tritium is being used in lieu of regular H^2O the suit compensates for the differences in the chemical makeup of the water and allows only what is needed for the human inside to continue breathing. The BAG suit will also control the temperature of the wearer. Because it is tied directly into the wearer in can control body temperature by the amount of oxygen it allows in. The more a person works the hotter he or she will become. The need for the body to circulate the blood faster and cool it down is imperative. If the amount of oxygen is regulated to the wearer then exertion will call for more oxygen and the temperature will not rise. If the diver goes deep into an ocean or a location where the water temperature is cold, the suit senses the outside temperature and begins to warm up by electrolysis. It removes oxygen from the water and using the electricity generated by the body of the human wearer it generates heat like a battery being recharged. In doing this the wearer stays at 98.6°F all the time.

The suit has another special feature and that is pressure compensation. No matter how far down you go in the ocean the suit will not let the person inside feel more than ten atmospheres of pressure. As the diver goes deeper the cells of the skin suit become compressed from the pressure and thus protect the diver from the extreme pressures at deep depths. The skin suit operates independently from the diver's skin even though it is attached to it. The genetic skin is a marvel of genetic engineering. The BAG suit is one of the greatest inventions for under water explorers since the Aqua-Lung and the self-contained underwater breathing apparatus. (SCUBA)

David often thinks of how it used to be but really likes the fact that it is much better now. David dons his bag suit daily and steps into the classroom and bubbles to be with his students. Teaching how to care and maintain the genetic material is really the life-blood of this project. If the material is damaged or is destroyed then it will be unlikely that the crew will survive on a new planet and the selection of mates may be limited and eventually would cause inbreeding which would destroy the genetic chain over a period of time. It is crucial to the survival of the Ark Ships that the genetic material arrives at the other side of the universe intact, fresh, and ready to be used. To this end Dr. David Martin dedicates each day to instilling in his students exactly how important their job is.

Learning inside the bubbles is repeated day after day after day so that any crewmember can stabilize any of the genetic material at any time during their journey. This course has also taught every crewmember how to swim and dive underwater.

To remove the BAG suit you enter the transfer chamber put your hands back into the depressions and wait for the door to close. The door closes and the tube fills with a material that looks like soapsuds. As soon as the tube is full, the outer skin starts to dissolve and drain into holes in the floor. The suds are then rubbed on the skin by the diver's hands. Their skin tingles a little and remains soft and supple.

Dr. Harold Boranum and his family spent as little time as possible in Dr. Martin's classes. He felt that it was ridiculous and a waste of time. His rage and ire ran deep and would not forgive Dr. Martin from shutting down the HRman project and essentially trashing all of his ideas pertaining to the Ark ships.

The training of all crews started in earnest and was now coming to an end in about three months. Next week the crew lists were going to be posted. The crewmembers with the best grades would be picked for the first ships to be launched. It didn't mean that if you were on ship twelve that you were not intelligent. It just meant that your grades weren't as good as the ship one crew. To put it in perspective, the grade spread was from 3.7 to 4.0. Everyone was bright and intelligent, they are all professionals, and they all knew their jobs.

Dr. Boranum and his family were assigned to Ark Ship #11.

President Farber made a personal telephone call to Dr. Martin. David picked it up on the second ring and was astounded to hear the operator say, "Hold for the President." When the President came on line he said, "Dr. Martin, I would like to congratulate you on your accomplishments in the design of the Ark ships and the training of their crews. I have been informed that your training has been exceptionally successful in guarding our precious cargo." David was a bit taken back and then he replied, "Well, thank you, Mr. President. I felt like it was my duty to do the best I could." The President said, "Do you mind if I call you David?" "Why, no, Mr. President," replied David.

The President continued, "David, I have a special favor to ask of you and I know it will not be an easy one, but after reading your background and your personality profile I think you are the only one who can accomplish this. By the way, reading through your files I see your middle initial is "M," but there is no mention of your middle name. What does the "M," stand for?" David cleared his throat and said, "Well, Mr. President, it is a very old family name. My great-great-great-great-great grandfather was named Mergrom. It was a name given to him by a king. Once given to him, from that day on he was only known by one name and that was Mergrom.

My mother found the name in some of our family history while she was still carrying me and thought it would be a good name to revive. We really don't know much about him except he became an advisor to the King that gave him this name. The rest is sort of shrouded in mystery and history. After he became advisor not much was written about him after that. Now what was this special favor you wanted to ask me?"

President Farber cleared his throat and said, "I would like to make you a crew member of one of the Ark ships. My request is selfish and a bit underhanded, but never the less I would like you to become the geneticist aboard Ark Ship #11."

David replied, "That ship already has one of the best geneticist in the world assigned to that ship. Dr. Boranum and his family are assigned to ship number eleven."

"Yes, I know," announced the President. "But I just don't trust him," he continued. "I know that he has developed the HRman and even his children are of this new race of beings. I just don't want him having the opportunity to take over the genetic portion of the ship once it has left earth. I would like to appoint you as head of genetics on ship number eleven. I know you and he have had your differences, but your personality profile assures me that you can deal with him. It would put my mind at ease if you would volunteer for this assignment."

There was silence on the phone as David pondered this assignment. Then he said, "Mr. President, of course I will do this for you if you think it is absolutely necessary. May my wife and family accompany me?" The President now spoke very solemnly, "No, David, I am afraid they cannot. I have already broken every rule in the book by getting you on board. I am very sorry, but they will have to stay behind with the rest of us. I will prepare a place for them in my personal underground bunker that is being built. That is the best offer I can make."

David contemplated all of this for several seconds before replying, "I will do as you ask, Mr. President."

"Thank you from the bottom of my heart," said President Farber. "You have in one word erased the fear of having all our efforts go in vain. Thank you again."

Then the connection was broken and David just stood there holding the receiver going over the entire conversation and thinking about his future and his family's future.

Chapter 11 - 2135 Launch of ARK SHIP #1

Construction on Ark ships one through four is complete and all ships crews have been trained and assigned to ships. Ships six through twelve are in various stages of construction and completion. All ships crews are ferried into space to live aboard their respective ships and familiarize themselves with all of its systems and components.

January 23, 2135, the crew of Ark Ship #1 has notified earth that they are ready for launch. All crew, provisions, genetic material, and spare parts are aboard. The order is given By President Farber, who is now in his third term as World President, "You are go for launch and may God and the fate of humankind go with you in peace."

With those words transmitted throughout the world Ark Ship One energized its blue hole and set course for the Andromeda Galaxy.

That's when things went haywire down on earth. All communications with all satellites went dead. Television stations all over the globe went black. Power outages swept around the world in a matter of minutes. Tidal waves were created in all oceans and earthquakes hit many inhabited countries. The world erupted in chaos.

The gravitational field created by the blue hole in a vacuum disturbed the earth's magnetic field. Effectively it tried to create a new magnetic field around the earth. Ark Ship One slowly accelerated away from earth and in a matter of two hours the intense field around the ship had dissipated from around the earth to the point that systems started to come back on line. Little by little communications were restored, television, radio, tele-communications were brought back on

170

line. Electrical generating plants began generating power once more. The real devastation took place along the coastline of all continents. Hugh tidal waves pounded the coastlines for hours killing thousands. Nothing but death and destruction was left in their wake. Earthquakes caused by the generated magnetic field soon subsided as the Ark Ship got farther from earth.

Immediately President Farber convened a panel of experts to uncover what had happened. As long as the ships blue hole was generating all communications had been lost with Ark Ship One.

The panel was made up of the best minds left in the world. Their immediate job was to explain why all that had happened on earth corresponded with the exact moment the blue hole was engaged on the Ark Ship. Their findings would not be available to the public for weeks. So in the meantime President Farber put a hold on future launches until precautions could be taken to protect the inhabitants of earth from the same effects as the first launch. Not knowing why everything went bad the moment of the first blue hole launch, was the most frightening of all.

It took the committee ten weeks to completely decipher what had happened. When they presented their report to the president this is what it said.

(The report was confidential and was full of scientific jargon and facts and figures that even the president needed advisors to explain it to him in layman's terms. So the description below is a summary of the report put into language that most people will understand. The full report can be read in the World Congress Archives titled "*Magnetic Anomalies Created by Blue Holes.*")

Blue Hole magnetic field strength - Once a blue hole is generated the field containment generator controls the size of the blue hole. Blue Hole magnetic field strength when Hole is engaged - Once the blue hole is

172

engaged in power generation the field strength continues to grow until equilibrium is reached. In the presence of an existing magnetic field, such as the earth's polar magnetic fields the blue hole field expands along the same lines as the existing magnetic field and increases its strength exponentially.

Blue Hole Power Generation - Once a blue hole is engaged it creates its own power through stellar fusion. The blue hole on Ark Ship One is capable of producing 10 to the 200th power megawatts. That type of power intensifies its magnetic field to keep the hole in balance with the universe.

The intense magnetic field created by the blue hole caused an imbalance in the earth's magnetic fields. This imbalance caused the earthquakes, and tidal waves. The power generated by the blue hole overloaded circuitry in satellites, generators

173

and transmitters. Once the power generator was removed from its location corrective actions could be taken to bring electronics back on line.

Some overloads cause by the immense power generated by the blue hole cause fires and instability in the power grid causing worldwide blackouts.

CORRECTIVE ACTIONS RECOMMENDED

Ferry Ark Ships ten thousand miles from earth prior to engaging the blue hole.

Install protective shielding on all satellites to protect against magnetic power generation.

Install magnetic grounds around all generating plants and tele-communications transmitters to neutralize stray magnetic fields.

Allow one year in between each Ark Ship Launch to give time for the earth to heal its magnetic poles.

Measure the earth's rotation and axis variance each time an Ark Ship is launched. Due to Anti-Gravity devices being use in the construction of the Ark Ships the magnetic field around the earth has become weakened by the continued use of its fields to lift heavy cargo into space. Loads lifted into space must be equally spaced throughout the globe to allow earth's magnetic fields time to heal and strengthen themselves from their continued use for lifting.

Well, you all get the idea, I hope. In a nutshell we used a new technology that knew very little about until we unleashed it. We have also weakened the earth's magnetic field by using if for something other than what it was designed to do. In our haste to leave this dying planet we are accelerating its demise by our new technology.

President Farber declared a moratorium on Ark Ship Launches for one year. Ark Ship Two will launch in January of 2126. All ships crews will stay on board their respective ships and will launch in order.

Ark ship one left our solar system thirty days after launch and was still accelerating as it passed Pluto. It appeared that the speed of light meant nothing to the blue hole. Once the coordinates were laid into the computer the ship accelerated to a form of slipstream. Physics as we know them are being changed daily as astronomers try and keep track of Ark Ship One.

On February 1, 2126 President Farber extended his farewell and God speed to Ark Ship Two. Ship Two was then towed ten thousand miles into space by a magnetic sled. Once they were sufficiently away from the earth they engaged the blue hole drive. Ark Ship Two will explore our own Milky Way galaxy.

176

This time when the blue hole was engaged the satellites did not fail and no blackouts occurred. Tidal waves pounded the coastlines once again, but people had been move inland to avoid loss of life.

Twelve minor earthquakes were recorded with little to no loss of life or damage. All of the world's experts keeping an eye on the earth's magnetic fields noticed a slight shift in the polar axis but nothing out of the ordinary according to recorded history. The earth often shifts a little on its axis to compensate for solar winds, sunspots and shifts within the earth's magnetic core. Moving the Ark Ships away from the earth seemed to help immensely from the first launch.

Launches of ships three, four, five and six went off without a hitch with the exception of a larger than expected shift in the polar axis of the earth. The earth did not seem to recover as much between launches as expected. Tides and climate were affected the most by this slight shift. But since the earth was experiencing large climate changes anyway the added changes due to the launches mostly went unnoticed by the populace.

February 1, 2132 came and the launch of Ark Ship number seven was scheduled for 8:00 AM Belgium mean time. (Since the polar magnetic shift the standard of international time and date along with 0° Longitude had shifted from Greenwich, England to Brussels, Belgium.) Ark Ship #7 was contacted and given permission to launch. At exactly 9:03 AM the ship disintegrated thirty thousand miles from earth. Debris was scattered over thousands of miles across space and an investigation by the new World President Scott Johnson was initiated to find out what went wrong.

It took nearly a year until the final report was handed to President Johnson. The panels finding was that the containment field around the blue hole had suddenly collapsed allowing the blue hole to expand well beyond the ship's hull. A considerable portion of the ship and its crew were sucked into the blue hole before it collapsed in on itself. This left bits and pieces of floating space debris to capture and try and determine what had happened. The board came to the conclusion after finding only parts of the ship that were not part of the engine housing. No parts of the engine housing or its auxiliary compartments where ever found. All of those parts of the ship were considered drawn into the blue hole, thus the conclusion that the blue hole caused the destruction of the ship.

President Johnson ordered and immediate thorough check of the entire remaining blue hole drives on each of the remaining ships. No problems were ever found in any of the containment fields on any of the remaining ships.

One year from the date of the disaster of number seven, number eight was ready to launch. At exactly 9:00 AM Paris, France mean time permission to launch was given by President Johnson.

The Blue Hole ISLSD was engaged and the ship launched perfectly. With each subsequent launch the earth seem to suffer more magnetic polar shift that was not corrected by the year in between launches. By the time Ark Ship #11 was ready for launch the $0°$ Meridian had shifted as far east as Moscow.

February 1, 2146 Ark Ship #11 was towed into the launching area fifteen thousand miles from earth. This precaution was taken because of the polar shifts taking place after each launch. It is also the distance limit of the new anti-gravity sleds used to ferry the ship to the launch point. All was ready on board and by now the crew had become accustomed to the ship and had been living aboard it for almost ten years. During that time Dr. David Martin had sincerely tried to develop a relationship with Dr. Harold Boranum and his family. The children were always friendly but Harold and Miranda kept their distance. David knew that his job was going to be a difficult one.

Last minute preparations were made for launch and everyone took their places in their assigned launch stations.

Permission to launch was granted and the captain crossed her fingers and engaged the blue hole drive. Immediately a shudder was felt throughout the ship as it started to move away from the earth. The vibrations decreased and the acceleration was smooth and swift. Ark Ship #11 was pulling away from earth never to return. Everybody on board breathed a sigh of relief when the ship passed the planet Pluto and left the known universe surrounding earth.

Meanwhile back on earth the launch of #11 caused destruction on earth of unimaginable proportions. One hundred foot Tsunami waves pelted most of the earth's coastlines. Earthquakes hit thirty percent of the populated sections of earth. Sixteen new or extinct volcanoes began to erupt pouring molten lava into the remaining oceans and into some populated areas. The world was thrown into utter chaos.

The population started to move into the underground bunkers that were being built to house the remaining survivors of earth. The launch of Ark Ship #12 was accelerated to launch six months after #11. Damage to the earth's magnetic fields was permanent and lasting.

President Johnson made the decision to launch #12 before it was too late and his mission was the same as President Farber's before him. Save the human race from extinction. On August twelve in the year 2147Ark ship #12 was launched. The launching causes a north-south shift in the earth's magnetic poles and the earth starts to wobble on its axis. Bunker construction is moving ahead at a fever pitch.

By 2150 the earth has been decimated by natural and un-natural phenomenon. Earthquakes, floods, volcanoes, and lightning storms the likes have never been recorded. The last of the survival bunkers are finished and what remains of the earth's population moves underground to protect themselves against the raging storms and climate. Shortly after that food and water shortages begin to plague the bunkers. Anarchy reigns underground. By the year 2155 all communications are lost between the bunkers throughout the world. Power and resources are depleting at a devastating rate. Finally power fails and the only hope for the human race are the Ark Ships.

Chapter 12 - Ark Ship Destinations

Each of the Ark Ships had their own destination. Each one would travel generations to reach their final destinations.

Air Bus - 1 - Explorer the Andromeda galaxy destination 300,000 light years.

Air Bus - 2 - Explorer the Milky Way galaxy destination 160,000 light years.

Air Bus - 3 - Explorer the Ursula Minor galaxy destination 230,000 light years.

Air Bus - 4 - Explorer the Born's Nebula galaxy destination 400,000 light years.

LBG - 5 - Explorer Fornum's galaxy destination 500,000 light years.

LBG - 6 - Explorer Blasteoff's galaxy destination 500,000 light years.

LBG - 7 - (Exploded on launch) was to explore Galileo galaxy destination 600,000 light years.

LBG - 8 - Explorer Sheppard's galaxy destination 1,000,000 light years.

Bell - EAD 9 - RE - Explorer Farnsworth's Galaxy destination 700,000 light years.

Bell - EAD 10 - RE - Explorer Bagroom galaxy destination 400,000 light years.

Bell -EAD II - RE - Explorer Fennel's galaxy destination 1,200,000 light years.

Bell - EAD 12 - RE - Explorer the Crimson galaxy destination 2,000,000 light years.

Each ship had a destination galaxy once they arrived in the galaxy then their exploration would begin to find a planet suitable for habitation or one that could be terra-formed to be habitable.

Generations would pass before any of the ships would reach their galaxies. So each ship got into their routine of suspended animation and revival. Each fifty years the crews would be awakened for a period of four weeks. Those crewmembers that became pregnant during that time would be left awake for the term of the pregnancy. Once the child was delivered then it would be raised by the awake crew maintenance teams until the child reached twenty years of age and then they would be put into suspended animation and the cycle would start all over again. Ships did reach their destinations and new colonies of humans were formed on distant and unnamed planets. For Ark Ship #11 almost 3,000 years passed until their galaxy was reached. During that very long time frame Dr. Harold Boranum continued his experiments on the lengthening of life through genetics and mechanics. During that time he perfected his HRman. He also discovered the elixir of life. Unbeknownst to some of the crewmembers he had injected this elixir into them while they were in stasis. The successful trials had the effect of not aging the person being given the genetic elixir.

The unsuccessful trials caused several of the crewmembers to perish. Their bodies were consumed by the ships systems for total recycle. During his awake cycles Dr. Martin would check his gene storage and take a complete inventory. So far nothing was out of the ordinary. He made sure his awake cycle coincided with Dr. Boranum's so that he could keep an eye on him at all times.

So in the year 4928 the crew of Ark Ship #11 was awakened. Their ships automated systems had located a likely planet for habitation. The ship put itself into a geosynchronous orbit around the planet and alerted the crew. Now the real work would begin. Each crewmember had aged approximately twenty-three years during their 2,892-year journey. None of them knew that they had all been given the elixir of life. All of them were completely stripped of the genetic preservation liquid and they all set about the myriad of tests to make sure this planet was suitable for habitation.

Dr. Boranum knew that he and his wife had not aged but about ten years during their voyage and his HRmen children had not aged one single day.

Dr. David Martin went about checking his precious cargo. He put on his BAG suit and checked every container personally as to their viability and survival. Every cask had made the journey intact. The outer shell of one of the bubbles had been penetrated by a small meteorite but the inner bubble was intact and its precious cargo was safe and sound. He repaired the damage to the outer bubble and refilled it with the heavy water and all was well in the genetic storage compartments. He extracted samples of genetic materials from each storage cask to be analyzed to see if any unknown radiation might have damaged any of the material. He was getting ready to withdraw his first sample when a new diver appeared beside him.

It was Dr. Boranum. Harold swam up beside him and said, "Do you mind if I help you checking these containers? It is a big job and it will go faster if two of us do it rather than one." David was a little taken back by Harold's chummy attitude all of a sudden, but in the spirit of extending an olive branch to make amends for almost three thousand years of petty jealously between the two of them he said, "I would love your help Harold." The two of them went to work and in no time at all they had extracted a sample from each of the casks. David said, "I see you remember all of your training from back on earth. Since I haven't seen you too much during the voyage I was surprised by your offer to help." Harold looked at him and said, "I have had many years to mellow my attitude David. Years spent in sleep seemed to have washed away all the bad

189

memories I have of us. Besides, here we are on the verge of discovering and maybe populating a new world and I would like to start anew with a clean slate with everyone. Miranda and I want to be part of the new population that helps develop this planet if it ends up to be one that we can work with."

David said, "I think that would be wonderful. It looks like a very big world down there and I am sure there is room on it for all of us. I think with your training and background in human genetics that you would be an ideal person to head up the new creations branch." Harold winced at that remark but said, "I will be glad to help in any way that I can. Who knows, maybe Miranda and I can set up our own little kingdom down there."

David just looked at him and didn't say a thing. They both went back to the BAG chambers and started to remove their suits. Once the transformation was complete and they were both standing there in their bathing suits David said, "We will not only have to develop creatures, crops, foodstuffs and new humans we will also have to develop a system of government and order. We have plenty of political science personnel to help handle the new earth structure. It will be up to people like you and me to be creative in our creations so they will blend in with this new environment." " Let's make a deal David," said Harold. "You can have the oceans and I will take care of the land creatures."

David just looked at him and said, "I think the ship's captain, Lydia Green, will make those kind of decisions once we decide if this is a viable planet or not. Let's not get too far ahead of ourselves until we know for sure what we need to do down there."

When you gazed down upon the planet from the view ports it was a beautiful sight. There are several large landmasses covered with green,

191

brown, and white colors. There was an abundance of white clouds. There were areas of blue green that could be oceans or seas. To the far north on top of the planet was a very large white area that could be a polar ice cap. With the orbit the ship was in it was hard to see the southern region of the planet. Some landmasses could be identified through the heavy cloud cover but no clear view was visible.

Chapter 13 - Planet 1 of the Fennel Galaxy

On the third day in orbit Captain Lydia
Green called for a meeting of all department
heads. She wanted to summarize all of the
findings from all of the laboratories on board to
ascertain whether or not she could send down an
exploratory expedition. When all were assembled
she stood at the table and said, "Well, ladies and
gentlemen, you have had three days to test and
dissect this planet to see whether or not we can
live here. What have you found? First I would like
to hear from atmosphere-weather and climate."
Martin Bell stood and said, "The atmosphere is
made up of 24% oxygen, 75% nitrogen, and the
other one percent is made up of argon, helium,

CO2, hydrogen and an element we have not identified yet. It seems inert but we would like to have at least another day to study it. The climate temperatures range from -60°F at the northern most readable zone to a very hot 130°F in what we think are desert regions. We have ascertained that there is rain and wind storms and have witnesses several storms at what we think are seas or oceans. We believe there will be four or five climate changes per year based on information for the Astro-metrics department. So in conclusion the air is very breathable maybe a little richer in oxygen that we are used to but still very breathable. The climate is similar or was similar to earth's way back when so finding a habitable spot will not be a problem." Then he sat down and Lydia said, "Now let's hear from Astro-metrics."

John Guilgood stood and said, "The planet is slightly larger than earth and is rotating slightly

194

faster than earth. The gravity is about the same as earths with the exception of several areas on several different continents. In those areas we have discovered anomalies that gravity may be turned upside down. We just can't explain it yet. These areas seem to be isolated and do not extend very far on the landmasses. We would like to put them off limits for the time being until we can study them from the ground. This planet that we have called planet 1 until it can be named is orbiting around a yellow-red sun that is about twice the size of earth's sun. In this solar system we have found sixteen such planets orbiting this yellow-red star. The planet we are orbiting is the eight planet from this sun. The orbit around the sun will take approximately three hundred and seventy days. The planet has an axis that is tilted at four degrees toward the sun during this portion of its orbiting travel. Solar radiation is slightly less than earth but this may be due to the type of sun and the atmosphere surrounding the planet. This also needs more study. We have found several bands of radiation that are unknown to us which warrants further study. Strangely this planet has two moons. The larger moon is shadowed by a smaller on held in place by the gravitational pull of the larger moon. Each moon is spinning on its own axis. The smaller moon is never seen it is permanently held in place by the larger moon. We don't know yet what all this means these are our first findings." John sat down and Lydia stood up and said, "Now what has geology found out?"

Francis Dorn stood and said, "From all indications the planet is about 400,000 earth years old. It has very dense forests covering more than 60% of the planets landmasses. Maybe that accounts for the larger amount of oxygen. There are several regions on the planet that have active volcano activity. Most of these are located in the northern hemisphere. We have not determined yet what that means and warrants further study.

We have not been able to take soil or plant samples as of yet but believe that the planet supports the type of and variety of plant life that was prevalent on earth some five thousand years ago. We have observed no indigenous life forms as of yet. Our cameras have located some animal life forms, but not very many. We have located some herds of animals to the north of a mountain range, but have not located any type of beings or any dwellings. It looks like a world on the brink of habitation. Francis sat down and Lydia said, "Ok, genetics, Your turn."

David Martin stood and said, "We have had our camera's trained on the planet surface for forty-eight hours now and have observed no bipedal life forms. We have seen flying creatures, grazing creatures and have seen the dense forests which we think contains not only deciduous trees but also conifers and there is one tree that stands out in one particular forest that must stand two to three hundred feet tall while all the other trees around it are shorter. We have sampled the atmosphere for germs, viruses, and bacteria that would be harmful to human life. We have found two viruses that we cannot identify, four germs and seventeen kinds of bacteria that we would like to identify and study. If precautions are taken by a discovery team I think most of the medicines we have on board will do the trick. I would like to be on the discovery team so that I can take the proper samples for our lab workup. I think the discovery team should use pressurized suits for their first mission. After all of us have had time to test the samples we will bring back I think we can make a better decision on habitation? I would also like to suggest that Dr. Harold Boranum be on the discovery team as well. His aid and input would be most valuable on obtaining all the genetic samples we will need from the planet's surface along with its flora and fauna."

198

David sat down and Lydia Green stood and said, "I will post the crew of Discovery Team One tomorrow morning at zero nine hundred. We will take shuttle module one down to the surface. We will all wear pressure suits and breathe our atmosphere until we know it is safe. We will also go through decontamination upon our return from the planet which means we will spend two days in isolation after we return while the medical team thoroughly goes over each and every one of us to allow us to return to normal ship's crew quarters. Dr. Bellemay the ships physician and surgeon will take the lead on our decontamination. I agree with Dr. Martin that Dr. Boranum would be a good addition to our initial investigation of the planet. He will be added to the discovery team roster. I will lead the first team myself. We will only spend six hours on the surface so prepare your tests and sample gathering accordingly. We have spotted a large river running close to a very dense forest and that is where we will land first. Soil and water samples will be gathered along with any plant and animal samples we can gather. No one is to remove their masks or suits while on the surface, is that clearly understood by everyone." Everybody nodded their heads in approval and Lydia concluded the meeting by saying, "We reconvene here at zero nine thirty tomorrow morning. Everyone check the posting board and notify your members by that time.

Harold caught David as he was leaving the meeting and asked him how it went. David covered all the reports with him and told him that he would be a member of the discover team and that they would be leaving sometime tomorrow morning and the team would be wearing pressure suits for this first mission. Harold said, "Why do we have to wear the pressure suits and be in quarantine for so long? Isn't this the planet we are going to habitat?" David looked at Harold and gave a little sigh and said, "These are Captain

Green's orders and I suggest we follow them. We don't know for sure what all is down there. We could bring something back that could infect the whole crew and all that we have onboard. I think she is just taking the necessary safety precautions to protect the entire mission." Harold said, "I just think this is all so un-necessary and I am going to have a talk with her!" Before David could say anything else Harold stormed off to see the Captain.

Chapter 14 - Discovery Mission One

     The next morning as promised the personnel list of Mission One was posted. Twelve people in all were listed. One name was not on the list and that was Dr. Harold Boranum. Promptly at 9:30 AM Captain Lydia Green entered the meeting room and took her place at the head of the table. She looked at each person before she said, "Are there any questions about the mission and the crew?" David spoke up and said, "Captain I thought you had intended to include Dr. Boranum on this mission?" She replied, "Yes, you are correct I was. That is until I met with him yesterday evening in my quarters and he explained how stupid and trite the idea of wearing pressure suits would be. He also said that if he had to wear one that he would rather not be part of the exploration team. So I accommodated him by removing him from the list. I think he was rather angry when he left, but I haven't seen him anywhere this morning so maybe he is cooling his attitude somewhere below decks.

Command shuttle number one will leave the Ark Ship in one hour. Have all of your gear transferred and stowed aboard in the next thirty minutes. We will all muster at the locking ring dock at that time for final instructions. This meeting is dismissed I will see you all in one hour."

In one hour all twelve team members gathered at the entrance to the shuttle with the Captain and her co-pilot Lieutenant Fred Bisselgrom. They went over the flight plan with everyone and told everyone to get aboard and start suiting up. They planned to be on the

planet's surface in less than thirty minutes. Just
as the command module doors were closing
Harold Boranum came running up the
passageway with his pressure suit in his arms.
The Captain stood in the doorway and said,
"Sorry, Dr. Boranum. You will have to set this one
out. Maybe next time you will not be so adamant
in dealing with me." She stepped back into the
door and closed it in his face.

The locking ring released the command
ship and the Captain started her decent to the
planet's surface.

Harold was still standing and staring at the
air lock door. He flew into a rage and raced back
down the hallway to his quarters. Miranda and the
children were sitting watching the command ship
pull away and head toward the planet on their
video wall. When Harold entered he told them to
pack some belongings and follow him to Genetics
Lab #5. Miranda said, "What are we doing, where

are we going?" Harold smiled and said, "Why, darling, we are going to our new home." They did as he requested and they all went to Genetics Lab #5. This was his own personal laboratory and no one had the key except him. They entered the lab and he opened a small cupboard that held four small wrist bracelets. He handed one to each of them and told them to place it on the arms just above the wrist. He cautioned them that there would be a slight pinch when they first put it on but after that it would be very comfortable. He placed his on his wrist and went to a computer station and turned it on. As each person put on the bracelet it identified each of them and stored their DNA sequence in his computer. They were all looking at him when he turned and said. "We are going down to the planet surface my way. Now I want us all to hold hands and stay that way until we are down there", as he pointed toward the floor. They all joined hands and Harold pushed a small button on his bracelet and there was a gust of wind that started spinning around them. It started spinning faster and faster and they began to blur and then all of them disappeared from the ship and within seconds they appeared on the surface of the planet still holding hands. When they landed there was another gust of wind that kicked up some dust which got in their eyes for a moment.

When the dust cleared they were standing in a meadow. Miranda said, "What did we just do?" Harold beamed from ear to ear and said, "I invented this device on our awake time during our trip here. It is a genetic transfer device that recorded our DNA and then broke it into molecules and transferred us to the location I entered into the computer. We are in the southern region of the largest land mass. I declare this to be our new home!" To the north of them they saw some gray mountains. All around them was very fertile grassland with some forests bordering it. Some of the trees were a purple orange color and some were green.

Gerald was the first to spy an insect of some kind flittering through the air. He pointed and called out to them, "Look, it looks like a cross between a bee and a butterfly." Gerald ran after it but was suddenly aware of another creature crawling in the tall grass. He called out, "Quick come over here and look at this." They all crowded around him to see what he was looking at. What they say looked like a bird but it was walking not flying. It had all blue feathers and legs like a human that were also covered with the same blue feathers. It had a very short orange beak and large round white eyes. It clicked and clattered at them as they stood their staring at it.

Harold spun around and said, "We have been here less than five minutes and we have already discovered two new species that live here." He suggested that all of them walk around for a while and try and discover all the new things they could. Miranda found a spot close to the forest that she thought was charming.

She turned to Harold and said, "Oh, Harold can we build a house right here in this spot? It has flowers; it has running water and is surrounded on three sides by the forest." Harold could see her excitement and said to her, "Yes my darling we can and will build our home right here." They had packed a light lunch which the leisurely ate while sitting on a fallen tree.

The children were running here and there finding new and exciting creatures at every turn. After spending about four hours Harold rounded them all together and said to them, "This will be our little secret. I don't want anyone to know how we got here and where we are. Little by little we will transfer our belongings to this area and when we have completed all of that we will permanently transfer down and start our own civilization right

208

here. Let the others settle where they want to, I claim this for us. We shall become King and Queen of our own Kingdom. I will transfer my laboratory down over there and we can start to transform this place as we see fit." They all looked at him in stunned silence and then cheered.

Harold called them together and told them to hold hands. When they were holding each other Harold pushed the button on his wrist and there was a swish of air and they disappeared from the planet and reappeared in Genetics Laboratory #5. Harold reminded them that they couldn't tell anyone what they had done. It would have to be their secret for now.

What Harold didn't know is that each of his children had brought a small pet back with them from the surface. It was a very tiny creature. It looked a little like a transparent monkey. It had six legs and had the ability to change its color and shape to mimic what the children were thinking it

209

should look like. It was so small that if fit in the tunic pocket of Melissa's cloak. Neither Gerald nor Melissa told them about their new pet. They called it" Pillowpod," which was a character from a book they both had read while being programmed back on earth.

They all left the lab and made their way back to their quarters without being seen and were in time to watch the docking of the Command Ship with the Ark. They watched as the twelve members of the discovery team were ushered into quarantine along with the Captain and the co-pilot. There they would remain for two days until they were approved by the medical team to re-enter the ships population. All of their samples they gathered were transferred to the separate laboratories in vacuum- sealed containers which would only be unloaded in the vacuum chambers of each lab.

Scientists from all nationalities started to study, dissect, probe, and analyze every bit of material brought up from the planet. Inside every vacuum chamber of every lab there was at least one electron microscope and mass spectrometer that could be remotely controlled from outside the chamber.

Within a matter of hours data started pouring into the central computer to detail every bit of scientific discovery of every sample.

Meanwhile in isolation, the discovery team had shed their pressure suits for drab and loose fitting medical gowns and tunics. They had access to all of the data that was being fed to the computer from all the different and diverse laboratories throughout the Ark. Every time a new bit of information was entered a cheer went up from the discovery team. It looked as though, as the reports kept coming in, that there was no killer bacteria, germs or viruses located on the planet that the human body could not contend with. The Captain was optimistic about the next mission being one without pressure suits but wanted to wait until all of the samples had been analyzed. All the reports seemed to be very positive. Several live specimens had been captured and returned to the Ark labs. Some were very strange and some were very similar to earth type creepy crawlers. No humanoid life forms had been observed or discovered during their mission. All the scientists speculated that with the growth observed and some of the insect life witnessed that there should certainly be some form of humanoid or bipedal life forms somewhere on the planet's surface.

The Captain had decided to make a thorough search of the planet's surface using infra-red imaging to see if they could find clusters of heat signatures which would indicate a gathering of some sort of life forms. She was

212

looking for a settlement or city or town of some sort that they could possibly observe and maybe land near to meet the inhabitants of this world.

The discovery crew had just completed forty-eight in medical isolation when the meteor struck the Ark. It was a very large one. It was about forty meters in diameter and of all places to hit, the impact was located just forward of the propulsion chambers. Which also cut off most of the labs and life pods except for Genetic storage. A considerable portion of the ship depressurized immediately killing eighty-five percent of the crew and crippling the Ark.

Chapter 15 - The Meteor

Alarms were sounding everywhere.
Pressure doors were shutting all over the Ark and
sealing off compartments and sections of the ship.
Fortunately the medical bay and lab were sealed
off immediately and everyone in isolation was
unhurt. Large chunks of the ship started breaking
away and drifting into space and some were being
drawn down toward the planet to be burned up in

the atmosphere. Several on the discovery team were knocked unconscious when the meteor struck the Ark. Captain Green shouted over the intercom to the doctor, "Get us out of here now!" The doctor replied, "That would be breaking your standard protocol Captain." Lydia took a deep breath and calmly said, "I order you to release us from quarantine. Do it now!" Reluctantly the doctor pressed the release button and the door to the quarantine pod slid open.

Captain Green went to the nearest intercom and said, "Command center this is Med lab what is the status of the ship? This is Captain Green." There was nothing but static over the intercom. Then finally a voice came over and said, "Captain, this is Harold Boranum I am in the command center and there is no one alive in here. Two of the crewmen are lying on the floor. I have checked them for a pulse and there is none. What do you want me to do?"

215

Captain Green calmly said, "Harold, go to the status board on the starboard side of the command center there is an array of red and green lights with a diagram of the entire ship. It displays all of the hatches and sections of the ship. Under each hatch is a red and green light. Red means it is closed and green means it is opened. Each pod and section of the ship is also indicated with a red and green light. Green will mean the compartment is pressurized and is normal in temperature. A red light by each compartment means it is depressurized or there is a fire in that section." In the background over the intercom all of them could hear alarms sounding behind Dr. Boranum's voice. Lydia continued, "I want you to start at the left end of that board and tell me every light that is red and every light that is green."

Harold said, "Can you tell me how to silence this awful sounding alarm up here?"

Lydia said, "Just to the left of the status board there are a group of buttons. One of them is purple and it is labeled MASTER ALARM SILENCE. Push that button and all alarms will stop for three minutes. Then it will sound again if there is still an alarm. If it sounds again keep pushing it. Now give me the status of my ship." Harold must have found the button and pushed it because the alarm went silent. Harold started to read all the indicator lights from front to back on the status board. Captain Green wrote down everything Harold told her. Then all at once the alarm sounded again and then went silent again.

Harold came back on the line and said. Everything after the medical bay is a red light or no light. Most of the lights are completely dark after the Med lab." Captain Green put her hand to her forehead and said, "It is worse than I thought. All the crew quarters are either gone or depressurized. Astro-metrics, Geology, Physics,

Health Sciences, and life pods are either gone or inoperative. The majority of the crew was back there. The only thing we have left is Genetics, Medical, provision storage, genetic labs and storage along with the command center and the forward eating areas. Since we are still breathing I suspect that all of the pressure doors have sealed off everything aft of our location."

She looked at the notes she had written from Harold's description of the status board. Then she said, "We can make our way to the command center via the port side access tubes. It looks like the starboard ones are either gone or damaged. I need to get to the control center and assess the damage to the ship. Dr. Martin I need you to go to genetic storage and assess any damage to the material in storage. Take three of the team with you. Don't be a hero, if there is a major problem back there then, do not try to open any sealed doors. If you cannot enter the storage

facility come forward to the command center."
She then got on the ship-wide announce system
and said, "Any crewmember who can hear my
voice make your way to the command center. If
you cannot get to the command center then call in
on the intercom. DO NOT OPEN ANY SEALED
PRESSURE DOORS. SOMETHING HAS HIT
THE ARK OR AN EXPLOSION HAS DAMAGED
US AND WE ARE ASSESSING THE DAMAGE.
Rescue teams will find you if you cannot make it to
the command center." She turned off the intercom
left the Med Lab and headed forward.

Dr. Martin and two other crewmembers
headed aft to the genetic storage facility. Upon
arriving at Genetic Storage Bay #1 the pressure
door was jammed shut and tight. It would not
open. There was a flashing red light above the
door indicating an automatic closure. Dr. Martin
looked through the small six inch round window in
the door and could see that two of the outer

bubble shields had been penetrated by metal columns that had been knocked free during the collision or explosion or whatever destroyed the ship. They continued onto bay #2 then #3 through #16. All of these storage bays seemed undamaged in any way. The bubbles were still intact and all lights were green on the monitoring systems. Once they were satisfied that most of the material was OK they made their way back to the command center.

Upon arriving at the command center David gave his report to Lydia and told her that they could not get into Bubble #1 storage but he thought the bay was secure. He described what he had seen she agreed with his assessment.

Then he said, "Have you discovered what happened?" She didn't answer him right away, she just pointed to the large video monitor in the command center which showed the rear section of the Ark. There was a huge hole in the rear section of the Ark. There was massive destruction of the ships framework, railings, pods, storage chambers, and living quarters. One of the blue hole drives was still connected to the ship the other two were completely gone. There were still minor sparks and arcs of electricity and metal debris everywhere. Then David saw the bodies, "Oh my God," he said. There were bodies floating in orbit with the ship, some still caught in the metal debris, and some of them frozen to the superstructure outside the ship. He turned to Lydia and said, "How many of us survived?"

Captain Green turned to them all and said, "It looks like only about twenty five of us survived. Of the twenty five survivors six are injured and have been transferred to Med Lab. Another 4 are trapped in part of the rear section. What you see here in the control room is the only hope for human kind for this planet below us. We still have life support, food, gravity, and water. The genetic material survived so we will use it down on the planet. Since Terra-forming and robotics were part of genetics we still have that. We also have the two best genetics people in the galaxy to help us colonize this planet. Now let's try and get to those trapped four crewmembers in section 321. Maybe we can use the command shuttle to get them free.

Harold turned to them and said, "I have a better idea. I have developed a genetic transfer device that I think I can use to get them back here to safety. If David will come help me I think together we can transport them to Genetics Lab #5." The captain looked first at David then at Harold and said, "I have no idea what you're talking about, but you and David give it a try. Let me know if you are successful."

Harold turned to David and said, "I will explain it to you on the way to the lab." Once inside the lab Harold set about putting in the coordinates for section 321 and continued to fill David in on what he thought he could do with his new device. Harold pulled four more bracelets from a drawer and put them in a small canvas bag he slung over his shoulder. He handed David a radio and said. Once I get to them, I will call you on this radio and tell you their names. When I tell you who they are, please enter their names into this computer in those four blank spaces. After you have done that hit enter and call me back to let me know everything is ready." David said he understood and would do as he asked. Harold pushed the button on his wrist bracelet and with a whoosh of air he vaporized inside the cyclone of air. A few seconds later he was calling David on the radio. He said, "David here are the crewmembers names, please enter them now." David entered the names then pressed enter and called Harold on the radio and let him know everything was ready. There was a bigger cyclone of air this time and suddenly five people started appearing in the cloud of air. When the air died down, there stood Harold and the other four crewmembers. David was flabbergasted. He had never seen anything like this before. Harold picked up the ships intercom and notified Captain Green that the crewmembers were all safe and where on their way to the command center.

After the crew had left David turned to Harold and said, "That was the most remarkable thing I have ever seen. When did you invent this and how does it work?" Harold said, "I built it on my awake times during our trip here. As for how it works, well let's say that will be one of my little secrets for now." David continued, "But Harold this can get us anywhere in the ship or even down to the planet without having to use the command module. This is worth sharing with Captain Green." " No," said Harold. "I am not ready to share this with anyone. The only reason I saved those worthless lives was to gain favor with the captain. Do you think I give two hoots about anyone on this vessel? You forget, I can create any human or HRman I want to. I can be King of this world if I want to." He turned to the computer and typed in David's name then went to the drawer and withdrew another bracelet. He slapped in on David's wrist and hit the enter button at the same time he pushed the button on David's bracelet. David disappeared in a cloud of wind. He waited for about thirty seconds and then erased David's name from the computer. Harold knew that he had to move fast now that he had transported David to the planet's surface. He didn't know exactly where he had sent him, he knew it was somewhere in the deep forest covering most of the northern landmass. He grabbed the rest of his bracelets and headed for the command center. When he arrived he passed out a bracelet to each of the remaining crewmembers telling them that it was used for keeping track of them genetically. Everyone put on the bracelet even Captain Green. Within a matter of two days all remaining crewmembers had been transported to the planet's surface except for the Boranum family. Harold turned to his family and said, "Now that we are alone, we can begin our work. With only four of us left on board there will be ample supplies and equipment for us to survive until we are ready to take our rightful place as rulers of this new planet."

They set about repairing what was left of the ship and the children set about cutting away portions of the ship that was damaged and together they transformed the huge ship into a smaller more compact one with one main engine and all of the genetic materials they would need to repopulate the planet below. Pieces of the ship that were going to be discarded due to damage were hauled into the remaining storage bays and Gerald and Melissa soon went about creating robots out of the materials salvaged from the ship

226

and some parts from the ships stores. They created physicians, engineers, along with some domestic helpers and finally they put together a warrior robot. Harold and Miranda started to prepare for the species that would be needed to serve them on the planet as well as some new comers that they would simply fit into the environment on the planet below. They found two-escape shuttlecraft that they repaired and were big enough to haul material and equipment to the surface to start building their home as well as their new laboratory. Miranda was the best wife and helper that Harold could have asked for. She agreed with most everything he said and was becoming a very good geneticist in her own right. Her records of new species and what was used to make them was impeccable. Harold had dubbed himself King Harold, Steward of the Ark Where Civilization Began. Miranda became, Queen Miranda, Holder of the Register of All Races. They spent nearly six months preparing for their launch to the surface. When all was ready Harold and Miranda transported to the surface of the planet using the bracelets and the children piloted the first shuttlecraft loaded with equipment and robots.

Upon landing they set about creating beings to till the land and grow crops. They would be known as Bengarie. They were very muscular and had been genetically engineered to toil tirelessly in the soil. They were assigned to an eastern portion of the southern region which was rich in soil water. Harold and Miranda entered their species into the Register of All Races. They were the first of the beings that would be created out of their fertile minds.

Chapter 16 - THE Bengarie (First Race - Second Nation)

The Bengarie were developed to be farmers. The male and female of the species look similar in nature. The female is the same height and build as the male and also has an infinite knowledge of agronomy. The female has two mammary glands protruding from her back just about were the shoulder blades would be located. Harold and Miranda put them there so that the children of the Bengarie could be carried on the backs of the females as they worked the fields. The children could feed and would not take time away from raising the crops. This would also keep them close to the land because they would be carried until they could help in the fields with the adults. They have very dark complexions from spending most of their time in the sun. Their skin deflects the ultraviolet rays from the sun. They have three toes on each of two feet. The toes help them dig in the field. One of the toes on each foot has a venom sack that can expel a poison that will disable a man in a matter of seconds. They are not warriors but are very skilled with a sling spear and sling axe. The tips of the spear and the blade of the axe are made from a black metal mined only in Bengarie land. It is one of their most highly regarded secrets. Their blades are said to be able to penetrate the doors of the Ark, but that is only a legend. No one really knows if that is true or not. They were bred to be somewhat docile but over the years have developed independence and an attitude of solidarity. They also have developed the art of foot fighting and taken it to a new level. They have been known to attack other beings with their feet and have immobilized them with their toe venom. The Bengarie is a matriarchal society and is ruled by a Queen. When challenged they are fierce fighters, but mostly to protect their lands and rights.

The Bengarie supply the majority of the food and fresh water to the southern region. King Harold and Queen Miranda have not interfered with the Bengarie and let them develop a society of their own. If they were to cut the food and water supply then Harold and Miranda would take steps to control them.

231

Chapter 17 – Transport of the Ark Crew

Harold Boranum made sure that he separated the crewmembers when he transported them to the planet's surface. The only two people he remotely placed close together were Captain Lydia Green and Dr. David M. Martin. Everyone else was transported all over the planet's surface. Green and Martin were both transported to the largest forest on the planet. Lydia was dropped into the middle of the forest and David was placed close to a lake on the edge of the forest. Each crewmember had been trained in survival and they immediately started to rely on that training.

Captain Green found the largest tree in her immediate surroundings and made it her home. This one tree towered above the largest of the forest greenery. She knew there was something special about this tree. At night it would ooze a honey like liquid from certain branches. This thick sap like material had healing and medicinal properties. While climbing the tree she scraped her shin. By accident some of this sap dripped on the scrape, immediately the pain disappeared and by morning the wound was healed.

After she had been in the forest for about three months she felt like she was being watched. She could never see who or what was watching her, but she just knew. It was one of those things like you just see something move at the very edge of your vision but when you turn nothing is there.

She constructed a very large and covered platform from downed tree branches or dead wood she had gathered from the forest. It was about one hundred feet off the ground. The tree had been very easy to climb since its branches started extending from the trunk of the tree about two feet off the ground. Her shelter was held together with vines that she had gathered from the surrounding forest. She made sure that when she cut a vine she only took part of it and left the rest to re-grow. It had taken her almost all of her time here just to construct her new home. From her tree house high up in this large tree she had sort of a bird's eye view of the entire forest. Of course it stretched on for miles and she couldn't see the edges from her tree house. It was like a sea of green that stretched out before her. She wandered the woods every day in search of berries or fruit that would sustain her.

She had lost several pounds of weight but her muscles had sculpted her body into a very lean and attractive female. She often wondered what became of the rest of the crew and dreamed of some type of revenge against Dr. Harold Boranum.

Lydia desperately wanted to find the other crewmembers, being alone was not her cup of tea. She had long ago discarded the bracelet that Boranum had tricked her and the rest of the crew to wear. She was lonely and in need of company. The forest would answer her wishes. It was as though the forest read her mind for one morning as she awakened from her sleep sitting at the foot of her bed was a short person. She rubbed her eyes at first thinking she was still dreaming. When she took her hands from her eyes the little fellow was still sitting there looking at her. She sat up with a start and the little guy fell off the end of the bed onto the floor.

He was dressed all in green leather material and stood just about four feet tall. He wore a green pointed hat with a leaf stuck into the side of it. His eyes were an emerald green with a slight almond shape and his hair which stuck out from under his hat was as red as the tree leaves in autumn. He had oversized large ears and a nose that seemed to jut out of his face. His cheeks were round and a little pink. His mouth seemed to be continually smiling. Over his shoulder was a leather strap from which hung a small leather pouch. His tunic and trousers looked like they were sewn together with spider web. His pointed leather moccasins came high up on his ankles and were closed with a strap wound around a seashell. They both just stood there and looked at each other without saying a word. Finally the little guy opened up his leather pouch and walked over to her table and poured out about a quart of strawberries. Lydia squealed with delight and went over and hungrily ate four of the largest

236

ones. Then remembering her manners, she picked up several of the berries and held them out at arm's length toward the little guy. He smiled and said, "Why thank you very much, I don't mind if I do." Lydia was amazed and fell back on a makeshift chair and just sat there and watched the little guy inhale the strawberries.

When he was finished licking his fingers she said, "Who are you and how do you know my language? Where do you come from? Are there many of you? Where is your home?" The little guy held up his hand and said, "Hold on my dear those are too many questions to answer. I suggest you follow me and I will show you the keepers of the forest. My name is Elmwook and I am a tree keeper. What is your name? What kind of tree keeper are you? Where did you come from? Why are you living in the Knanga Tree? It is the oldest tree in the forest."

"My name is Lydia Green and I am the captain of the explorer ship Bell-ADA-1RE. I come from the stars in hopes of making this my home. I picked this tree because it offers me the most safety and the best view of the forest."

Elmwook just looked at her and tilted his head sideways as if trying to understand all that she had said and then replied, "You may want to put on some clothes before you meet Captain Firfare." He just motioned for her to follow him. She didn't realize that she had been standing in front of him in her underwear and quickly threw on a tee shirt, trousers, and shoes along with her tattered Oriole's baseball cap and then followed him down the tree to the ground. She had thought she had pulled the vine ladder up the night before, but evidently she had forgotten too and that is how Elmwook found his way up to her tree house.

Once on the ground Elmwook was very light of foot and took off at a very fast pace

through the forest. Lydia had to jog to keep up
with him. After about twenty minutes of jogging
they came to section of the forest that was
absolutely beautiful. The forest itself was thinned
out somewhat letting sun filter through the upper
most branches and there were wildflowers growing
everywhere. Elmwook turned to Lydia and said,
"Welcome to Greenhaven." He pointed toward the
clearing in the trees. As Lydia looked she could
now see the village he was pointing too. There
looked to be hundreds of vine-covered homes in
the shape of pointed domes everywhere. They
would be almost impossible to see from the air.
They were perfectly camouflaged by their ivy and
flower coverings. There were children and people
moving everywhere. She could see crooked
chimneys poking out through the ivy coverings on
the tops of the homes. On the ground she could
see people cultivating the flowers and land and
then she saw what looked like gardens growing
melons, corn, carrots, turnips, lettuce, cabbage

and all sorts of vegetables. Elmwook started moving down the path toward the settlement and Lydia jogged after him. When they got to the base of one of the trees he put two fingers in his mouth and whistled so loudly that it hurt Lydia's ears. Almost immediately a wooden platform was lowered and Elmwook motioned for her to get aboard. Then he said, "I am taking you to the Captain of the Tree Keepers. She does not speak your language yet so I will have to be your talker. If you tell me what you have to say I will tell her and when she answers I will tell you in your language. She is sort of our Queen, but prefers to be called Captain. It is polite to slightly bow when you meet her. It is a sign of respect. Just follow my lead and everything will be just fine." He gave another shrill whistle and the platform began to ascend up into the trees. As they rose into the canopy Lydia could see many upturned faces looking at them from the ground.

240

Elmwook said, "They are very curious about you. We have been watching you since your arrival. They think you are a witch because you just appeared in a cloud of wind and dust. I was assigned to watch over you and to learn your talk. Do you know you do a lot of talking to yourself?" The platform stopped and two more Tree Keepers that looked very much like guards came forward and helped Elmwook and Lydia from the platform and onto a very large flat tree limb. Each of the Tree Keepers grabbed hold of one of Lydia's arms to steady her and they all walked toward a large arched shaped hole in the tree trunk. Once through the doorway the guards let go of her arms and she followed Elmwook up a circular staircase that had been carved into the tree. After climbing for a minute or two they emerged into a dwelling built in the canopy of the tree. It was a large circular room that was open to the forest on all sides. Shutters were propped up giving a panoramic view of the forest.

Sitting at a table in the center of the room was a woman with long flowing white hair. Her hair hung down below her shoulders almost to her waist. She was wearing the same emerald green leathers that Elmwook wore only they looked less weather beaten and more regal somehow. On her head she wore a laurel wreath with flowers woven into it.

As they approached her Elmwook slightly bowed and so did Lydia. The woman rose from her chair and spoke to Elmwook in a language that sounded more like birds talking than a spoken language. They twittered and squawked back and forth for a few minutes and then he turned to Lydia and said, "I have introduced you to our leader. Her name in your language would be pronounced Firfare. She asked me your name and I told her you were called Lady of the Green. I also told her you are a Captain and came from the stars to make this place your home. She asked me if you

242

were alone or if there are others like you in the forest? I told her you were the only one I have observed. Is that correct?"

Lydia said, "I am not alone, there should be more of my kind somewhere in this world. My crew and I were separated when my ship was damaged by a large rock high above your planet."

Elmwook tilted his head to the side again and turned back to Firfare and started chirping again. This conversation went on for a while with questions and answers back and forth.

Elmwook turned back to Lydia and said, "Firfare wants to know if you would like to look for the rest of your kind? She has also invited you to partake of our mid-day meal with her." Lydia said, "Tell Firfare that I would be delighted to eat with her and yes I would very much like to look for my crewmembers. My problem is I don't know where to look and I don't have any means of transportation."

Elmwook turned back to Firfare and started chirping again. Firfare moved forward and took Lydia's hand and directed her to the table where she had been sitting. Lydia was a good foot and a half taller than Firfare or Elmwook. When she sat down at the table her legs barely fit under the table. The chair was lower to the floor and she looked very uncomfortable. Firfare turned to Elmwook and chirped and twittered.

Elmwook turned to Lydia and said, "Firfare would like to know if you would feel better standing to eat or if you would like to sit on the floor on a cushion?"

Lydia's cheeks blushed a little and said, "A cushion would be nice." Two servants came forward and removed the table and chairs and brought a small center table and three cushions.

All three of them sat down around the small table as food was delivered and placed before them. Firfare started to twitter to Elmwook again and then pointed to Lydia's head. Elmwook turned to Lydia and said, "Firfare would like to know what type of head piece or crown you are wearing." Lydia was embarrassed that she had forgot to remove her hat as they entered the room. Lydia said, "Where I come from this is called a ball cap. The emblem on the front is a mascot of the team or group of people it represents. In this case it is a bird called the Baltimore Oriole. It is the symbol of a team that comes from the city of Baltimore. She reached up and took the hat off and handed it to Firfare. Firfare took her crown off and handed it to Lydia. Lydia watched as Firfare place the hat on her head with the brim facing back over her neck. Lydia bowed slightly and placed the laurel wreath upon her head. Firfare smiled from ear to ear. Elmwook clapped his hands together and said, "You have exchanged crowns with Firfare. She is

245

very happy and you are now her friend." Firfare turned to Elmwook and chirped and twittered and then pointed to Lydia again. Elmwook said, "Firfare would like me to offer the Lady of the Green her protection and wants to know if you would like to take up residence with the Tree Keepers while we look for your crewmembers?"

Lydia was dumbfounded and didn't know how to thank Firfare. She reached into her pants pocket and pulled out her pocketknife. She slowly slid it across the small table to Firfare. She turned to Elmwook and said, "This is one of my most prized possessions and I want to make a gift of it to Firfare. I will be glad to live with the Tree Keepers while we look for my crewmembers." Firfare had picked up the knife and was looking at it wondering what it was. Lydia extended her hand and Firfare put the knife in her hand. Lydia opened the knife and cut an apple in half that was lying on the table. Then she folded the knife back into its case and handed it back to Firfare. Firfare opened the knife and ran her finger along the blade and just barely cut her finger. Lydia was about to say be careful when she watched the cut disappear as fast as it had appeared. Firfare stood and walked over to a cupboard where she opened the door and took out what looked like a broom. She walked back to the table and handed her the broom. She turned to Elmwook and twittered and chirped and pointed to Lydia again.

Elmwook shook his head in amazement and said, "Firfare has just given you one of her most prized possessions. It is called a flying stick. She also has told me that I must teach you how to use it. She said that since the Lady of the Green is also a Captain that she will move you and me into her quarters until we find your crewmembers." Lydia looked and Elmwook and said, "I don't think there will be much to teach me about this broom. We also have these where I come from. They haven't been used in centuries. They were used for cleaning floors and walkways."

Elmwook smiled and said, "This is not for cleaning, Lady of the Green, it is used for flying. With that Elmwook stood and said, "Boomba," and the flying stick rose into the air and just hovered there. Lydia jumped up from the table and reached out and touched the stick. It resisted her touch. She pushed down on it and it took her weight. She was amazed. Elmwook repeated the command and the stick gently floated to the floor and came to rest. Elmwook said, "So you already know how to fly and command the flying stick?" Lydia shook her head and said, "No I have never flown one of those. You will have to teach me."

They all sat and ate the rest of their meal with Firfare twittering and cutting everything on the table with her new knife and Elmwook acting as her translator. The day passed so quickly and finely Elmwook said, "Would you like to go to your tree house and retrieve your belongings or would you like me to send for them and my people will bring them?"

Lydia said, "I will go and gather my things, but I would like some company if you don't mind." Elmwook said he would be delighted to go with her and help her bring back the things she had collect from the forest. Lydia knew that in her tree house was a laser pistol that she had been wearing at the time of her transport to the planet and she felt that she didn't want to show these seemingly gentle people the destruction it could cause.

Together Lydia and Elmwook left the village and made their way back to the Knanga Tree. They climbed the ladder and Lydia hurried about gathering all of her belongings and put them into the long sleeve shirt she was wearing when she was ejected from the ship.

While going back to their village Elmwook explained to Lydia about the Knanga Tree. "It has stood for thousands of cycles and its tree water has remarkable healing properties. The Tree Keepers use its healing liquid for just about everything. When a new child is born to a tree keeper family the family is given a gift of the healing tree water by Firfare. When the child is old enough to drink, other that its mother's milk, it is given a tree water to drink. Elmwook remarked, "We Tree Keepers live a very long time and we think it is because we drink the healing tree water. No one really knows, but Firfare is now reaching her four hundredth cycle of life. So if she is any indication of what its healing waters can do then we all shall continue to drink it."

The sun was just about down when they reached the Greenhaven settlement. Lydia could smell the cooking fires and see the lights of the houses in. That is when she noticed that some of

250

the houses must be two stories tall because some lights seemed to be issuing high up in the domed houses. There seemed to be as many lights glowing in the houses as stars in the sky. When they arrived back in Firfare's quarters Lydia was led to her own private room with a shower. Her bed was filled with fresh pine needles and the smell of dinner filled her nostrils. Boy was she hungry.

Upon leaving her, Elmwook told her that he would return in one moon arc and she would have dinner with his life mate, Flower Maiden and his young son Soil. Lydia was excited about meeting other Tree Keepers.

In about one hour by Lydia's watch Elmwook returned and they left to eat their evening meal. Elmwook led her through the tree branches to the elevator and down they went to the forest floor. They started walking through rows of the houses until they came to one that was covered top to bottom with wild flowers. Elmwook noticed that Lydia was admiring the beauty of his home. Elmwook said, "My wife Flower Maiden grows them for the entire village. Her hands are magic when it comes to growing the most beautiful flowers in the village. These are some of her creations. Not one person in our village can match her skill with flowers. My son will someday become a Soil Master like his Grandfather. But he is still very young and has much to learn before we can call him a master." Upon entering Elmwook's house Lydia could smell something very delicious that smelled like freshly baked bread. Flower Maiden was standing in what Lydia thought was the Kitchen. Elmwook called her name and she was startled and almost dropped what she had just taken out of the oven. It was a roasted chicken. Sitting next to the chicken was a loaf of freshly baked bread. Flower Maiden was wearing leather clothes like Elmwook except hers were dyed an autumn red. She bowed slightly when

252

introduced as did Lydia. Elmwook turned to Lydia and said, "She speaks a little of your language. She helped me learn the words at night by repeating them to me over and over until I got them just right. Flower Maiden reached out her hand and touched Lydia's right cheek with the open palm of her hand.

Lydia pulled back a little but Elmwook said, "That is how we greet and receive strangers into our homes. It is our custom. Does it offend you?" " No," said Lydia. Flower Maiden then said, "I am pleased to meet you Lady of the Green. I have been learning your talk from my life mate. He has taught me many things about your customs and ways. I hope I please you with the food I have prepared. Elmwook told me you liked to eat fowl and I have prepared one of our egg hatchers for our meal. Please sit and I will bring in the food shortly. Would you like to have some chilled tree water to drink while you are waiting?" "That would

253

be wonderful," said Lydia. She turned around and Elmwook was motioning her toward pillows on the floor around a small table. In a few minutes Flower Maiden returned with a tray of horn goblets filled with tree water and sat it down in front of Lydia and Elmwook. Lydia said to her, "You have learned my talk very well from Elmwook. You must be able to learn very quickly." Flower Maiden said, "Since you arrived and my life mate was given the task of watching you and learning your talk he has been obsessed with you. Every day we would repeat each word until he had it right. It is he that is a very quick learner. I learned because of repetition." Lydia nodded and picked up her goblet. It was cold to the touch and she placed the brim to her mouth and took a big sip. The tree water tingled her tongue as she swallowed. It tasted a little like apple cider and had the after taste like fine wine. She smiled and said, "That is very good." They all smiled and Flower Maiden left the table and went to fetch the food. Elmwook started chirping and squawking and very soon a young boy entered the room. Elmwook turned to Lydia and said, "Lady of the Green this is our son Soil. He does not speak your talk yet but he is trying to learn from me." Lydia reached out with an open palm and touched his right cheek. Soil blushed and quickly sat down on his pillow. Elmwook smiled in appreciation of Lydia's understanding of their greeting custom.

Flower Maiden returned with a tray of food consisting of roast chicken, fresh bread and carrots and peas. She also place on the small table a bowl of yellow paste they called putter. Lydia watched as they all joined hands and bowed their heads and chirped a rhyme together.

Elmwook took the bread and passed it to her and said, "While I was observing you, you often said that a loaf of bread and some roast chicken would taste wonderful." But all you ate were berries and roots. You do have a fire stick

255

that I saw you use to cut down vines with. I always wondered why you never used it to kill one of our many flying creatures and eat their meat. The yellow paste is called putter. It is especially good when layered on the bread."

Their dishes were made of leaves and their eating utensils were carved from wood. Lydia was surprised to hear he had witnessed her using her laser pistol, she had always thought she had been very careful to use in only when she thought she was alone. Then she said, "I am a stranger to your land and I do not know what is good to eat and what is not. I didn't want to end a life if the sustenance of life I end would not be acceptable to my body. So I just kept eating what I knew would fill me up and thought over a time I would learn what was good and what was not."

Elmwook and Flower Maiden nodded their heads in approval and they all ate and drank their fill. When they had finished all the food on the leaf

Elmwook rolled it up and took a bite of the end of it and said, "Sometimes I think this is the best part. All of the flavors of the food are stored in this final bite." Then he placed the leaf in a bowl on the table. Finally little Soil rolled off his pillow holding his bulging tummy and chirped that he was full. Elmwook dismissed him from the table and he went back to his room.

Flower Maiden started to clear the table and Lydia said, "Let me help you with those." Flower Maiden turned and said, "No guest or Captain in my house will help clean up the meal!" Lydia looked at Elmwook and said, "I hope I didn't offend her by offering to help." He smiled and said, "You are a Captain, Lady of the Green and that type of work is below your status when you are with our people. When you are alone it is alright for you to clean up after yourself." Lydia nodded that she understood and was feeling a little light headed then said, "I am very tired and so full I feel that I could go to sleep right here." Elmwook chuckled and said, "You are feeling the effects of the tree water. I will take you back to your room with Firfare and I will greet you in the morning after you wake up."

When Lydia awoke the next morning the sun was already high in the sky. She stretched and yawned like she had been asleep for days. She couldn't remember the last time she had slept that soundly. She honestly couldn't remember Elmwook bringing her back to her quarters last night. She looked around her room and there sat Elmwood in one of the small chairs reading a book. She looked at the book closer and it was her ships logbook. She remembered having it under her arm when she had disappeared from the ship and reappeared on the planet's surface. But she hadn't seen it since then. He looked up from the book and said, "Good morning Lady of the Green. I hope you slept well." Lydia just stared at him and said, "Where did you get that book? I couldn't find it anywhere."

He grinned and said, "When you appeared in the forest you startled a group of our hunters. While you were clearing the dust from your eyes, one of the hunters picked up the book and brought it back to Firfare. After they described what happened in the woods, she sent for me and gave me the book and told me to learn your talk. I started with this book. It must have been very important to you because you wrote in it a lot. It seems very old. Not much makes sense to me, but it helped me learn your talk. I now return it to you." He walked over to her and handed her the ships log. Then he said, "How old are you Lady of the Green?" She looked at him and grinned and said, "That's not a question you ask a lady Elmwook! But if I were to hazard a guess I would say that I am over three-thousand of your cycles. We call a cycle a year where I came from.

He rubbed his chin and said, "You are older than anyone in the forest or anyone who we know of. Maybe the dragons are older but I don't think so." "Dragons," Lydia said. "Did you say dragons?" "Yes, but they live far in the north to the colder area where the mountains that spit fire are located. They haven't ventured into the forest for almost one hundred cycles or years as you call them," said Elmwook.

He continued, "Come, and have a bite to eat and then we start your flying lessons."

Chapter 18 - Dr. David M. Martin and the Woggles

David was transported into Deep Lake about ten yards off the southern shore. Oddly enough when he was genetically recombined he was about one foot off the surface of the lake and had just enough time say, "Oh crap," before he plunged into the lake. The lake was cold and boy did it stink. He almost got sick to his stomach from the smell.

Because of the chill from the water David's body involuntarily gasped for air. The lake water entered his mouth and he swallowed one or two mouthfuls while keeping himself from choking on the retched foul smelling liquid. When he bobbed to the surface he quickly got his bearings spat out the remaining water and quickly began swimming to the southern shore which he could see was thickly wooded.

Crawling out on the shore he quickly stripped down to his underwear and hung his clothes on some low hanging branches to dry. His sneaker type deck shoes were soaked so he took off his socks and put his shoes back on to scout the area. He turned back to the lake to see if he could decide what made it smell so bad. It looked stagnant because it had some kind of scum standing on most of the surface. He decided that maybe some underground hydrothermal vents were spewing forth quantities of sulfides and other chemicals giving the lake its smell and disgusting taste.

He looked across the lake to the eastern shore and could see some crudely built houses. He didn't see anyone but if there were houses there were people he thought. He looked into the lake and saw his reflection in the water. "What on earth," he muttered. He looked again and then at his hands and arms. They had been stained a bronze color, almost metallic in appearance. He tried rubbing it off and it could not be removed. At first he thought it might be the mud he climbed through getting out of the lake, but no his skin had changed color and his hair was now completely white. He had always prided himself on his black head of hair. He never had the slightest tinge of gray in his dark head of black straight hair. Now it was totally white and somewhat stringy. It was also longer than he thought it should be. His hair was now shoulder length and looked to be still growing. He was bewildered by his new appearance but didn't know what to do so he just sat down on the bank of the lake and stared across it at the houses on the other side.

All of a sudden he felt dizzy and light headed and laid back on the moss covered ground under a fir tree and fell fast asleep. He awoke with as start and thought he heard voices. He couldn't be sure they were voices because what he heard was a lot of clicking and clacking and a few whistles. They were not close or what he was hearing were whispers he couldn't be sure. The noises seemed to come from all around him. He sat very still like a scared rabbit. He slowed his breathing and didn't move a muscle. He knew he was well under the boughs of the fir tree and would be difficult to see. He sat in silence for a very long time as the voices continued their clicking and clucking. Gradually the voices trailed off in the distance and the forest was quiet again. The only sounds he heard was the water lapping on the shore of the lake and some unknown night creatures chirping and buzzing in the forest.

Slowly he move to a sitting position and peered into the nighttime forest. Nothing seemed to be moving, but just for good measure he sat there for another fifteen minutes without moving. His eyes were adjusted to the night and the moonlight reflecting off the lake gave him a good field of vision. He wondered how the lake could reflect light with all of the scum on top of it and looked out into the lake again and all the scum was gone. He couldn't smell it anymore either. That is really weird he thought. He slowly stood under the tree and found his clothes neatly folded in a pile sitting by the tree trunk. They were dry and had even been washed and seemingly pressed. His sneaker shoes were no longer on his feet. They were gone. Sitting on top of his clothes was a pair of leather slippers with the toes curled up like the shoes he had seen as a child on the feet of a genie it the tales of "Aladdin and his Magic Lamp." There was also a pointed leather cap with stars and moons tooled into the very soft leather. Both the shoes and hat were sitting on top of his freshly cleaned clothes.

He cautiously picked them up put on his clothes and socks and new slippers. The hat reminded him of a cone hat worn by ladies in waiting in medieval times. He noticed that his long white hair had grown down to the middle of his back now and he had to pull it out of his shirt after he put it on. Once dressed David looked across the lake again and could see what looked like small fires close to the houses he had seen during the day. He was about to move when he noticed a large staff leaning up against the tree with a very regal looking cloak hanging beside it. He felt the cloak and it seemed to be made of cloth of some kind. He couldn't be sure of what kind of cloth had made such a fine cloak but he was happy to have it because the forest had cooled down considerably from its daytime temperature.

The staff was like a big walking stick with a rock mounted on the top of it. There were some carvings in it as well but in the dim moon light he couldn't make them out. He could only feel them with his hands. Throwing the cloak over his shoulders and tying it in front he grabbed the staff to steady him and slowly started walking around the lake toward the village on the other side. He thought he could hear whispers coming from the forest but then dismissed the thought as the wind rustling through the leaves. He stayed close to the lake and made good progress toward the village.

The closer he got to the village, the more he swore he could hear whispers coming from all around him. He was now in sight of the first campfire. Carefully and cautiously he moved toward the fire. He stopped behind a large fir tree and peered around it at the fire. There sat three figures around the fire poking at it with long sticks of wood. They were talking to each other but not anything he understood. It seemed there language was made up of clicks, clacks, clucks, and whistles. David summoned all his courage and slowly advanced. Once out of his hiding place he gained a little more courage and started making noise in the brush as he advanced on the fire. Suddenly all three of the Woggles stood up, turned, and pointed their flaming sticks in the direction of David. From where he stood they looked like they were all holding flaming spears. He froze where he stood and thought about turning tail and running in the direction he had just come from. David looked back over his right shoulder only to see six more of these creatures standing not more than twenty feet behind him.

267

They were all holding the same type of wooden stick by their side, only these were not on fire. He was trapped. He was afraid to go forward and now he couldn't retreat the way he came. Summoning all of his courage he started walking toward the three beings holding the flaming wooden sticks. As he approached the campfire the three beings dropped their sticks and got down on their knees and bowed toward him. He turned around and the six behind him was doing the same. He walked up to the first kneeling being and grabbed him by the shoulder and pulled up slightly which caused him to stand. He repeated the gesture for the other two.

Once they were all standing facing him, David extended his right hand in a gesture of friendship. When he did this, they all backed away from him. David took another step forward and again they all took one-step backwards. Suddenly one of the beings started squawking and clicking

268

to the others. They all backed away from David but motioned for him to come and sit by the fire. One of the beings put a blanket on the ground by fire and motioned that David should sit there. David complied and as soon as he was safely on the ground all of the others followed suit and sat on the other side of the fire facing him. In the firelight David could see the humanoid features of these creatures. They stood about five feet seven inches. They all seemed to speak the same strange language. They were slimly built with long arms and legs. Their hair was dark and long. It hung below their shoulders. They were wearing some kind of uniform. They all had something that looked like and axe hanging from a leather belt.

They sat there in silence for the longest time until David said, "Can you please tell me where I am and who you are?" Well this brought on a group squawking and clicking and suddenly one of them jumped up and ran into the woods toward the village. David sat there in utter silence as did the others. Finally there was a rustling in the bushes and the being that ran toward the village returned pulling another being in tow. She was dressed all in fur from head to foot but instantly David knew she was a female of this species. She was adorned in jewelry and face paint. She also walked with a stick. He could see she had the curves of a female under her furry clothes.

As she approached the group they all started squawking and pointing at David. She moved closer to him and extended her right hand with the palm facing toward the sky. It looked like she wanted him to give her something. David stood and reached into his pockets and all he could find was a partially melted chocolate bar. He pulled it out of his pocket, unwrapped the foil from it, and put the chocolate in her hand. She pulled her hand back and sniffed the chocolate and tossed it into the fire and pointed at the foil wrapper he still held in his hand. She again put out her hand and waited. David placed the foil in her hand and she smiled. She took the foil and touched it, smelled it and then tasted a little of the chocolate left on the wrapper.

She came closer and took off one of her bracelets and handed it to him. David took the bracelet and put it on his wrist. Then he smiled and bowed. She started chittering and squawking like they were old friends. Then she reached out and touched David's face and hair. She turned around again and squawked to the others sitting on the ground and they all stood and bowed to David. David in exasperation said again, "Who are you and where am I?" The female jumped back and got down on her knees and bowed to David. "Well this is getting us nowhere," David muttered to himself.

With that he started walking toward the village. As soon as he started walking they all stood and fell in behind him in a single line. As he approached the village he could see more of these beings hovering around the entrances to their homes. Small fires were burning everywhere. He could only wonder why none of the instrumentation picked up these fires during their orbiting scans of the planet. As he approached the center of town he saw a large stone circle with a chair sitting in the middle of it. The stone circle was surrounded by small burning torches. This lighted the area so well that David could see the rest of the village quite well. As he approached the circle a door from a nearby house opened and another female being entered the circle and sat in the large chair in the center. She was not dressed in furs, but dressed in very fine cloth. Her jewelry looked like real gold and David could swear she was wearing lipstick. Her ebony black hair was pulled up onto the top of her head and was held there by four golden pins. Around her neck she wore a string of beads that looked like diamonds. Her feet were adorned with golden sandals. David entered the stone circle and stood there just taking in the beauty of this female. She approached him and said, "Welcome Mergrom, we have been awaiting your arrival for many years. My mother told me of your coming when I was just a little girl. Until yesterday when you suddenly appeared over the lake I thought you only a myth." Her voice was very exotic in its tone. It had a slight island melodious quality to it.

David shook his head because he thought she had spoken English to him. He said, "Pardon me, would you repeat that again? I don't think I heard you properly." The beautiful female threw back her head and started to laugh. "Come now Mergrom you know the legend of your coming. It has been foretold for many years. It was said that one evening when the sun was particularly bright and in the evening sky that you would appear over the lake and you would come to help us rid ourselves of this small area that we inhabit and we would spread across the land. We have had your shoes, cloak, and hat ready for you for more than two hundred cycles. I made sure that your legendary tales were told every day. Our people never lost hope in your arrival."

David said, "Pardon me, but how do you know my name and where did you learn my language?"

She smiled, took his hand, looked into his eyes, and said, "My name is Merelana I am the high priestess of the Woggle. My entire life, my mother's life, and her mother's before her were all high priestess of the Woggle. All of my life I have studied the ancient scrolls that foretold of you and your exploits. It is said that you come from the sea and someday you will return to it. But for now you have come to help the Woggle take our rightful place in the structure of this world. It is our destiny to rule this world. We have only waited by this lake until your return. Now it is time to take back the forest of our ancestors. Bless you Mergrom for coming and bless you for helping us. While you are with us I will be your mate, spouse, concubine, mistress whatever you desire. I only wish my mother had been alive when you arrived she was much more beautiful than I. She would have made you a wonderful mate. Then I would be of your seed and a sorceress as great a sorcerer as you are.

David shook his head in disbelief. They must have mistaken him for this fellow Mergrom they speak of. I know Mergrom is my middle name, but how could they know that. He touched the breast pocket of his shirt and his identity badge was missing. It had a picture of him and his full name on it. They must have removed it when they washed his clothes.

Merelana must have been reading his mind. She reached into a small leather pouch and withdrew the identity card. "Are you looking for this David Mergrom Martin," she asked as she read his name off the card. She continued, "We did not realize that you had three names. All we know you by is Mergrom."

David said in bewilderment, "You must have me confused with someone else. I come from the stars from a place very far away. I came here to make this place my home. I have no special powers. I am not a sorcerer, I am a marine geneticist. I think you have the wrong man."

Merelana just smiled and said, "We are told that you are a very modest sorcerer and that you do not like to be praised for your work. But the scrolls have never been wrong. You are the Mergrom we have waited on it says so on this card with your picture. Come now, we will feast and talk in my house. I will tell your people that their savior has arrived." She stood and turned to the throng of people that had gathered around the circle of stones and started chirping and squawking, gesturing and whistling. When she was finished the crowd started cheering and squawking and then everyone got on their knees and bowed toward the circle.

David just scratched his head and nodded toward the crowd. Merelana took his hand and together they walked from the circle and entered her home. Once inside she pulled the four pins from her hair and let it fall across her shoulders. She turned to him and pointed to a bed and said, "This is now your home and I am yours."

The next morning you would have thought a team of lumberjacks had moved into the village. David was awakened by the sounds of falling trees. When he went outside to see what the commotion was he saw hundreds of the Woggles cutting down the forest next to the settlement. They were felling the trees as fast as they could move from one to the other. He also noticed that the odor from the lake had returned and a scum had formed on the surface.

Chapter 19 - The ARK of Civilization

Harold, Miranda and the children wasted no time in creating a home for themselves. They had made several trips back to the Ark explorer ship and brought down much needed supplies laboratories and one of the command shuttles. Together with the army of robots they had created they built what they called the Ark of Civilization. The genetic labs were now manned with robots that had been programmed to produce whatever the good doctor and his spouse saw fit to make. Right after the labs were set up and the Bengarie had been produced, then Miranda wanted a race of beings that would be like servants to them. Harold and Miranda had come up with a genetic scheme to produce a race of people that would be known as the First Facers.

The First Facers were designed to be the servants to the King and Queen. They were genetically engineered to be a stout but not too bright race of beings. The peculiarity with the race is that as a First Facer grew older their face would slowly migrate down from their head to their chest area. While this was not particularly visually appetizing while the facial skin was migrating downward it only took about three days and it only happened every fifteen years.

This was an anomaly that happened after the first two beings were developed. The male and female pair that was originally made did not display this characteristic their faces remain the same until their reign is over. During their life cycle, which is very long, two children are picked from the First Face nation and genetically altered in the Ark of Civilization to keep their faces and are placed with the existing king and queen as their children. When the current king and queen's life cycle ends their children take over as rulers. All other First Facers make the face change. To see how old a First Facer is you need only look at their chest and see the number of old faces residing there. They were the second race created, but they are called the first nation. King Harold thought it prudent to develop the Bengarie first to provide the food for what was yet to be more races of people.

The next race of beings that came out of the Ark was the Pillowpods. They were genetically engineered to be amorphous. They could assume almost any shape and color they needed to. Their outer skin was made up of very fine scales that could reflect the sun and almost make them invisible to the human eye. In their original form they had four legs to propel them very fast. They were bred to tolerate almost any climate they encountered. They preferred very hot and dry climates so King Harold set about changing the landscape to suit his new creations. The genetic labs of the Ark worked tirelessly around the clock producing and growing Harold and Miranda's new creations.

Through their experiments they created Nightwalkers, Reed Walkers, Gizmaths, Merkoots, Wind Walkers and some new forms of Dragons. Last on his list of creations were humanoid creatures like he and Miranda. But eventually he got around to creating human beings modeled after some of the DNA that was aboard the Ark Explorer. He had long sense forgotten about the rest of the crew he had abandoned years before. He was too busy repopulating and terra-forming parts of the planet to suit his master plan. He and Miranda were quite comfortable in their new surroundings. They had robots, First Facers, and all of their creations who worshiped them as King and Queen. If one of the races or individuals protested their rule or judgment they would invite them into the Ark of Civilization and one of two things would happen. They would never be heard from again, or they would leave with an entirely new attitude. With the supplies aboard the Ark Explorer they would have an unlimited supply of DNA and materials to last for eons.

Ten years passed then twenty then fifty then one hundred and still the labs kept pumping out new people and beings to inhabit the planet.

282

Harold and Miranda also took to burying cargo containers throughout the planet of memorabilia collected from the Ark Explorer thinking that someday they would need these containers. Most all were usually buried deep in the mountains or caves throughout the planet. All of this was done just in case the Ark Explorer was unexpectedly struck by another meteor and was destroyed. Eventually all that was left on board were the empty laboratories and cavernous storage bays that survived the first meteor encounter. The ship was still operational and in orbit. King Harold and his family could visit it any time they wanted to and frequently used the magnetic hovercraft to shuttle themselves to and from the mother ship.

Decades passed and civilizations flourished on the planet. To the far north the Merkoots had established their empire. In the center were the humanoids that spread both east and west but never south. They developed a culture similar to

283

medieval times back on earth. They were ruled by a King and Queen as well. There were several feudal states surrounding the center of their culture. The largest city in the north was Belledrade. Their kingdom was called Belleadaire. Their King was a descendant of King Harold's DNA chain but he was unaware of it. The first king was King Gerald Boranum. Harold thought it was only fitting to name the first humanoid king after his son. The tradition was carried on from generation to generation and all of the kings of Belleadaire were named Gerald.

Kingdoms were established north, south, east, and west of Belledrade but never far enough south to encroach on King Harold's kingdom. He had terra-formed the area south of the Deep Forest into a huge desert of blowing sand and very hot temperatures. This provided a natural barrier of sorts from other beings trying to cross the desert to see what lies beyond. The Pillowpods protected their desert domain and usually did not let explorers wander to far south.

Chapter 20 - The Lady of the Green

Lydia was taught to fly by using the flying stick given to her by Captain Firfare. Elmwook taught her all of the Boomba commands and in less than two weeks she was flying like a professional. Every day she would fly in larger and larger circles looking for her crew that had been sent to the planet. After spending ten weeks scouring the forest and countryside she abandoned all hope of ever finding them. Captain Firfare had adopted her like a long lost daughter she never had. She was picking up the English language and Lydia was learning tree talk. They would spend hours and hours talking about the forest and its mysteries as well as its beauty. When they were talking and didn't understand each other they would send for Elmwook and he would always translate for them.

Lydia was now known only as the lady of the green. No one ever called her Lydia. One day as she and Firfare were talking about the forest and its mysteries Firfare said, "Lady, if you are willing, I would like to train you as my successor? I know by our conversations that you love the forest as much as I and you would do nothing to harm it." Lydia was surprised at her question and said, "Firfare you still have a long life ahead of you, and I am not of your kind. I don't think the tree people would want a Captain that is not of their people, an outsider." Firfare looked at her and smiled, then continued, "Look at yourself Lady, you are one of us. You dress like us you speak our talk and you care for the forest and all the living things within its protection. Why would you think we would not welcome you as one of our own? I know you miss your own kind and we have searched the forest from end to end and top to bottom. They simply are not here. I want to teach you the ways of forest magic. There are spells, herbs, animals, and trees that are magical and help me in maintaining the woodlands in their pristine shape. I simply want to pass on this knowledge to you so you can carry on after my passing." Lydia didn't say anything right away so Firfare said, "Good, that is settled and your training starts tomorrow. I will ask Elmwook to assist in our training because there are words that

287

have no meaning in your talk. He will have to find your words to match ours."

Lydia started to cry softly and tears streamed down her cheeks. She reached across the table and gently grasped Firfare's hands and said, "Earth mother you have treated me like a daughter and now you flatter me by choosing me to be the next Captain of the forest. I don't know what to say or how to thank you?" Firfare smiled and said, "Don't thank me yet daughter you have no idea what you are in for. It took me more than ten cycles to learn what I had to just to start becoming their leader. You have years of training and hard work ahead of you. If I didn't think you could do it, I wouldn't even spend my time trying to place all of my knowledge into your head. You have shown me that you are the one. If you were to ask Elmwook he would also agree with me. You don't have to ask him, I already have. His reply to me was, "What took you so long to see that she is the right one?" Lydia felt elated and also emotionally drained by Firfare's decision. She left Firfare that evening feeling good about the training she was going to be given. It had been a long time since she had something to concentrate on except survival and looking for other crewmembers. She thought this new undertaking would be just what she needed to become at peace with her surroundings and her mind.

When Lydia arose from her bed the next morning laying at the foot of her bed was a beautiful emerald green cloak with a hood, a pair of sandal boots, and a dress that was like a gown you would wear to a ball or party. It was a beautiful pale green with embroidered flowers and leafs across the bodice and over the shoulders. She couldn't remember the last time she had seen a more beautiful dress. She also couldn't remember the last time she had worn a dress. A shirt and trousers had been her uniform of the day for so many years she had almost forgotten how people dressed when they were going to a fancy ball.

Hanging next to the fancy dress was a set of green leather outerwear, green moccasins and a wooden staff about six feet tall that was made from a tree root. Hanging beside these was a green leather cloak with a hood. She quickly dressed in the green leather outfit and walked up to Firfare's quarters to have their morning meal.

Upon arrival she saw Firfare dressed in a similar set of clothes. With the exception of the Oriels baseball cap and her height they could have been twins. They sat and talked while eating and finally Firfare said, "Go and get your flying stick and I will meet you at Elmwook's home. He will be traveling with us today. I am going to take you to the most treacherous part of the forest where evil lives and must be continually monitored so it doesn't spread beyond the limits that I have set forth." Lydia went to her room and grabbed her flying stick and was soon circling down to gently land in the flower yard of Elmwook and Flower Maiden's home.

When she arrived she saw Firfare and Elmwook twittering away. As she approached she could hear Elmwook protesting their destination. He was saying, "I don't think it wise to take her there so soon. The Woggle are not friendly to us and they want more of the forest. She does not know magic yet and may not be able to defend herself." Firfare replied, "Then we will have to make sure we defend her. This is all part of her training. She must find out that all is not well with the forest. She must learn to defend the forest against all intruders!" Elmwook bowed his head and said, "As you wish my Captain." His faced turned into a smile when he saw Lydia gently gliding down to them. He did not know she had heard what they were talking about.

291

Lydia landed and quickly dismounted and walked to them with her flying stick neatly tucked under her arm. Firfare turned to her and said, "Stealth is one of the best protectors we have in the forest. Your landing did not make a sound and you made not dust or noise. I see you have been taught well and fly like a master of the stick. Today we will test your skills of flying. We are headed to the east toward the deep lake in the land of the Woggle. They are not our friends and will not welcome us with open arms. In fact it is most probable that we will be met with open hostility. The Woggle, by my command, live on the edge of Deep Lake. They have been told not to cut the forest for profit and they may not expand their realm. Word came this morning that they are destroying the eastern forest as fast and they can fell the trees. It is said that their great sorcerer Mergrom has returned and will protect them from me. So they have started to expand and are killing my forest to line their pockets with the

292

bounty that fresh wood and lumber will bring from the surrounding kingdoms. We fly there today to appeal to them one last time. If they do not stop then they will suffer the consequences. I take you with us only to show you what evil and destruction look like and what it is doing to my forest. You will stay close to me and Elmwook because you have not yet learned the magic of the forest. I hope I can appeal to their high priestess Merelana to stop this madness and destruction.

Before Lydia could say anything Firfare and Elmwook mounted their flying sticks and took to the sky. She followed suit and before long all three of them were flying in formation eastward toward the still rising sun.

Just after mid-day they could see smoke on the horizon and a lot of it. As they drew closer the sky became filled with the smell of burning foliage. They made a detour to the north to avoid flying into the smoky cloud being created. Flying in from the north they saw why the large cloud of smoke was happening. Almost ten acres of forest had been clear-cut to the ground. Limbs and brush were being piled high and set ablaze to clear the land of debris. All they could see from the sky were the remains of stumps and burning brush. Logs were floating in deep lake is such abundance that you could walk from side to side on the floating logs.

Firfare blurted something to Elmwook that Lydia could not interpret or translate. Suddenly she pointed her stick toward the ground and shot down out of the sky like a meteor. Lydia could see a large bubble forming around her. Once the bubble was formed she started throwing lightning bolts at the ground and woodsmen below her. Immediately they scattered and started running toward the settlement and the protection of their houses. Once she had them on the run, she concentrated her barrage on the village. Lightning bolts were being tossed at houses and people on the ground. One of the bolts landed in the middle of the stone circle and completely destroyed the throne that was sitting there. Firfare directed her flying stick toward the circle and landed in the middle of it still encased in her golden bubble. Several of the Woggle threw spears at the bubble but they just bounced off and landed harmlessly on the ground.

Merelana came running out of her house with her staff in hand and stamped it into the ground and a small earth tremor emitted from its tip and flowed across the ground to where Firfare was floating inside the bubble on her flying stick. The earth shook a little and jostled the bubble but that was all.

Firfare looked at Merelana and said, "If that is the extent of your magic priestess then you are in for a rude awakening!" Firfare released a small fireball from her hand and aimed it toward

Merelana. Merelana snapped up her staff and swung it like a club and knocked the fireball right back at Firfare. The fireball hit the golden bubble and just exploded against its outside. Firfare conjured up a small lightning bolt and threw it at Merelana. This time she wasn't as lucky. The bolt struck the staff and instantly Merelana fell unconscious to the ground. Firfare just floated there waiting for the next challenge. Meanwhile up in the sky Elmwook had moved next to Lydia and said, "She will motion for us to come down when she is ready and when she thinks its safe enough for us to land." In about five minutes Firfare waved her hand in the air still inside her bubble and Elmwook said, "That is the sign follow me and stay behind me." She did as she was told and followed him. They landed just behind and to the backside of Firfare. No one approached and all of the Woggle got down on their knees and just sat waiting for what was to happen next.

Out of Merelana's house came a tan skinned man dressed in a white robe with long white hair wielding a wooden staff with a glowing rock on top of it. Firfare became very rigid on her flying stick and said, "Mergrom I have no reason to fight you, so do not give me one. My displeasure is with the Woggles not with you." Mergrom spread his arms as wide as they could go and slowly brought them back together above his head. As his arms started to get closer together a blue globe started materializing between his hands. The closer he brought his hands the more intense blue the globe became and then tiny lightning bolts started crackling out of it. When his hands were about one foot apart he spoke. "Who are you and why have you attacked our village?"

Firfare's globe turned from gold to green and she spoke in an eerie low voice and said again, "Mergrom my fight is not with you, extinguish your blue sphere, or be destroyed!"

297

Lydia jumped from her flying stick and ran in between Mergrom and Firfare and shouted, "David it's me Lydia don't your recognize me?" Mergrom stared at her for a moment then put his arms down and ran to her and threw his arms around her and hugged her tightly.

He backed up from her and said, "Oh my god, Lydia where have you been and what is this all about?" She backed up and looked at him and said, "I didn't recognize you when I first saw you, your appearance has changed completely, but your voice is the same. As far as what this is all about, it's about destroying the forest. Firfare is the Captain of the forest. She is in charge of it and responsible for every living thing that depends on it. Your people are destroying it for profit. From what I understand they have been warned before and were given this land next to deep lake to live on, but they were not to expand. Now look what they have done to all of these beautiful trees," as she pointed toward the lake. David bowed his head and said, "I guess I got caught up in this Mergrom character and got carried away with the power that the Woggles taught me and the readings of the earth that I have read and learned since arriving. As for my appearance, that happened after Harold dumped me into deep lake. It is polluted and after swimming in it my skin turned this color and my hair grew long and white. I was just fortunate I only swallowed a little of it. No telling what that would have done to my insides."

Firfare walked up behind Lydia and said, "Do you know Mergrom? I thought you were a stranger and didn't know anyone down here on the ground? How do you know Mergrom?"

Lydia turned to Firfare who was still in her golden bubble and said, "David or Mergrom was a member of my crew. He is a human just like me.

He came from the same ship as me, he is my friend."

Slowly the golden bubble around Firfare disappeared and she walked up to David and said, "You are the oldest and strongest wizard on this world except for me. I am glad you decided not to challenge me to a fight. It would have been long and destructive."

"No, no," said Lydia, "This is David Martin he was or is one of my crewmembers."

Firfare grasped Lydia's hand and pulled her back away from Mergrom and then she said, "Mergrom please tell her who you are and how old you are. She has you confused with someone named David Martin. Clear it up for her so we can all sit down and discuss the forest devastation and the future of the Woggle." David opened his mouth and said, "I am Mergrom, protector of the Woggle, and advisor to King Gerald of Belleadaire

300

so say the ancient scrolls. I wield the power of the earth and all that is sacred to it. I have lived on this world and others for over three thousand cycles, so say the ancient scrolls. I was here at the birth of the forest, so say the ancient scrolls." He winked at Lydia or The Lady of the Green and said, "We will meet again Lady of the Green and with that meeting all will be understood." He reached out and took Captain Firfare's hand and together they walked back into this house and shut the door.

Elmwook darted up beside her on his flying stick and said, "Do you really know Mergrom?" Lydia just looked at him and said, "Well I thought I did, but looks like I was mistaken, I do not know this man."

Firfare and Mergrom talked late into the night and not one soul moved from around the circle. At dusk the fires were lighted and still the people remained sitting on their knees. A little before mid-night the door to the house opened and Firfare walked out holding Mergrom's staff but without Mergrom. She entered the circle of stones and held Mergrom's staff above her head after tapping it in the ground three times. Then she stated to chant. Her voice became deep and guttural. Lydia could not translate or understand any of the words coming out of her mouth. Suddenly a green mist began to form in the air and a slightly green rain started falling over the village and all of its inhabitants. As the mist surrounded them they all started screaming and yelling and clucking and chirping. Then their voices turned to clicking and clacking. They were all writhing on the ground now groaning and flopping around as though they had lost control of themselves. Lydia could hardly see them because the green mist was becoming thicker and thicker. Firfare continued chanting and swaying to her own chant.

A light rain started falling and clearing away the mist and dousing the campfires. Closer to the forest the rains were harder which started putting out the fires of burning tree limbs and brush. White smoke started rising into the air. Eventually it became too dark to see what was happening to the Woggles. All Lydia could hear was moaning and clacking, coughing and moaning. She desperately wanted to see what was happening to the Woggles so she started walking out of the circle of rocks toward a writhing pile of Woggle. Firfare and Elmwood grabbed her by the arms and Firfare said, "Do not leave the circle until the transformation is complete. We will wait here until morning and then we will speak to their next leader now that the High Priestess Merelana is gone. With that she snapped her fingers together and her golden bubble appeared around all three of them and they all sat down and fell asleep using their flying sticks reed end as pillows. Lydia turned to Firfare and said, "Where

303

is Mergrom, what happened to him?" Firfare patted her hand and said, "I will explain everything in the morning. Do not be frightened by what you see tomorrow because you will have to keep the spell in place long after I am gone." " What do you mean," Lydia said. Firfare just patted her hand again and gently said, "Go to sleep now, and everything will be clearer in the morning."

Morning seemed to come early and as the sun rose steadily over deep lake the odor from the lake seemed to carry with it a pungent smell of decaying algae. Lydia opened her eyes and saw Firfare sitting with Elmwook talking quietly to themselves. She sat up quickly and looked around the stone circle. Lying on the ground before them were creatures that were not there last night. The tan skinned humanold beings were all but gone. In their place were creatures with long arms with their fingers webbed together. Their mouths had been replaced with beaks.

Their eyes had been replaced with large insect type eyes. No longer did hair grow on their heads but had been replaced with thick orange fur that starts just above the large eyes and continues down to their lower backs. A small band of fur encircles their waist and then covers their front and stops just above the knees. Below the hair on their back was a tail. All of the Woggles were trying to stand and were having trouble because their feet had been replaced with cloven hooves. The male and female were almost indistinguishable. The males were slightly larger and the females had protruding breasts. The orange fur on their backs that continued around their waist and down their front covered all distinguishable sexual differences.

Firfare stood in front of the murmuring throng and said. I have cast a changeling spell upon you and you will now be known as Woggs. If you ever hope of regaining your original forms you must lose all greed and remove it from your make up. Secondly you will not leave this area of the forest and you will replant all that you have destroyed. Your lake and water supply has been changed to keep you here. Daily you must drink from its waters if you do not, eventually you will go mad and die. You will never be more than six hundred in numbers. Your food habits will have to change from solids to mostly liquids. Lastly you will have to learn your new language because now you all speak differently.

The door to the house where Mergrom (David Martin) had been living opened and Mergrom stumbled out into morning sun. Lydia thought he looked like he had been drinking. Mergrom looked at Firfare and said, "What have you done? Where is my staff?" Firfare still in the protection of her bubble held up Mergrom's staff and said, "Here is your staff and the Woggles have been changed to Woggs. If you still want to protect them go ahead. But I think you will have a difficult time in acclimating them to their new bodies. They have been told not to stray away from this village. I am sorry that I had to disable you last night but it couldn't be helped. I knew that you would have battled me for what I needed to do and as I said before, my battle is not with you!" She tossed Mergrom's staff at his feed and then turned to the Woggs again and said, "Heed my warning Woggs if you persist in destroying my forest then you will leave me no alternative than to destroy you."

She motioned to Elmwook and Lydia to mount their flying sticks and still in her bubble they flew up into the sky. Once they were over the forest here golden bubble evaporated and they flew in silence until they reached Greenhaven.

Once on the ground Lydia asked Firfare if she would explain to her what had happened at Woggrace. Firfare just smiled and said, "This will be explained during your training to replace me. Do not try to understand all that was done last night. Eventually you will learn the changeling spell along with many others at my command. Now come and tell me about this David Martin (Mergrom) person. You say he is one of yours and I say that next to me he is the strongest wizard in this world. I know he wields good and bad earth magic. His training is very old and he is very strong. I don't think he can best me in a fair fight but I didn't want to take the risk last night. While we were talking about the Woggles I slipped some Penari root into his drink and he fell fast asleep. I took his staff so his powers of the earth could not help him if he recovered before I was finished. So come now child and we shall talk about this man you call David Martin. I want to know all about him."

They ascended to her chambers and sat down and talked the rest of the day about her ship and crew. Lydla described as best she could who people were and what they could do. She described in detail all she knew about David Martin and then she went on to explain about the evil Harold Boranum and his family. She tried to get across to Firfare how dangerous Harold Boranum was and what he could do to the land and its inhabitants. She told Firfare about Terre-forming and genetic manipulation. Finally she said, "This Dr. Boranum can also do what you did last night. The difference is his spells are permanent and cannot be reversed. From what I heard you tell the Woggs and me, is they could be restored to normal if they follow your orders. Is that correct?" Firfare nodded and said, "All spells can be reversed. Spells must be kept in place by us using our mind power. If my mind should not remember a spell then the spell dissolves. I try not to use too many of them because the older I get the harder it is to remember the spells I have

309

cast to keep them in place. So I use them sparingly and only after a lot of forethought."

They talked late into the night when finally Firfare said, "Lady of the Green I am tired from our ordeal yesterday. I would like to continue our discussion tomorrow if that is alright with you?" Lydia said, "That is fine with me I am rather tired myself. Sleeping on the ground last night was not like sleeping in my own bed." She excused herself and went to her quarters.

She did not sleep soundly that night. She could not help but remember what had taken place the night before. She dreamed of David Martin and the character Mergrom. She could not for her life understand why he was impersonating a wizard or sorcerer. She woke up out of her fitful sleep and was determined to fly back to Woggrace and talk with David. She would leave at daybreak. She tossed and turned the rest of the night and awoke just before sunup. She dressed in her green leathers and pulled the cloak over her because there was a morning chill in the air. She commanded her flying stick and away she went toward the rising sun.

Chapter 21 - The Lady of the Green Meets Mergrom the Magnificent

She had flown almost three hours when she came upon Woggrace. As she flew over the village it looked like utter chaos below her. There were Woggs scurrying around bumping into each other and seeming to argue with each other. There were animated squawks and clicking of their beaks. No one seemed to understand the other. Standing in the middle of the stone circle was Mergrom (David). He was trying to calm them down enough to speak to them. He looked up and saw Lydia flying overhead and thought it was Firfare coming back for another go at him or the Woggle. Using his staff he formed a blue globe of fire and threw it at her. She easily dogged the ball of fire and dropped out of the sky and landed in the center of the circle.

Upon landing she said, "Hold you fire David it's me not Firfare." She threw back the hood of her cloak and Mergrom saw Lydia standing before him looking very much like Firfare. He did not

312

smile and did not acknowledge who she was. He pointed his staff at her and a bolt of lightning flew out of the end of it and struck her flying stick. It blew apart in thousands of pieces that went scurrying about them and then disappeared into the air above them. "Why did you do that," Lydia exclaimed?

"Now you can stay here and see what havoc you have caused," Mergrom said. He continued, "These beings are utterly devastated by what you have done to them. You and your mistress have rained utter destruction and chaos on these people. Since I am their sworn protector you are now my prisoner." His eyes flashed red as he talked. He pounded his staff into the ground and enveloped her in a red globe of confinement. From inside the globe she pounded on the wall of the sphere and screamed for him to stop and come to his senses. She could not be heard outside the red sphere. Once enveloped by the

313

globe she floated off of the ground and floated to a nearby house and popped through the front door. Once inside the door slammed shut and a red beam of light surrounded the door. The bubble vanished and she dropped to the earthen floor like a rag doll.

Outside she could hear Mergrom giving orders in a language she had never heard before. There were clicks, clucks, and squawks. Finally the murmuring from the crowd died down and Mergrom continued his oratory. His speech seemed to go on for almost an hour. When she could no longer hear him she chanced a peak through a crack beside the door. As she approached the door her skin began to tingle so she didn't touch the door, just looked through the crack. There was now a bevy of Woggs crowded around Mergrom. He seemed to be very animated and was still talking in the strange language but with a quieter tone. He kept pointing at the house where she was being held prisoner and pointed to two of the Woggs. The two went to the house and stood by each side of the door making sure they didn't touch it. Once they took their places as guards, the red light around the door faded and disappeared.

It was several hours later when the door swung open and Mergrom entered and stood in front of her. Lydia tried again to communicate with him by saying, "David don't you recognize me? I am Lydia, Captain of the explorer ship, don't you remember?"

David looked at her with completed indifference and said, "The Lydia I knew would not have done this to these people. What has happened to you since we were stranded on this planet? Why did you team up with Captain Firfare?"

Lydia started to tell her story and Mergrom just held up his hand and told her to be quiet. He continued, "Why have you turned evil?"

Lydia took immediate offense to his statement and said, "I am not evil. Your people were destroying the forest and had to be stopped." Mergrom gave a snort and said, "Nonsense, what are a few trees to this world. They have an abundance of them. This planet would not miss the ones we chopped down. In time they would grow back. The Woggs needed goods to expand their population and the only way to do that was to sell wood or technology. While they are great thinkers and do study everything, they could not afford to expand for lack of funds. Wood seemed to be in abundance and that is what we used to give us the resources to expand."

Lydia responded by saying, "David, this Mergrom character has gone to your head. Just listen to you what are a few trees," she sarcastically said?

"Quiet." He exclaimed loudly.

She continued, "I think Firfare was perfectly within her rights to stop the devastation of the forest. I believe in the forest and have been asked to continue on when Firfare retires. I will be known as the Lady of the Green. Then you will answer to me.

Mergrom threw back his head and laughed. "You will not be taking over for anyone. I am going to hold you prisoner until Firfare dissolves her terrible spell she cast on the Woggles." Lydia was getting angry now and said, "Get out of my way and let me out of here!" Mergrom stood in her way and said, "You are going nowhere. You have no magic to match mine!"

Then from behind him came a voice that he knew all too well, "Ah, but my magic can match

317

yours, "said Firfare. She continued, "I thought my daughter might come back here today to see you. When I awoke this morning I waited for you to come to breakfast and when you didn't come I went in search of you. When I saw your flying stick and leathers gone I thought you might want to see David again. But I will bet you didn't think you would get this kind of reception?" Firfare continued, "Come my dear and we shall leave this retched place for now. Stand aside Mergrom and let her pass!"

Mergrom stepped aside and said, "She can go with you now, but this is not over yet!"

Lydia walked briskly by David and out through the door. Firfare handed her another flying stick and they both took to the sky.

As soon as they were flying away from Woggrace Lydia pulled up beside Firfare and said, "How did you know I would be there and what is

wrong with David err Mergrom and why is he
acting the way he is?" Firfare turned to Lydia and
said, "I knew you wanted to see Mergrom again.
He is not the same person you once knew. He as
consumed the water from deep lake and he is now
thinking like a Woggle. He is completely
consumed by the tales and spells of Mergrom.
For all practical purposes he is now Mergrom and
the David you once knew is no longer. I am sorry I
didn't explain that to you. It would have saved you
from the unplesantries you suffered at his hands.
Mergrom is not a bad wizard when he is away
from Woggrace. In fact he is a very good wizard
and advises King Gerald all the time. Mergrom
was born of the soil and knows a lot of worldly
magic. He is a strong wizard and is a champion of
any downtrodden people. He will help the Woggs
as much as he can and get them organized again
and living within their new bodies. Now we must
start your training for I fear he will blame you for
the Woggs problems. So I must train you as fast

319

as I can so you will be able to counteract or ward off any of his earthen spells. Eventually he will see the error of his ways and once again treat you as a friend, not an enemy."

The flew on in silence for a long time then Firfare said, "We will not stop at Greenhaven we will continue on to the darkest part of the forest for that is where your training will begin. You must also be aware that my scouts have detected some rather strange beings coming from the southern regions to inhabit areas of the northern realm. We will have to keep our eyes on them as well and see if they are friend of foe to the forest."

They flew over Greenhaven and flew on until the trees were so close together their canopies obliterated any sight of the ground. Late in the afternoon there was a small break in the canopy and Firfare dropped through it like a rock. Lydia followed closely behind her. Firfare flew low through the trees for a short while and then came to a tree with a large hole at its base. She landed by the hole as did Lydia and now Lydia could see there was a door deep inside the hole. The forest was so dimly lighted that she could hardly make out the shape of the tree and doorway. Firfare snapped her fingers and a flame appeared at her fingertips. She flipped the flame toward the door and the small flame hit a torch beside the door and instantly it burst into light.

"Now that's better," she said as she walked forward and touched the door with one hand. Lydia noticed the door did not have any handle or latch. Firfare said, "Doorway of today, doorway of tomorrow Firfare is here requesting entry!" Lydia could here several latches opening inside the door. Once the clicking had stopped the door slowly opened. Firfare stepped inside and immediately snapped and flicked small flames in all directions. Each of the small flames found a torch and before long the inside of the tree was ablaze with light. Firfare led the way through the entry hall and into the next chamber. Lydia could see another room after this one and another after that. How is this possible she thought? The tree is not that big.

Firfare turned to her and said, "Your chambers are through that door over there." She pointed toward a large ornately carved wooden door to her left. "My chambers are directly across from you," and pointed to her right. The door looked the same has hers except it had no doorknob; Lydia's door had a doorknob and shined as though it were made of gold. Firfare turned to her and said, "Training starts in earnest tomorrow morning. You will find clothes that fit you in your room. No leathers tomorrow dress casually and we will start with simple spells and conjures. Have a good night's sleep and I will see you at sunup tomorrow for food." Firfare turned and walked toward her door and whispered

322

something as she approached the door and it opened, she went inside and left Lydia standing in the middle of the second room. Lydia turned and walked to her door, turned the knob and the door didn't budge. She tried again and the knob would not turn. She looked back over her shoulder to see if Firfare was still there and she was gone and her door shut.

Lydia stood there for a moment and said, "Doorway of today, doorway of tomorrow, Lydia is here requesting entry." Nothing happened. Lydia thought to herself for a moment and then said, "Doorway of today, doorway of tomorrow, The Lady of the Green is requesting entry." She heard the door click and the knob started to turn and the door slowly opened. Lydia had a little surprised grin on her lips as she stepped into her bedchamber. The room was dark and she could not see clearly with just the light coming from the doorway. She snapped her fingers and a small light erupted from her fingertips. Startled and a little afraid of being burned she flung her hand sideways and the flame leaped off and immediately landed on a chair and went out. She snapped her fingers again and another flame appeared. She quickly looked around the room and saw a candle. She walked over to it and gently put the flame to the candlewick. Instant light she said to herself and smiled. Picking up the candle she started wandering about the room lighting other candles as she went. Finally the room was ablaze with the warm glow of candlelight. Looking around she found a wardrobe cabinet and looked inside. An entire ensemble of clothes had been put there and they looked to be just her size. On a table was a bowl of fruit and a pitcher of cool water. She went to her bed and pushed on the mattress. It was soft as though it was full of feathers. She could hear water running somewhere and wandered around until she found a small room off of the bedroom with a small

324

stream of water coming through the ceiling and splashing on the smooth stone floor then slowly flowing out a trough cut into the stone and exiting the room. She held her hand under the stream of water and surprisingly it was luke warm.

There were several bottles on a shelf next to the falling water. She lifted several to her nose and each one held a different fragrance. One was rose, one was lilies of the valley, and the last one was gardenia. She stripped of her leathers and walked into the stream of water and just let it cascade over her body. Taking the bottle that smelled like roses she poured some of the thick liquid in her hand and started rubbing it against her skin. It lathered up beautifully. Soon she was covered from head to toe in bubbles. After rinsing off she found a cloth and dried herself and went into her bedroom. There was a chest against one wall of the wood covered walls and she pulled open a drawer and found several sleeping gowns.

325

Putting one of them on, she stretched, and walked around the room blowing out the candles. With the only candle left burning beside her bed she lay down on the bed and was asleep almost before her eyes closed.

She was awakened by a gentle knocking on her door and could hear Firfare calling her name. With no window in her room she couldn't tell whether it was day or night. She assumed that it was morning and Firfare wanted to start her training. She called out, "I will be right there."

Lydia jumped up and lighted a candle with the snap of her fingers. Feeling refreshed and found a long pale green robe that she quickly threw on and found a dark green cord she tied around her waist. A pair of sandals was sitting beside the bed and quickly slipped them on and went to the door. When she opened it she was expecting to see Firfare sitting at a table but instead of just Firfare being there Elmwook and

326

another being was sitting there as well. This new being looked something like a bird. It had wings and a beak like a bird with large yellow eyes with black centers. On the top of its head was a cover of orange fur. Just above its beak was a patch of orange feathers. Most of its body was covered with feathers until you got to its legs which changed back to fur. It wore a loincloth around its waist to cover its private parts.

Lydia was startled at the new being and just stood in her doorway staring at this new guest. Firfare said, "Well don't just stand there child come and have some food. Our new guest is ORNG and she is a Gizmath. Today's training will start with forest survival. ORNG is one of the oldest creatures of the forest and can teach you where food can be found and what you can and cannot eat. You will spend two days with her. Elmwook will accompany you and help you communicate with ORNG. I expect that you will pick up their language very quickly because they like to mimic what you say."

During breakfast Lydia explained how she had opened her chamber door last night and how she started flames on her fingers. She showed them and snapped her fingers and a small flame started at the end of her finger. She blew out the flame and showed them again. "How is this possible," she said?

Firfare looked at Elmwook and then back to Lydia and said, "You have been drinking tree water. That is how it's possible. Not everyone can make fire. I knew when I met you that you had great power of over your mind. This tells me I was right. Tree water will help you unlock the power of your mind. After seeing what you can do now, your training may not be as long as I thought. You will learn quickly and have control over many things." Elmwook nodded his head in approval and said, "Lady of the Green, it pleases me to see that you have already learned more than we tree keepers. I am very proud of you.

Lydia shook her head in disbelief that just drinking tree water would make her able to light a flame with her fingers, yet, she can. If she can light fire, what else can she do, she thought.

They ate and talked then Firfare said, "I have to leave now and will return tomorrow. Stay with ORNG and Elmwook and I will see you then." She grabbed her flying stick and walked out the entrance of the tree and was airborne in a flash.

Chapter 22 - Training the Lady of the Green

      Lydia turned to Elmwook and ORNG and said, "Shall we get started?" ORNG wasted no time in getting up and walking toward the door. She paused at the door and picked up her long bow and a quiver of arrows and briskly walked through the door. Elmwook and Lydia followed. Upon exiting the tree the door slammed shut and Lydia could hear it lock. She wondered to herself if she could command the door open again but that thought was soon forgotten when she saw ORNG and Elmwook disappear into the forest greenery. She quickened her pace and soon caught up with them as they made their way through the dense undergrowth along forest floor. Not a word was spoken for the longest time while ORNG agilely threaded her way through the forest. Lydia had been watching ORNG and could see how the four-clawed toes on each foot made it easy for her to dig in to the soil and push her way through the dense growth. Her tail would flop left and right and sometimes it would even hold small branches out of her way. It was almost like having a third arm. They had been walking for hours when ORNG suddenly stopped and pointed to a bush with lush berries hanging from its limbs. ORNG turned to Lydia and said, "Noooo eattth." Lydia reached out to touch one of the berries and ORNG slapped her hand away and said, "Noooo feelllth. ORNG removed an arrow from her scabbard and sliced the large berry. Out of it crawled one of the ugliest bugs Lydia had ever seen. It was about as long as your hand is wide and had pinchers on its head and a rather large stinger on the other end. Its body was segmented and looked armored. It had several legs on each side of the body which allowed it to rear up and use its pinchers. ORNG pointed to it and said, "Homeeee in fruithhh. Verryyy badddd." Then ORNG pointed to Lydia's head and said, "Learnnn,

331

understandthth." Then she pointed to the leaf and then touched Lydia's head and said, "Rememberrrrr." Lydia studied the leaf and plant and berries without touching it. ORNG then said, "Newwww to woodssssss." ORNG took the arrow and stabbed the worm. The worm squealed and curled around the arrow and dug its stinger into the arrows shaft. ORNG scrapped the worm off of the arrow, put it back into the quiver, and was off again. ORNG pointed out plants, birds, animals and other flora and fauna as they proceeded through the dark forest.

After walking for another hour they came to a small clearing and ORNG sniffed the air through holes in her beak and spread both wings and stopped. Slowly she took her bow, strung an arrow, and stood perfectly still. In a few seconds Lydia could hear something running through the underbrush close by. ORNG suddenly turned and loosed the arrow. A high-pitched squeal was heard and then silence. ORNG sprinted off in the direction of the arrow and slung another arrow in the bow while on the run. Cautiously Elmwook and Lydia followed in the direction she had darted. When they pushed aside a small tree branch Lydia saw ORNG standing over a large blue humanoid with pale blue skin and long white hair. The creature was very muscular with extra-long arms. An arrow was sticking out of his chest and a bluish liquid was leaking from around the arrow. ORNG threw back her head and squawked so loud that Elmwook and Lydia had to put their hands over their ears to block out the sound. ORNG turned to them and said, "Merkoottttt, veryyyy baddddth. Newwww to woodsth. Frommmm northhh of silverrrr mountainssssth." Then she said only one word which explained everything, she said, "Killerrrrr." Then Lydia saw the large club lying beside the downed Merkoot. ORNG reached down and pulled her arrow out of his chest and

333

returned it to the quiver. She pointed to Lydia and said, "Learnnn and rememberrrth."

The trek through the forest lasted the rest of the day with ORNG pointing out good and bad plants berries and where to find water. Elmwook had been strangely silent through this entire trek through the woods and finally Lydia asked him why he had not spoken since they left the tree.

Elmwook turned to her and said, "I am also being trained to be your aid after Firfare passes back into the earth." Lydia didn't quite know what to say so she just looked back at him and smiled while gently patting him on the shoulder. Even though the forest was dimly lighted Lydia's eyes had adjusted and she could see quite well. All around her the forest buzzed and crawled croaked and creaked with the insects and animals that called the forest their home. The woods were alive and thriving.

As the sun started going down the forest became dimmer and dimmer. Finally ORNG stopped and said, "Sleepppp here tonightth." She started to gather pine needles and pine boughs to make beds while Elmwook and Lydia gathered dead tree branches and to make a small fire. Once they had established their camp ORNG started looking up in the tree canopy. Finally spotting what she was looking for she carefully strung an arrow and pulled back her bow. Lydia was looking up in the tree and could see a very large bird like creature but could not see it clearly enough to describe it. As ORNG concentrated on the shot and slowly said, "Gum-Gum flierrrrr, very gooddddth." She let the arrow fly and just before it struck the bird hopped to another branch and the arrow flew by. Lydia stepped forward to ORNG and said, "May I try?" ORNG handed her the bow and a new arrow.

335

When Lydia was in college she was the captain of her archery team. She and her team had won the state championship three years in a row. Even though she had not pulled a bow on almost three thousand years, she told herself it was just like riding a two-wheeled bicycle. Once you knew how you never forget. She concentrated on the spot where the Gum-Gum bird had been and strained her eyes. Finally she could just make out the shape in the tree. She waited and anticipated the birds jumping from branch to branch. She pulled back the bow and followed the bird with her eyes and turning slightly each time the bird jumped. Finally she took the shot just as the bird jumped to the next branch and the Gum-Gum literally flew into the arrow. It screeched and fell to the ground. ORNG quickly ran to the bird and brought it back to the fire. Expertly and deftly, using her finger claws she gutted and skinned the Gum-Gum then put it on a spit over the fire. ORNG looked at Lydia and said, "Noooo teachhth bowwww."

They all ate their fill of Gum-Gum and slept quite soundly that night. When morning broke and the sounds of the forest came alive Lydia awoke with a start then remembered where she was. Elmwook was sitting by the rekindled fire and eating what was left of the Gum-Gum. She looked around for ORNG but she wasn't in sight. She called to Elmwook, "Where is ORNG?" Elmwook said, "She is gone but she left you a message scratched in the soil over there," and pointed to a patch of bare earth. Lydia walked over to where he had pointed and looked down. Two words were scratched in the soil. Go Home!

She turned back to Elmwook and said, "What does that mean?" He replied, "I think that means find your way back to Firfare's tree. I hope you paid very close attention to how we got here and what not to touch and eat along with what we can. We are also going to need water for our trip back."

Lydia thought for a minute and said to herself this is just like the survival training we all had to take before we left earth in the explorer ship. I can do this. She sat down and had a little of the left over Gum-Gum, and took a small drink of water. Once finished eating she turned to Elmwook and said, "Let's get started." She stood up and made sure the fire was out then started off through the forest with Elmwook close behind. They had traveled for about four hours when Lydia became a little confused in her directions. She said to herself what would Firfare do in a situation like this. She thought to herself that Firfare would just create a bubble and float up in the air to look down at the forest and see where they wanted to go. Then she remembered the comment that Firfare had made in the tree the morning before.

338

Tree water makes your mind stronger and you can do what you want with your mind.

Lydia sat down on the ground than envisioned a golden bubble around her and Elmwook. She shut her eyes and pictured it in her mind. Then she pictured them floating up above the forest canopy. When she opened her eyes she and Elmwook were floating in a golden bubble above the treetops. Elmwook had a death grip on her arm and was beginning to shake. As she looked around she was surprised and a little afraid of what would happen if she stopped thinking about the golden bubble. So she kept thinking about it and started imagining it floating northward. When she did this, the bubble started floating northward.

She looked down at Elmwook and said, "Now, this is easier than walking isn't it?" Elmwook nodded his approval but still didn't say anything. After floating about an hour over the trees she saw the tree with a door in it. Now she imagined the bubble floating down and landing softly in front of the door and they did. Once on the ground she dissolved the bubble and they both just sat there for a minute or two. Elmwook loosened his grip on her arm and finally said, "When did you learn to do that?" Lydia answered, "Firfare said I could do what my mind wanted, so I wanted to fly in a bubble and here we are." Elmwook just shook his head in disbelief. Lydia got up and walked to the door and said, "Doorway of today, doorway of tomorrow, The Lady of the Green requests entry." She heard the familiar clicks of the locks unlatching and the door swung open.

Chapter 23 - Mergrom Becomes Mergrom the Great

Mergrom finally taught the Woggs how to communicate with each other and they started complying with Firfare's wishes. Saplings were starting to be planted for all the trees cut down and life was getting back to a semblance of normal among the Woggs. Mergrom now had the time to study the old scrolls depicting his life and times in the history of the Woggles. Ensconced deep in the ancient scrolls were the earth spells and conjures he used to use in a life he couldn't remember. His daily intake of the water from deep lake dwindling. Slowly but surely his memories were returning. He would send Woggs to Deep River, at the edge of the forest, to bring its crystal clean water back to him. He thought its water was the reason his memories of the past were returning to him. He stayed up late at night and studied the scrolls until sleep would overtake him and he would fall asleep at the table where he read by candlelight. He found his staff had magical powers and could take him anywhere he wanted to go. All he had to do was tap it three times on the earth and think where he wanted to go and he would be there almost instantly.

He had become the advisor to King Gerald of Belleadaire and shared his time between the Woggs and the King. Gerald was setting up a new kingdom and needed all the advice he could get to keep his people safe and prosperous. Since the founding of Belledrade, a great number of people had been moving into the city for the chance of a better life. More and more people were arriving with new skills and trades. A new city on the coast of the big sea was founded by ship builders. The port of Portington was established and its people started to fish the sea for food and profit.

342

Mergrom honed his trade as a wizard and was renowned and feared in some places. His spells and magic could not be matched. He had developed a secret hiding place for the sacred scrolls of the Woggs and kept an eye on them as well. He found that ideas would pop into his head that were many years advanced than the current time. He did not know where the ideas came from or sometimes even what they meant. Some of his ideas he would pass along to the King and some he kept to himself. When it came to governing he had many ideas he shared with King Gerald. When it came to weaponry he kept many ideas to himself.

New cities were cropping up to the north and west of Belleadaire and people began flocking to them in droves. Mergrom would visit these new cities on occasion to see what direction their Kings and Queens were taking to preserve the well-being of their subjects. Even though more and more people came to the newly formed kingdoms Mergrom had always preached balance between people and the environment.

Years passed and Mergrom watched the Kings and Queens grow old and die and new successors took over the kingdoms. Belledrade seemed to be the most progressive and successful of these new cities of commerce. Though they were all ruled by Monarchs the population flourished and people had good lives and food.

Chapter 24 - Uglias the First

Far to the north, a kingdom had been established by a Merkoot King called Uglias the First. The Merkoots were a race of people that had suddenly appeared north of the silver mountains. The land was fertile and covered by a dense forest. Immediately the Merkoots started to chop the trees to build their capital city of Mercatia. They had total disregard for the land that provided them with food and shelter. Mergrom knew that in time they would need to hunt for more land and resources. Luckily for the people south of the silver mountains that the only passage available to pass from one side of the mountains to the other was Ravenslock Pass. It was called this because at one time there were

345

thousands of Ravens that made this pass their home. They had built nests all along the escarpment and their incessant cawing was deafening to people trying to pass through. Their bird droppings covered the walls of the pass along with bones and treasures that Ravens inevitably bring back to their nests. Over the years as the nests had fallen and been rebuilt a lot of the bird treasures found their way to the floor of the pass.

Uglias the First was a ruthless king and ruled his kingdom by fear. He had even bred mutant Merkoots called Gringles. They were very large Merkoots. Their bodies were almost twice as big as a normal Merkoot. They were strong and muscular. Their minds however left a lot to be desired. They were what you would call slow-witted. Yes they could think, but not very fast. Uglias had developed them as the Kings Guards. No regular horse could carry them for a long distance and so the King bred and animal called a

346

Bicap to carry them. You could say the Bicap was a cross between a buffalo and a grizzly bear. Their heads were part of their front shoulders which kept their heads low. Their teeth were as sharp as bears fangs, and boy did they have a mouth full of nasty teeth. When you saw a herd of Bicaps charging you being ridden by Gringles your best bet was to run or ride the opposite way as fast as you can. They were ferocious. Mergrom watched and wondered where all these new beings came from but his visions could not see where they originated. Maybe that was from the water he had consumed from Deep Lake, or maybe time had dulled his memory to any of his life before this one.

Once the Merkoots had started to outgrow their lands they made raids through Ravenslock pass to pillage anything they could from the surrounding countryside south of the mountains. King Gerald had sworn to protect the people in this

347

area so time and time again he and his knights had battled the Merkoots and pushed them back through the pass. Since so many battles had taken place in the pass or on either side of it, most of the ravens had moved further westward along the mountain chain.

Mergrom knew that someday there would be a great battle and the Merkoots would be defeated once and for all. But as yet his visions could not tell him when that would be. For now he could just help King Gerald defeat Uglias's evil Empire.

Chapter 25 - Mergrom Growing Older and Wiser

Mergrom was the first to introduced King Gerald to metal. First came copper then lead after that came bronze and iron. Gerald's knights were the first to sport metal armor on the outside of their body. Prior to metal leather, wood and wool had been their outer protector. Then came layers of leather for body protection. Once introduced to metal a new profession had quickly found its way into everyday life. The skill of the blacksmith was born. Then to refine the job of a blacksmith to the next level an armorer was developed. This person just made body armor and made weapons of metal. To aspire to the king's armorer was one of

349

the highest privileges a blacksmith could earn. King Gerald's armorer was the best in all the land. He worked at his trade until his armor was sought after by knights from all the kingdoms. His suits were nothing less than perfection. He developed the articulated joints and panels to protect parts of the body that had to move during battle. He learned to color the metal to make blues, reds, gold's, and blacks. Each knight could have their own distinctive suit if they so desired and had the money to pay for them.

Mergrom would introduce technology in order to protect one kingdom from the other but he especially liked King Gerald.

Because of his longevity he watched as several generations were born, grew old and inevitably died. Mergrom himself didn't seem to age at all.

Many years passed and he finally made friends with the Lady of the Green and mourned the passing of Firfare. Firfare had even shown mercy to the Woggles for a while and let them return to their previously normal shapes. Promises were made by the Woggles to Firfare that they would change and follow the ways of the land. But it only took one generation for them to return to their old ways and started to destroy the forest for profit.

One of Firfare's final spell was to permanently change the Woggles back to Woggs. They would never return to their normal bodies again. Mergrom had warned the Woggles what would happen if they defied Firfare, but his warning and heeding fell on deaf ears. Even though his magic was powerful Firfare's was greater. Mergrom often thought that her final spell had weakened her so much that it wasn't long after that she passed into the earth and The Lady

351

of the Green became the guardian of the forest. Once a sorceress dies, her spells cannot be undone by anyone.

Mergrom had met Lady of the Green many times during his visits to the forest and several times when she was visiting King Gerald. He thought her a much kinder and gentler guardian of the forest than Firfare. Somewhere deep in his memory he swore that he knew her before she became Firfare's protégé. But the thoughts were so far buried he couldn't make any sense of them. Still, there was something familiar about her. One day he would figure it out. She also should be very old, but she was like he, she didn't age as others do. They had formed somewhat of a pact to protect the kingdom of Belleadaire as long as the ruling monarch cared for and gave back to the land. It was to that lineage that a son was born and as before him his given name was Gerald.

His mother Queen Alexandra was a matron of the forest. She loved everything about it.

So it came to pass when young Prince Gerald became seven cycles old that his mother summoned the Lady of the Green and Mergrom to Belledrade. This was to be a momentous occasion. The day of their meeting was in the early season right after the cold days. It turned out to be a particularly beautiful day. The sun was shining. It was warm and the heads of the flowers could be seen just breaking the ground.

Birds were beginning to build their nesting places. Small animals were scurrying about looking for new places to live. The sky was that beautiful spring blue color we all love and look forward to after a particularly cold season.

Chapter 26 - Educating young Prince Gerald

Mergrom arrived early in the morning and was in session with the king. At precisely mid-day a golden bubble appeared in the sky carrying the Lady of the Green to the Belledrade castle. She floated into the throne room through one of the open windows high up in the catwalk surrounding the large royal space. Sitting on their thrones were King Gerald and Queen Alexandra. Standing to the right of the king in his royal purple wizards robe was Mergrom. The hall was adorned with the banners and standards of all the king's knights as well as several tapestries that Queen Alexandra had made herself. A contingent of the king's knights flanked the hall on either side leaving the center of the room void of any obstruction or furniture. The exception was a large round cushion chair that was placed directly in front of the raised throne platform. Softly and delicately the Lady of the Green floated her way down to the floor before dissolving her bubble. She was dressed in the palest green gown that Mergrom had ever seen. Flowers adorned her head with small branches of fir and maple leaves encircling her head. As her bubble dissolved she courteously bowed to the king and queen. King Gerald spoke and said, "Rise dear lady you have no need to bow to us. Please take your seat and let us talk as we enjoy our mid-day meal. Instantly servants brought in a low table and three more cushions and set them in front of the Lady of the

Green. Immediately the king and queen along with Mergrom descended the steps and sat down with her. Food was brought in along with spirits, milk, and water. Together they sat and ate and talked of times past and how Belleadaire was turning out to be the leader of all the surrounding kingdoms.

The Lady of the Green enquired as to the whereabouts of young Prince Gerald. Alexandra said, "He is here in the castle, awaiting to be summoned by us. The king and I have a proposal we would like to discuss with you and Mergrom.

We would like to surrender the Prince's care and teaching of the forest and magic to you and Mergrom for the next few seasons. Dear Lady of the Green we would like you to teach him the ways of the forest and all of its inhabitants. He has exhibited the ability to listen and talk with the animals around the castle and we would like you to introduce him to all the creatures of the forest.

356

He needs to learn why the forest is sacred and one of our most useful resources. He needs to learn how and why plants, trees, and living things grow as they do. What better person than you to teach him all of these things dear lady? We know you both know the ways of magic and spells. We don't want to turn young Gerald into a wizard or sorcerer what we do want him taught is how to use magic only for the good of everyone. He needs to be able to heal the sick and infirmed by using herbs and potions. He needs to see how everything can be in harmony and balance. He also needs to be able to correct that harmony when it goes out of balance, but more importantly he must be able to detect when it does. We want our young king to be the greatest of all the Kings of Belleadaire. Without your help and teachings he will not be able to achieve that goal. I know it is a lot to ask of either of you but as his parents, we both feel that you are is his best chance for success. We can teach him how to be good and

357

forthright and when to fight and when to walk away, but we cannot teach him the ways of this world like you two can."

Alexandra sat back and looked at Mergrom and the Lady of the Green as if expecting them to answer immediately. Neither of them did. Mergrom stroked his beard and looked off into the distance as though he were solving a problem and the Lady of the Green looked down and fidgeted with her fingers in her hands.

Finally the Lady of the Green spoke and broke the silence and said, "I have never had a child nor have I ever been a mother or teacher. My duties to the forest and all of its inhabitants and creatures take up all of my waking time. I do not know how I will find the time to teach young Gerald."

Then Mergrom spoke and said, "While the Lady of the Green is looking for the time to teach, I will take the young sprout and begin his training in the earth magic. I will show him what can be done when earth magic is used correctly and not out of vengeance or retribution." He said this kind of acidly looking at the Lady of the Green. "Young master Gerald will accompany me everywhere I go and watch and learn everything I do. I will care for him as if he were my own and keep him safe and away from any harm. He will be away for long periods of time and away from the two of you during his teachings. Should you ever want him for any reason what so ever I will empower one of your flying sticks to summon me. All you need do is tap the stick end it in the earth three times and I will hear you and come immediately.

The Lady of the Green spoke and said, "While I was contemplating the training regimen for young master Gerald I believe that he should first learn the magic and ways of the forest. His teaching in earth magic would be a natural follow up to the forest magic. I can teach him to listen to the animals, the wind, the rain, and what healing can be found in the plants all around him. If Mergrom agrees, I will take him first to the forest and then Mergrom can continue his education into the magic of the earth and the ancient teachings of the scrolls."

Mergrom replied by saying, "I believe the Lady of the Green is correct. I also think that the forest should be the first place for Prince Gerald. I offer my services to her if there is any training or education that she thinks should be done in conjunction with her training."

The Lady of the Green raised an eyebrow and looked at Mergrom suspiciously.

Mergrom continued, "Prince Gerald's training in earth magic, potions and spells should take the better part of two cycles of the seasons."

The Lady of the Green said, "Prince Gerald's training of the forest will take at least that long as well. I suggest that he comes and lives with me until his training is finished. I will prepare a place in my lodge for him. Should he need to return to Belledrade for any reason, I shall bring him here myself. During his time with Mergrom and me he will also learn to fly using the flying stick for transportation. When I return in two days I will bring you a cage of white homing birds. If you need me to return with the prince release one of the birds and the prince and I will come."

Alexandra spoke then and said, "So the two of you want to take my son for five cycles of the seasons. You both realize that he will be almost fifteen cycles old upon his return to us. That is a long time for a son to be away from his mother and father. He will get homesick and lonely being gone that long. Is there no other way? I know we want him educated, but I guess we didn't think it would take that long. We will get lonely for him as well. What can be done to shorten his training?"

Both Mergrom and the Lady of the Green spoke up in unison, "His training will take as long as it takes."

The Lady of the Green continued, "We will schedule trips to Belledrade during his training so that your relationship with him will flourish. We promise!" She looked at Mergrom and he nodded his approval.

Gerald stood and said, "Good, then it is settled, Gerald will start his training in two days with the Lady of the Green. Once she has taught him the ways of the forest then he will continue his training with Mergrom in earth magic. His safety and wellbeing I trust into your capable hands. Treat him as you would me for someday he will be your king. We will get him ready for you and pack what he will need."

The Lady of the Green held up her hand with the palm forward and said, "King Gerald that will not be necessary. Dress him as you would for an outing in the forest and we will take care of the rest. Just pack him some food for him to snack on during our trip but nothing more."

Gerald nodded in approval and The Lady of the Green formed her golden bubble around her and ascended to the ceiling of the room and out through the window where she had entered. Mergrom tapped his staff three times on the stone floor and started dissolving in a whirl of wind and dust scattered off the floor and was gone as well.

Alexandra turned to Gerald and started sobbing. Gerald gently held her and said, "There, there my love, everything will be all right and our son will be the best King Belleadaire has ever had. Scribes will write volumes of his days on the throne. He will move our people into a new and abiding time of peace and prosperity like they have never known. I believe Mergrom and the Lady will care for him emotionally as well as physically. Besides, we can go visit him as well. It would do us good to fly into the forest for a few days each season to watch his development." She smiled at him and buried her head on his shoulder and said, "You always seem to know what to say at the right time. I will miss him terribly. Do you promise that we can go visit him?"

" Yes I promise," said the Gerald.

Chapter 27 - Prince Gerald's Forest Training

As promised, two days later the Lady of the Green returned to pick up Prince Gerald. Alexandra had spent the last two days preparing him for what was ahead. He seemed a little frightened at first but the more he thought about it the more he thought it to be a great adventure. He was going places he had never been before. He would see and meet people who were forest dwellers as well as all the animals that made the forest their home. By the time the Lady of the Green arrived he was eager to start this new chapter in his life. As the Lady of the Green arrived in the throne room as she had on the previous visit Alexandra, Prince Gerald and King Gerald were all waiting on her. As she floated to the floor in her golden bubble, she could see the excitement in Prince Gerald's eyes. He was dressed in beige leather pants and pullover shirt. Dark brown moccasins adorned his feet. His hat was of red dyed leather pointed at both ends with a white feather to its right side. It was tilted low on his forehead and his sparkling green eyes could be seen staring out at the Lady of the Green.

As her bubble dissolved she walked forward to the young prince and held out her hand. For a moment Gerald just stared at it and then extended his hand and grabbed hers. She said, "Gerald, I am Lydia but they call me the Lady of the Green. Over the next few cycles I am going to teach you the ways of the forest, its animals, and it's magic. You will be very busy during that time and will find the forest an exciting place. During your time with me you may call me Lydia or Lady of the Green, when we are alone, whichever you prefer. When we are around other beings or people please refer to me as The Lady of the Green. Do you understand?" Prince Gerald nodded yes and slightly bowed at the waist. She continued, "For all practical purposes I will be your mother and father during this time. If you need anything, anything at all just come to me and let me know. For instance, if you would like to come and visit your mother and father all you need do is tell me and I will make it happen. So go and say your good-byes to your mother and father and we will be on our way. We have a long way to go and I would like to arrive before night." She gently brushed his cheek with her hand and turned him around toward his mother.

Alexandra opened her arms and said, "My dear son, please be a good boy for the Lady of the Green. Learn all that you can about the forest for some day when you are King it will aid you in guiding your subjects into a time of great prosperity, growth, and peace. I will miss you with all my heart while you're gone. Write me when you get lonely and I will write you back or come and visit." Gerald replied, "I will mother I will write you every day." She hugged him tightly to her breast and kissed him gently on the cheek.

Gerald turned to his father and ran and embraced him and began to become teary eyed. King Gerald bent down and looked into the eyes of Gerald and said, "My son this is a great day for you and Belleadaire. Never has any King been as knowledgeable as you will be. You will be the greatest king of all. The Lady of the Green will care for you as we would. Learn from her as much as you can, for this opportunity will never come again. We love you and will watch you grow and become the leader of the future. When you see a white dove flying to you, you will know it is a message from your mother or me." The Lady of the Green raised her arms and a green globe floated in through the window carrying a cage of twenty-four white doves. As they floated to the floor and the bubble dissolved and you could hear the cooing of the caged birds.

Alexandra took a small leather pouch and hung it over Gerald's shoulder and said, "Here are some fresh fruits and nuts to eat while you are traveling. Share them with the Lady of the Green."

Gerald kissed his mother again and turned and took the hand of the Lady of the Green and said, "I am ready Lady of the Green. We can leave now." Lydia moved her hands in a circle and a golden globe appeared around them and started floating up to the ceiling and out through the throne room windows. This was the first time

369

Gerald had ever flown so he was a little apprehensive at first but then he started to smile and laugh and wave goodbye to his parents. They floated out of the castle and up into the sky where Gerald could see all the surrounding countryside. He could see the large expanse of the forest that stretched as far as the eye could see to the south and to the north he could just make out the silhouettes of the Sliver Mountains. He was excited to see all of this land from above. He shouted, "Higher, higher." The Lady of the Green smiled and up they flew above the clouds. Now all he could see was an ocean of white fluff. Above the clouds he could also see the stars of the heavens. He could almost reach out and touch them.

He turned to the Lady of the Green and said, "Miss Lydia, will I learn to fly in a bubble like this?" She turned to him and said, "No, my dear, you will not, but you will learn how to fly a flying stick. I only use these bubbles to go great distances or when I am going to be carrying a passenger like I am now. Usually I use a flying stick to fly around the forest. You will have one of your very own."

Gerald squealed with excitement. They descended back down through the clouds until the forest and land came into view. They were flying over the forest and Gerald could look down and see birds and animals and oh so many trees of all different varieties. Still they flew on until Gerald's stomach started to growl. He took an apple out of his pouch and offered it to Lydia. She accepted it with a thank you and he pulled out a handful of nuts. Once they had finished their snack, Gerald said, "I'm thirsty Miss Lydia, can we stop for some water?" Lydia looked down and winked and said, "How about some tree top water? It is the cleanest water of all. When it rains the leaves high up in the trees curl up and catch the falling

371

rain like tiny little cups." They swooped down out of the sky and flew just above the treetops until Lydia saw what she was looking for. There stood a giant tree with all of its top leaves curled up. She slowed the bubble and stopped it just above a cluster of the leaves. Slowly she extended her hand through the bubble and gently pulled a leaf from the branch. She pulled it into the bubble and handed it to Gerald. He put it to his lips and drank until it was all gone. He smacked his lip and said, "Thank you Miss Lydia that was delicious." She retrieved a leaf for herself and after she had finished the water she also said, "I agree, that was delicious." They lifted higher over the trees and started heading south. Gerald was tired of standing and was now sitting in the bottom of the bubble looking at everything as it passed below them.

The sun was just going down over the horizon when they came to Greenhaven. Lydia landed the bubble softly because Gerald had fallen asleep during their flight and was sleeping very soundly. Lydia had landed the bubble in her tree house and gently lifted Gerald into her arms and walked him to his bedroom. Laying him softly on his bed and covering him with a white sheet. She took off his hat and placed in on the corner post of his bed so he would be sure to see it when he awoke.

When Gerald woke up the next morning he was a little confused and disoriented for a moment wondering where he was. This place did not look like a castle; instead it looked very much like a cottage. He could see the thatched roof above his room. Every wall had open windows in them showing him a panoramic view of the forest. Sun was streaming in through them.

He jumped out of bed and rushed to one of the windows and peered out to see what was beyond. He could see treetops and smell the smoke from fires. He wondered if the forest was on fire but could not see any large smoke or the flaming fingers of fire. He scanned the forest and ran from window to window to assure himself that the forest wasn't burning. He looked around his new room and saw that it was just his size. All the furniture was smaller than adult furniture. He sat down in several chairs and at the table that was just right for him. He was absolutely giddy with excitement. Now that he had made friends with his surroundings he began to look in drawers and closets to see what else this wonderful place had to offer. He found new clothes and shoes, hats and belts, and a magnificent cloak with a hood. On the shelf in his closet he found a hat with a bird on it. He tried it on but it was too big. He had never seen a hat like this before. It had a word he had never seen before. The word was Orioles. The hat looked very old and it was somewhat tattered around the edges. It had a brim that went out over his face. As he was fondling the hat his

374

door opened and the Lady of the Green entered holding a broom in her hand. She smiled when she saw he had found her old hat. Gerald rushed to her and said, "Thank you for all my new clothes and this hat. I really like it but it's too big for me. He handed it to her and she adjusted the back strap and made it smaller. She placed it back on his head and it fit just right. She smiled and said, "That hat used to be mine a long time ago. It brought me good luck. I think it will do the same for you." She held out the broom she was holding and said, "This is for you and your first lesson is about to begin. He took the broom and started sweeping the floor. Lydia started laughing and said, "I hardly think you have had time to get the floor dirty. Besides, that is not a broom that is a flying stick. While you are in Greenhaven that will be how you will fly around. But before we start your first lesson, let's have some food and talk about the forest. Bring your flying stick with you and we will begin after we eat."

She led him down a spiral staircase in the tree trunk until they came to her quarters. Here the furniture was normal size. She motioned him to sit at the table which was loaded with fruits, berries and something she called cheese. He had never tasted cheese before and loved it the moment he popped it into his mouth. There was cold milk and a liquid she called tree water. She instructed him to drink at least one glass of tree water every day. She knew that if she were to develop his mind that the tree water would help with this task. He tasted the tree water and wrinkled his face a little with his first gulp but the second drink tasted better. He finished his food and couldn't help but burp when he was finished. She looked at him scornfully and said, "I see we will have to help you with your table manners as well." Gerald blushed a little because he knew that burping was not polite but that sometimes you just couldn't help yourself.

After their meal an elderly short person arrived and said, "Dear Lady of the Green, did you send for me?" For which she replied, "Yes, Soil, I did. This is Prince Gerald and I need to have someone teach him to fly." Soil snorted and looked at her and said, "My Lady, I have not flown for seasons now, surely you do not want me to teach him to fly!" "No, Soil, I didn't mean you. I thought you might know someone nearly his own age that could teach him the fundamentals and then you watch over them to make sure he doesn't get hurt." The Lady of the Green looked at Gerald and said, "Soil is my trusted advisor, he has been so for many seasons now. His father Elmwook was my advisor before him. Go with Soil and he will find you a young tree keeper to teach you to fly. Once you have mastered the flying stick then we can start our travels to other parts of the forest to round out your education.

Soil put his arm around the shoulders of Gerald and walked him down the center of the tree to the elevator. Once on the ground Gerald took a closer look at Soil. He was about the same height as Gerald but would probably be taller if he were able to stand up straight. He walked stooped over. He was dressed all in dark brown leathers from head to toe. His boots were curled up at the end and ended in a point. His hands and fingers were darker brown than his clothes as though he had spent many seasons with his hands and fingers in the soil. His eyes were a sparkly emerald green. His ears seem to come to a point on top but they were mostly covered by his fiery red hair that hung out of his hat.

They walked in silence for a while making their way through rows of houses and finally Soil turned to Gerald and said, "My grandson Garden Tender is about your age and size and he is very good with a flying stick. I will ask him to teach you

378

how to fly." They continued down the path between the houses until they came to a house that was overgrown with flowers and vines. Beautiful and fragrant flowers encircled the doorway. As they entered the house Soil removed his hat and his intense red hair fell down over his shoulders. They were greeted by Rose Woman and Pin Oak. Soil said, "Rose and Pin, I would like to introduce you to Prince Gerald Boranum. He is heir to the throne of Belleadaire and the only son of King Gerald and Queen Alexandra. He will be spending the next few season cycles with us to learn the ways of the forest and all of its inhabitants. The Lady of the Green has given us the honor of his first training. I would like Garden to teach him how to use the flying stick. I know he is very good at flying and I thought since they were about the same age and size that he would be the perfect teacher. What do you think?"

Rose and Pin looked at each other and then Pin said, "Well yes, he can fly very well but I don't know whether he can teach it. Remember, he gets into a lot of trouble when flying by buzzing people on the ground, flying through tree branches, landing on houses or playing knock over the scare dolls in the fields. I just don't know if he is mature enough to be a teacher. He is still a boy with the energy of two people and I must say he has your mischievous streak." Soil nodded and said, "Yes, yes I know he just skirts trouble but he loves to fly. I think he would like to be a bird if he could. Why don't we ask him if he would like to teach young Master Gerald and let him decide? I will oversee the training because I have been asked to keep him safe."

Just then the door flew open and a young boy came running into the room. When he saw Soil and Gerald standing there he stopped in his tracks and reached out with his right hand and touched the cheek of Gerald. Gerald drew back and then Soil said, "That is our way of greeting people and welcoming them into our homes." Gerald reached out and touched the young boy's cheek and they both started to Laugh. Garden spoke first and said, "My name is Garden Tender, what is your name?" Gerald said, "I am Prince Gerald Boranum but you can call me Jerry if you like." Garden looked him over and up and down and then said, "Well Jerry my full name is Garden Tender third class but most people just call me Sprout." Gerald reached out his hand and grabbed Sprout by the hand and shook it up and down and then said, "Sprout that is the way we greet each other in Belledrade." Sprout looked him in the eye and said, "But we are not in Belledrade, we are in Greenhaven of the forest. We follow different customs here." Gerald said, "I didn't mean to offend you Sprout, I just wanted to show you our greeting of welcome."

Chapter 28 - Learning to Fly

"Why are you here?" Sprout said. Before Soil could say a word Gerald said, "I need to learn how to fly and I am told that you are the best around. Do you think you could teach me how to use a flying stick without me breaking my neck?" Garden looked at everyone in the room and then a smile spread across his face from ear to ear.

382

Then he said, "I may not be the best, but I am the fastest! I can out climb, turn and dive faster than anyone in the village." Soil spoke then and said, "Gerald has never flown before. You would be teaching him from the ground up. He must learn the commands and balance. I believe you can teach him very well, but he must not be hurt or injured while you are teaching him, the Lady's orders."

Garden looked at Gerald and said, "I will be happy to teach you how to fly Jerry. Go and fetch your flying stick and we will start today with the commands. Gerald rushed out of the little house and ran back to the big tree with the elevator. He was lifted to the top and then he sprang up the stairs to his room. He grabbed his flying stick and started back down when he ran into Lydia standing on the stairs.

She said, "Did Soil find you a teacher?" "Yes," said Gerald, "his grandson Garden is going to teach me to fly!" She winced a little and then said, "Fly safe and listen to Sprout. He is a good flyer. If you learn to fly as good as he can, your first lesson will be over. The next trip we take will be aboard our flying sticks. I have to leave for two days but will return and then we will start your next lesson providing you learn how to fly in two days."

Gerald grabbed his flying stick and ran back to the house with the flowers surrounding the door and didn't bother to knock but rushed through the door. Sprout was waiting for him and together they rushed out the door to begin his first lesson in flying. Soil followed after them but could hardly keep up.

They found a clearing in the village and Sprout said, "Your first command is "Boomba" this will bring your stick to a stop and hover." Gerald tried the command with his stick and the broom rose to a horizontal position and stayed there just hovering. Sprout commanded his broom to hover and then he straddled it with his feet touching the ground. Gerald did the same. Sprout got off of his flying stick and said, "To make the stick go forward you say "Boomba-fo" to make it go in reverse you say "Boomba-re" and to make it come down you say "Boomba-do." When you say Boomba-fo you pull up on the front of the stick. You can come down by pushing down on the front of the stick or you can say Boomba-do. Once in the air, your stick will continue to go forward. If you want to go faster you repeat the command. The more you repeat a command the faster you will go until the stick reaches its maximum speed. To stop or slow down just say Boomba. Gerald was listening to all the commands and trying to get them all straight in his head. He was still straddling his stick and said in a commanding voice, "Boomba-fo." His stick took off like a shot making him pull back on the front of the stick so naturally it zoomed up into the air.

Not use to flying, he soon found himself upside down pulling down on the front of the flying stick causing it to rocket toward the ground. He looked over his shoulder and saw the ground coming up very fast. He yelled, "Boomba," and his stick stopped causing him to slide off the front of the stick and fall to the ground. Looking up he saw his broom slowly hovering down to the ground until it was in the start position. Sprout flew up on his stick and seeing Gerald on the ground he circled and came to rest about one body length above him. Sprout said, "Are you all right?" Gerald nodded his head and straddled his flying stick again. Sprout said, "The louder you say a command the quicker your stick will respond. Try your commands with a little less authority until you are used to flying. That should keep you from crashing again. Gerald said the word "Boomba-fo" in a calmer voice. The flying stick started inching forward. Gerald pulled up on the front of the stick and it rose into the air. He watched as Sprout leaned forward on the stick and crossed his legs under the stick and buried his feet in the reeds at the back of the stick. This position locked him and the stick together while his feet kept him from turning upside down. Gerald assumed the same position and together they flew up and over the forest. They flew west for about one arc of the sun and then Sprout turned and started flying back the way they had come.

During their flight Gerald had tried all the commands and was getting the hang of faster, up, down and left and right. When Sprout started flying back the way they had come Gerald commanded his stick to fly faster and faster. Soon he shot by Sprout like he was hovering. Sprout immediately took up the challenge of a race. Sprout leaned forward until he was completely lying flat on his stick. With a mighty commanding voice he shouted, "Boomba-fo" three times. His flying stick took off like a comet leaving Gerald in

387

his wake. He flew so close to Gerald that he almost blew him off his flying stick.

Gerald mimicked Sprout's position on his broom and shouted the same command four times. Within moments he had caught Sprout and was passing him. Sprout pulled back on his stick and shot up through the clouds. Gerald followed him. Above the clouds the played tag with each other. First one then the other would zoom down into the cloud cover and then pop up again somewhere else. The two of them were having the time of their lives. They were shouting at each other. Then one would tag the other and say, "You catch me." They flew on for at least two more arcs of the sun until Sprout suddenly slowed down and stopped and began hovering. He had not seen Gerald in a while and stopped to look for him. When he didn't see him above the clouds he flew down until he was below them and stopped again. Far down below, just above the treetops he

388

thought he could see movement. He put his stick into a steep dive and headed for the forest. The closer he got to the tree tops he saw Gerald darting in and out of the tree branches turning left and right going up and down. Chasing him was a very large Kargara bird.

The Kargara is a predator and cairn bird. It prefers it prey already dead, but when they are really hungry they will hunt and destroy what they need to survive. Very cleverly camouflaged the Kargara's mottled green and brown feathers make it blend in with the treetops of the forest. It's huge pointed red beak and large black taloned toes will rip a prey to shreds in the time it takes to blink.

Sprout watched as Gerald was weaving his way through the uppermost branches of the trees trying to lose his pursuer. The Kargara was gaining on Gerald every time he would dart down into the treetops and then rise back up again. Sprout pointed his stick directly at the Kargara and

389

nosedived toward its back. Sprout knew he had the element of surprise because the Kargara was focusing on Gerald. Sprout knew he had no weapons to fight off the bird so he carefully aimed his stick at the bird's right wing. He was almost in free-fall now going as fast as he could. When he was about two rods from the bird the Kargara saw him but it was too late. Sprout flew by the Kargara and reaching out grabbed a handful of the long feathers of its wing. At the speed he was going the feathers pulled out of the wing with ease. That split second it took to pull out the feathers almost dislodged Sprout from his flying stick and he swerved. His stick was headed for the treetops. He was going too fast to and was going to crash. Just before the collision with the tree Sprout felt him being lifted off his stick and watched as his flying stick crashed into the uppermost branches of a Garber tree. He was still holding the handful of feathers when he looked up and saw Gerald holding him by the neck of his leather jacket.

390

Gerald winked and started heading for the forest floor. They landed softly on the ground and started laughing. "Boy, that was fun," said Gerald. "What kind of bird was that?" He said. Sprout told him all about the Kargara and what kind of bird had been hunting him.

Then Sprout offered him one of the large green-brown feathers he had plucked from its wing. The feather was a little longer than the length of his forearm. They both continued to laugh and talk until sprout said, "Give me a lift back up to the top of that tree, and let's see if we can find my stick. I don't believe the Kargara will give us any more trouble today." They both flew up and found Sprouts stick. Some of the reeds were broken but it seemed to be in good flying order. They both took to the sky and headed for Greenhaven.

Flying over Greenhaven they saw Soil jumping up and down shaking his fist at them.

391

They couldn't hear what he was saying, but they both knew he was not happy. Soil was absolutely livid when the two landed. He first scolded Sprout and then turned his attention to Gerald. He said, "Don't you know the Lady of the Green put your safety into my hands? Do you know what would happen to me if you are injured or hurt in any way?"

Gerald turned to him and said, "With all due respect Mr. Soil we did not get hurt and we are not injured in any way. Sprout is a very good teacher and I now know how to fly like a bird. He held up the feather Sprout had given him. Soil said, "Where in heavens name did you find those feathers? They are from a Kargara. It is one of the most feared predators of the forest." Just as nonchalantly as he could Gerald said, "Sprout plucked them from the wing of the one chasing me." Soil clutched his chest and immediately passed out and fell to the ground. Gerald bent down but didn't know what to do to help him. Sprout rushed up and bent beside his grandfather and pinched a small branch off of a vine covering one of the cottages and held it under his nose. Shortly thereafter Soil's eyes fluttered open and before he could say anything Sprout said, "I was going to tell you about our brush with the Kargara, but you didn't give me time to." Sprout and Gerald grabbed Soil under each arm and helped him to his feet.

He was still catching his breath when Sprout said, "Jerry, tomorrow we will fly to the south and I will show you the changing area." "Oh, no you won't," said Soil. "You two are grounded until further notice. I am not going to have to explain to the Lady of the Green how you two disappeared exploring the southern region. There is a great upheaval going on to the land to the south of the forest and you two are not going to be involved in whatever is going on there. That is where the Lady of the Green is right now. She is trying to determine why and how the land is being transformed into something it never has been. It is too dangerous for you to fly there now." Sprout nodded and said, "How about we fly east to Woggrace, and I will show Gerald the Woggs?"

Soil shook his head and said, "Why don't you just fly above Greenhaven tomorrow and teach him how to maneuver through the trees. Gerald and Sprout looked at each other and started laughing. Sprout said, "After seeing him fly today to get away from the Kargara, I think he already knows how to fly through trees." Soil then got a little more forceful and said, "I prefer you to stay around Greenhaven tomorrow, is that understood?" They both nodded their acceptance and then they both winked at each other.

Gerald bid his goodbyes to both Soil and Sprout and returned to his quarters. When he arrived he found food already on his table. He didn't realize how hungry he was until he started eating and drinking a little of everything. He still thought the tree water tasted a little strange but drank a full glass of it to wash down the bread and cheese he had just consumed. He felt tired and sleepy but he also wanted to clean up from his exciting day of flying. He took the two Kargara feathers and put them in the band in his pointed green cap. He thought they looked just right there.

Searching his room he found a small room which had a small stream of water coming out of the roof and draining into a hole in the stone floor. He put his hand in the water and it was warm. Not hot, it was just right to bathe in. Looking around the small room he saw a shelf with several bottles sitting on it. He picked up the first bottle and smelled the liquid inside. It had the odor of ginger and cloves. The second bottle smelled like the white flower that grows wild in the forest. The last bottle smelled just like his mother. It was the smell of roses. She loved them. He picked that bottle because it made him feel closer to home. He stripped off his clothes and stood under the stream of water and let it splash down him from head to toe. Using the rose scented oil soap he washed his hair and body. When he was finished he dried himself on a cloth that was hanging in the small room. Once dry he walked out and found a long nightshirt to wear and put it on. It fit perfectly. Except for the candle burning on the table the room was completely dark. Drawing the table closer to his bed he laid down, blew out the candle, and fell fast asleep.

He awoke the next morning to someone pounding on his door. He jumped up and opened it to find Sprout standing there with his flying stick and dressed in a leather cloak with a hood on it. Gerald recognized it because he had one just like it in his closet. Sprout said, "Hurry up and get dressed, we can be in the air headed south or east in a matter of minutes. Soil never gets up this early. We can be gone before he wakes up."

Gerald rushed around and dressed quickly and then turned to Sprout and said, "Won't he be angry with us if we disobey his order to stay over Greenhaven today?" "Why of course he will Jerry," said Sprout. "But he will love us all the same. He is my grandfather and he knows I will keep you safe. He is just worried about what the Lady of the Green would do to him if you got hurt or injured. He will be fine once he gets over being angry," said Sprout. He continued, "Where would you like to go today Jerry? We could head south and see what the land is trying to do there or we can fly east and I can show you the Wogg village of Woggrace." Why can't we do both", said Gerald? Sprout thought for a minute and said, "I guess we could fly south-east and then fly back north over Reedland and its marshes and then over Woggrace and back to Greenhaven. It will be a long ride, but if we fly fast I think we can see it all." Gerald grabbed his small leather bag and put in some bread, cheese, nuts, and four apples. They would have to find water along the way. Gerald jumped on his flying stick and commanded it to fly and shot out through one of the windows of his bedroom, followed by Sprout. They made one circle over Greenhaven just to see that everyone was still asleep. When they saw no one stirring or walking they both shot off toward the southeast.

Flying low and fast over the forest treetops they made good time. Gerald was constantly scanning the surroundings looking for more Kargara birds.

The sun was about midday when they reached the southern boundary of the forest. Sprout pulled up on his stick and commanded it to hover Gerald did the same. Sprout said, "This land used to be green and lush. Now look at it, it is a desert for as far as the eye could see. What has happened here? He cried out." Gerald just shook his head. All he could see was sand and the blinding sun. "Not very pretty," said Gerald. "It used to be," said Sprout." He continued, "Maybe the Lady of the Green will have and explanation once she returns. In the meantime, I suggest we find ourselves a place to land and have some food. I don't know about you, but I am about starved."

They circled al little bit before Gerald found a place to land. They landed and Gerald handed Sprout an apple, some cheese, and a hunk of bread. They ate in silence and Gerald knew that Sprout was concerned about the southern region. Finally to break the silence Gerald said, "Tell me about the reed marshes." Sprout looked up and said, "The reed marshes are where the flying reeds grow. The reed walkers harvest them twice a cycle to make flying sticks. The reeds are then given to the Wind Walkers who make and train the

399

flying sticks. Very few people have ever seen the inside of Sticklacia where the flying sticks are actually made.

Sticklacia is buried deep in the coastal mountains where the sticks grow. I don't know of anyone who has ever seen how the sticks grow. Maybe someday when you are king the Wind Walkers will invite you to Sticklacia to see the whole process."

Gerald looked at him and said, "What are Wind Walkers?" Sprout turned his head toward Gerald and said, "They are people that can fly on the wind without the aid of a flying stick. They have a sack of skin that grows down from their waist with some kind of bones in the skin that can be raised and lowered. They are good archers. It is said that they can shoot arrows faster and straighter than any forest or city dweller." " Wow," said Gerald, "I will have to meet them some day and see how they fly.

Sprout just smiled and then said, "If we leave now, we will have just enough time to fly over the reed marshes and make it back to Greenhaven before nightfall." They took to the sky without hesitation and flew northeast. In about two arcs they could see the reed marshes. Once over the reed marshes they started to fly northwest. Sprout figured this course would take them over Woggrace, he was wrong. One arc after the reed marshes a thunderstorm blew up with lighting and very heavy rain. All their visual sightings were gone. The heavy clouds blocked the sun and the pelting rain made it almost impossible to see. Both boys put their hoods up and tied them tightly under their chins. This didn't help their vision any, but it did keep them a little dryer. They continued on their northwest heading until sprout suddenly turned due west. Gerald flew up beside him and yelled over the wind, "Why are we changing course?" Sprout yelled back, "We should have seen Woggrace by now. I am going to head for

401

the bird caves and get out of this rain. If it doesn't let up we will have to spend the night in the cave of the birds." "Soil will not like it if we do not return home tonight," said Gerald. "I know," said Sprout. "But it is better than to be hit by lightning bolts," he continued.

They flew on for another arc and the storm was getting worse. Small pellets of ice started hitting them as they flew on. Finally Sprout dove down toward the forest. Skimming the treetops he saw what he was looking for. In a small clearing he could see a giant hole leading down into the earth. He dove straight into it.

Chapter 29 - The Cave of the Birds

Gerald followed close behind. Entering the cave Gerald could see all kinds of smaller caves surrounding the large entrance. Each of the smaller caves seemed to have an endless string of every type of bird the forest had to offer flying in and out of them. The stench from their droppings was horrendous. Gerald followed Sprout into one of the cave openings and they both landed in a feather-lined nest. It was a very large nest with no eggs. Sprout turned to Gerald and said, "We will rest here for tonight and dry ourselves. Do you have any food left in your pouch?"

Gerald produced a handful of nuts and two pieces of cheese. "This will have to do," he said. They took off their capes and hung them over the entrance to the cave-nest and finished the nuts and cheese. Sprout started to tear a hole in the bottom of the nest until he had an opening about one arm length across. He piled up a few of the twigs in the center of the hole until he had the beginnings of a fire. He hunted around the cave and found a small piece of the cave rock and brought it back to the pile of twigs. Taking out his small knife he struck the rock with its blade and a spark jumped from the blade to the pile of twigs. Nothing happened. He looked at Gerald and said, "Take your shirt out of your pants and let me cut a little off the bottom. Gerald did as he said and Sprout cut about a finger width of shirt off the bottom. He sat about unraveling the shirt until he

404

had a handful of string and put It under the twigs. Again he hit his knife with the stone and a spark jumped into the pile of string. Sprout began to gently blow on the spark and soon the string was ablaze. He pushed the pile of burning string under the twigs and before long had a small but warming fire going in the middle of the nest. The smoke curled out the opening of the cave and up into the evening sky. Sprout turned to Gerald and said, "Let's keep the fire burning throughout the night so whoever lives in this nest will not return. Whatever kind of bird lives here is very big. But we should have enough wood in this nest to keep the fire going until sunup. If the rain has stopped by then we will fly back to Greenhaven and take our punishment."

Very soon the cave had warmed up and Gerald started to get sleepy. Smelling the smoke was a lot more appealing than the bird poo. Sprout said, "I will stay awake first and you get some sleep. When I get sleepy I will awaken you and you can keep the fire going. Pull the twigs and branches from the nest to keep a good blaze. The smoke and fire should keep the rest of the birds at bay also. Since the nest was lined with feathers as well as wooden sticks the stench from the fire was almost as bad as the stench from the poo. The feathers made a nice soft bed an soon he fell fast asleep listening to the thousands of birds chirping and singing their evening songs.

When Sprout woke him up it was pitch black outside the cave entrance and most of the birds had gone to sleep. He didn't know what time it was but it was his turn to tend the fire. He noticed the rest of his clothes had dried and his cape was also dry even though it smelled like smoke and burning feathers. He would have to wash it when they returned. He stoked the fire with some more of the nest and settled down close to it to keep warm. He added more wood to the

406

fire to create more light and heat. Looking around the cave outside the nest he saw a lot of animal bones. Some of the skeletons were rather large so he could only imagine how large the bird must be that lived here. While looking deep into the cave at the edge of the darkness he thought he saw some movement. He wasn't sure so he just stared at where he thought he saw something move. There it was again. He was sure this time he had seen something move. He poked a rather large stick into the fire until the end of it was burning like a torch. Pulling it out of the fire and holding it in the direction of the movement he had seen he saw two sets of little eyes reflected in his torch light. Carefully and gently he crawled to the edge of the nest and saw to small furry animals that looked like they were wearing masks over their eyes. Their fur was gray and black and their tails were ringed with gray and black stripes.

Each one was staring at the other to see if they were friend of foe. Then he thought he heard one of the creatures speak. No it couldn't be he thought to himself. Then in the gentlest voice he heard, "Are you going to eat us?" Gerald hesitated for a minute and then shook his head no. "That's a relief," said one of the creatures. "We thought you were going to eat us like the bird that captured us and brought us here. "Where are my manners," he said, "My name is Ray and this is my wife Ronda. We were caught near the deep lake where the Woggs live. You wouldn't happen to have anything to eat would you?" Gerald shook his head no again as if he had been struck dumb and couldn't speak. Ray turned to Ronda and said, "I don't think he speaks or he doesn't understand us." Gerald said, "I understand you very well, I just didn't know that the forest dwellers could talk." Ronda broke in and said, "All of us can talk honey, all you have to do is listen." Gerald replied, "Would you like to come close to the fire and warm yourselves?" Ray said, "That is mighty hospitable of you. Don't mind if we do. Are you sure you don't have anything to eat?" Gerald reached into his leather pouch and pulled out two very large nuts he had been saving for later and held out his hand with the nuts in his palm. Ronda took one and sniffed at it and then tasted it and turned to Ray and said, "It's not much darlin, but it will have to do for now." Gerald pulled back and they both crawled over the edge of the nest and curled up by the fire.

He was going to say something when Ray spoke up and said, "Are you leaving in the morning when the sun comes up?" "Yes we are," said Gerald. "Do you think Ronda and I can hitch a ride with you when you leave? We don't want to be here when that bird comes back." Gerald smiled and said, "We are on our way to Greenhaven, not Woggrace." Ronda who was getting sleepy said in her nicest forest drawl,

"Honey, we will go where ever you take us as long as it's away from here." She turned to Ray and said, "You two go ahead and talk for a while. I think I need my beauty sleep." With that she closed her eyes and curled up against Ray and fell fast asleep. Ray was not tired yet and wanted to know all about his benefactors. Things like where did they come from and where were they going and why did they sleep in the bird cave? He was just full of questions. Gerald finally said, "How is it that I can understand you? I don't know how to speak your language?" Ray answered him by saying, "Each animal, bird, insect, or creature that lives in the deep forest has a language. Sometimes people think they can hear us but really never do. Every once in a while a person, such as yourself, comes along and is able to understand the speech of all creatures. This person is said to be in tune with the earth. I only know of two others that can understand us all. You are the third. The Lady of the Green and

Mergrom are the only other people who can talk with us. The tree water is supposed to open your mind to all that is around you but if you didn't already have the ability the tree water would not help you. If anyone else is listening to us they would not understand what we are talking about. They would just hear our natural chatter, squeaks, squawks, and clicks." Ray said he was getting tired and would sleep now but if Gerald needed company he would stay awake and help him tend the fire.

Gerald told him to go to sleep and he would awaken him if he got sleepy. Oddly though Gerald was wide-awake and his brain was reeling with all the information that Ray had just told him. Now he listened hard to the soft chatter of the birds in the other caves. It was like eavesdropping on others conversations. He felt a little embarrassed at first but then he started tuning in on various conversations and suddenly was aware that all

411

creatures like people had very similar problems and situations. One conversation was how to raise their children and another was where the next meal was coming from and so on and so on. Gerald smiled to himself as he put more of the nest on the fire. His mind was racing with his newfound talent. He stayed awake the rest of the night amazed at all he could hear and understand.

Sprout stirred a little before daybreak to find Gerald still tending the fire. The cave was toasty warm by now and very comfortable in the cool morning air. Birds were starting to wake up from their night's sleep and all around Gerald could hear the conversations. He just smiled to himself. Sprout said, "Who are these two creatures?" Gerald simply replied, "That one is Ron and the other is Ronda. They were hiding in the back of the cave. They would like us to rescue them this morning when we leave. I told them we would take them to Greenhaven." " Sure you did," said

Sprout. Gerald smiled and said, "Ron and I passed the night away talking with each other." "Sure you did," said Sprout. "No, really we did," said Gerald. Sprout just looked at him and said, "Well then if we are going to rescue them we had better wake them up and be on our way before the owner of this cave returns. Whatever belongs in this nest is not going to be happy that we burned most of it and stole it morning meal." Gerald woke Ron and Ronda and placed them in his leather pouch. They donned their leather cloaks and mounted their flying sticks and took to the sky. Along the way Sprout could hear Gerald chattering away with his passengers but could not understand any of it. He just shook his head in amazement.

They had flown for about three arcs of the sun when Sprout caught sight of Greenhaven. They swooped down out of the sky and could see a crowd gathered on the ground below them.

413

Sprout turned to Gerald and said, "It looks like we are in for it now. Even the Lady of the Green is waiting with them." When they landed they both took off their hoods and bowed to the Lady of the Green and to the others gathered with her. Before she could speak, Gerald said, "I am the reason we are late and disobeyed Soil's orders. I wanted to explore the forest and see more of the countryside as well as become more competent flying this stick. Do not blame Sprout; he was just fulfilling my wishes. We spent the night in the cave of the birds where I met Ron and Ronda." He pulled up his leather pouch and two little furry heads popped out. Seeing the Lady of the Green they both bowed their heads in respect. Gerald continued, "They were going to be the feast for a very large bird we did not meet, thank goodness. But the most wonderful thing happened, I talked with Ron and Ronda and they with me. I understood them. After they went to sleep I could listen to the birds. It was wonderful!"

The Lady smiled with pride. Then her smile turned into a frown and she said, "Gerald you must promise me that you will not run off unattended again. You and Sprout had us so worried that we sent search parties out in that terrible weather last night to try and find you. We thought you lost or even worse. Please promise me that you will not take off again without an adult with you. The forest can be very dangerous if you don't know where to go and how to act. I am very glad that you learned to talk with the woodland creatures. They will all be your friends and can help you anytime you are in the forest. Each one of them has special skills that can help you if you just ask for it."

Gerald looked at her sheepishly and said, "I promise that I will not leave Greenhaven unattended. Please do not punish Sprout for doing what I asked him to do. He is my best friend besides you, and I don't want him to get into any trouble because of me. The lady looked at Sprout and then to Gerald and said, "There are always consequences for your actions young masters. Your deeds of the past two days do not warrant a free pass. Many people risked their lives looking for you. We are fortunate this time that no one was lost. I think a week of turning compost is a just punishment for your mischievousness this time. But if it happens again your punishment will be swift and severe. Do I make myself clear?" While you are in my care you will obey me or whomever I put in charge of you. Is that understood master Gerald?" Both Gerald and Sprout nodded their agreement. Before Gerald could speak The Lady of the Green grabbed Gerald and Sprout by the shoulders and turned them to face the gathering of people and said, "Now I want you both to apologize to these people for your selfishness. Especially to Soil who is very old and cannot take the kind of stress you both made him suffer."

Both Gerald and Sprout sincerely apologized and promised they would not run off unattended again. They took hold of Soil's hands and promised they would be better children. He snorted and said, "Now off to the compost bins with both of you they will need to be turned every day for the next week."

After their week in the bins and with their punishment over Gerald and Sprout were inseparable. They went everywhere together and Sprout was teaching him the fine arts of horticulture.

Training continued through the next few seasons with Gerald learning about every plant and tree that grew within the deep woods. He learned each of their special strengths and weaknesses. He kept up his regiment of drinking at least one glass of tree water every day and sometimes two glasses. He didn't realize there was so much to see and learn from the forest.

The Lady of the Green gave him a journal for him to start recording the things he learned. He had one journal just for the medicinal plants that could be found in the forest. He had another journal for the trees and another for the animals. When time permitted he would draw a picture of each of the species and would note what they were for and their special attributes. He would spend late at night rereading each entry until he had memorized all of his writings. About once a season a white dove would arrive from his mother or father and he would return home for a few days to renew the family bonds between parents and siblings. He was so enthralled by the forest that his father had asked him to start mapping the forest so that people would not become lost while traveling through it. He let his parents read his journals and they would spend countless hours discussing them.

He was growing up and his abilities with a flying stick were making him the talk of the kingdom. He was known as the fastest flyer in Belleadaire. Some of his tricks made his mother's heart skip a beat or two, but he was always very careful and had only had one or two bad falls.

His body was becoming more muscular and his skin was a bronze color from spending his days in the sun. He would talk to all the animals in the castle and tell his parents what they were saying. They would just watch in amazement and then thank him for letting them know. Both King Gerald and Queen Alexandra could see that he was flourishing under the tutelage of the Lady of the Green. His manners had improved, his table manners and all of his thought patterns showed marked improvement. It was always a sad time when he had to depart and go back to the forest. But as he grew older his parents could see that his time in the forest was building him into a man who would be the best King Gerald Belledrade had ever seen.

Chapter 30 - Woodsprites

Upon returning to the forest this time the Lady of the Green was not there. Soil told him that she would return in a few days. Then he said, "In the mean time you will be taught the fine art of hand to hand combat. To do this we are going to travel to Spritedom. This is the home of the Woodsprites. Let me explain to you about the Woodsprites and the reason they do not reside in

Greenhaven. The Woodsprites are very private beings. They are the protectors of the forest. They reside for the sole purpose of protecting the trees from harm. Their loyalty to the Lady of the Green is unparalleled. If someone is trying to harm a tree the Woodsprites have been given full authority to do anything they need to do to protect the forest. When the Woggles started cutting down the forest close to Woggrace hundreds of Woodsprites lost their lives trying to prevent the Woggles from harvesting the forest. Finally they turned to the Lady of the Green for help. They are fierce fighters and can bring down a grown man with ease. They only use their hands, feet, and teeth to defend the forest. They have no hardened weapons, bows or magic, just the bodies. When up against spears, arrows, swords, and the like they may sacrifice themselves in numbers to try and overcome the weapons being used against them. This is what happened with the Woggles. The Woggles were armed with axes, spears, swords, and knives. Like I said, hundreds of the Woodsprites perished during that battle. They are small and spindly in nature but they are fierce fighters. They do not get along very well with outsiders because there whole life is spent in training with other Woodsprites. They have been ridiculed because of their height and the way they look. So they prefer to live with their own people and not mix with the rest of us forest folk.

I have talked to William their leader and he has agreed to teach you how to defend yourself with your hands, feet, and teeth. He knows who you are and what you will become someday. He has asked that you come alone. You must take him a gift when you go. It is our custom. Also you must take a supply of tree water for you but under no circumstances do you let the Woodsprites drink it. Do you understand?"

Gerald nodded his understanding and then said, "If a Woodsprite drinks the tree water what happens?"

Soil sighed and said, "Eventually it will kill them. The tree water will try and make their bodies grow bigger and they will eventually explode. So remember what I said, no tree water for the Woodsprites!"

"I understand," said Gerald. Gerald continued, "How will I know when I am with a Woodsprite? What do they look like?"

Soil nodded and said, "Oh, you will know. They are only about a quarter of a rod tall and very slender. Their skin is sort of a pale green in color. Their ears are high set on their head and end in a point just above the top of it. Their eyes are big yellow eyes that never blink. They have no eyelids. When a Woodsprite is asleep you will never know it because those eyes are still looking

423

at you. In between those big yellow eyes is a small pointed nose that is made out of bone they also use as a weapon when needed. Below their nose is a mouth full of very sharp teeth. Even though they are not big, if they bite you they will hang on to you while hitting you with their clawed four fingered hands. So if they don't beat you, they will shred you and let you bleed to death. Finally we get to their legs and their four toed, clawed feet. Woodsprites never wear shoes, so the soles of their feet are like the toughest boot leather. The soles of their feet are so tough they can stop a knife from cutting it.

If they attack in numbers one person has no defense against them. When you encounter even one of them do not underestimate them, they are a formidable foe. The males are the fighters and the females stay at home and raise the children. Each Woodsprite is allowed to have one male and one female child. The females are a little larger and bulkier than their male counterpart. In all my years, I have never seen a female Woodsprite. Their clothing is mostly green to help them blend into the forest, and is usually worn below their waist. Oh, one more thing, never touch the greenish silver hair of a warrior Woodsprite. If you do, you are challenging him or her to a duel to the death." Gerald said, "I think I have it. Now how do I find them?"

Soil continued, "Fly into the forest and find a clearing and pretend you are going to sleep there for the night. The Woodsprites will find you. When they approach, hold your hands out with your palms up and your fingers extended. This is a sign to them that you are not armed and mean them no harm. When they surround you tell them you were sent to meet with William." Gerald said, "OK, I had better go pack and find a gift to give William."

He went to his room and packed several sets of clothes and then looked around for a gift that would mean something to the leader of the Woodsprites. Finally on the upper shelf of his closet he found the old tattered Oriels hat. He thought that would be a perfect gift for William. He stuffed the hat into his leather bags he hung over is flying stick, filled two bladders with tree water and then set off to find Sprout and Soil to bid them farewell.

Once he had said his goodbyes he mounted his flying stick and shot off to the western sky. He circled the forest for quite a while before he found what he thought was a perfect spot to camp for the night. There was a meadow with short grass surrounded by fir trees of every varicty. He knew the pine scent would be wonderful once on the ground. Running through the meadow was a small brook with water so clear you could count the fish swimming with the

426

current. He angled down and eventually landed about two rods from the brook. He hauled some rocks from the stream and placed them in a circle. A short walk into the woods supplied him with enough dead tree branches to make a fire and keep warm at night. He made several trips into the pine trees and carried back more firewood. On his last trip he swore he saw movement just at the edge of his left eye. When he turned there was nothing there. He carried his wood back to his camp and began to start is small fire. Grabbing a handful of dried pine needles he placed them in the center of the ring and then small twigs. Taking a rock he had kept from the bird cave he struck it against a small metal knife he always carried in his boot. A sparked jumped from the knife blade to the pine needles and before long he had a small but warming fire going in the ring of stones. He unrolled his blanket and small pillow beside the fire and laid down on it to test the ground beneath. He got up, grabbed his

427

blanket and walked under the nearest pine tree and filled the blanket with needles. Walking back to the fire he dumped the needles on the ground and spread them out. Then put his blanket over them. Now when he lay down, he said to himself that is much softer. Pulling his cap down over his eyes he pretended to go to sleep. The place was so peaceful and serene that he did indeed go to sleep.

When he awoke it was almost dark and his fire was almost burned out. He jumped up and put more wood on the fire because the night air had a chill in it and the heat of the fire felt good against his skin. He had not seen any movement or heard any rustling in the woods since he awoke from his nap so he set about fixing him something to eat. He took a dried ear of snapping corn from his leather pouch and set it close to the fire and kept rolling it so all sides of the corn would get hot. Before long he could see the kernels of corn

428

expanding on the cob. Then they started to snap and fly away from the cob in all directions. Gerald scooped them up as fast as he could and put them in the fold of his shirt where he had created a small pocket. The corn continued to pop and go in all directions. Finally all kernels had been cooked and the snapping stopped. He picked up the remaining corn and put them in his makeshift shirt bowl and sprinkled a small spattering of salt on top of them. Eating his corn and drinking tree water from his water pouch he sat and stared at the fire and was soon mesmerized by the dancing of the flames. Now that his belly was full he wondered when the Woodsprites would find him. He put some more wood on the fire and lay back down on his blanket. With the warmth of the fire and the fullness in his tummy, he swiftly fell fast asleep.

He was awakened by a scuffling noise around the fire. He opened one eye cautiously and saw a Woodsprite gathering up the uneaten kernels of snap corn. He was eating them when he became aware that Gerald was awake and looking at him. He turned in a flash toward Gerald and opened his mouth and hissed at him so loudly that spat the remains of the corn all over Gerald. Gerald sat up with his hands out stretched and palms up. Both he and the Woodsprite stood there and looked over each other. Then Gerald said, "I am Gerald Boranum and I am looking for William, can you take me to him?" The Woodsprite just stared at him and didn't say a word. Gerald repeated his request and this time the Woodsprite nodded his head yes. Then he went about picking up the remains of the snapping corn and popped the kernels in his mouth and smiled.

The Woodsprite started to walk away and Gerald said, "Wait till I put out this fire and pick up my things." The Woodsprite kept right on walking as though he hadn't heard a thing. Gerald shouted, "Wait!" The Woodsprite turned and sat down. Gerald quickly covered the fire with dirt and packed up his blanket and food pouch, picked up his flying stick and walked in the direction of the Woodsprite. When he got close the Woodsprite jumped up and ran for the forest. Gerald took off in a run after him but couldn't catch up with him. The Woodsprite quickly disappeared into the dark forest and was gone. Gerald called out, "Where are you, wait on me." No response and the forest was pitch black. Fire ashes would not have been blacker. He yelled again, "I can't see you, where are you?" This time he heard a whisper, "Listen to the forest with your ears, not your eyes, and listen carefully."

Gerald closed his eyes and listened. He could hear the rustle of leaves above him blown by the gentle breeze in the treetops. He listened again, this time he thought he heard the gentle fall of footsteps as they plodded through the undergrowth of the forest. He could hear the bushes being pushed aside as someone was moving away from him. Opening his eyes but still concentrating on the sounds he moved off in the direction he thought the sounds were coming from. Slowly he was gaining on whatever was making the noise. Several times he bumped into trees and low hanging branches. He thought he heard a low chuckle each time he banged his head into something. But it was soon gone. Finally he emerged at the edge of a clearing where he could look up at the night sky and see the thousands of stars dotted there. There was just enough of a light from them that he could see the clearing he was on the edge of. In the dim light he thought he could make out shapes darting left and right. Standing very still and closing his eyes he could hear the footfalls of many things. It was a real rush for his auditory senses. Whatever these creatures were, there were a lot of them. They seemed to be moving closer to him so he stood very still. When he opened his eyes he could see hundreds of big yellow eyes staring back at him.

He lifted his hands palm up with his fingers extended and said, "I have come to find William will you take me to him?" From the midst of the crowd came a soft-spoken almost childlike response. "I am William. You must be the young king that Soil told me would come. He wants me to teach you to protect yourself. He wants me to make you feared amongst your kind. What do you want?"

Gerald resisted the urge to laugh at the tiny voice, but he cleared his throat, and said, "I am here to learn what you want to teach me. I want to be a leader to all people and beings. I do not want to be feared by anyone, I want to be just, fair and capable of understanding all sides of any dispute or problem. I want to bring all species, races, and beings together as one family. That will be my goal when I become King."

The tiny voice spoke again and said, "We will teach you how to defend yourself and the forest. The other you will have to learn elsewhere. We have never been close to your kind because of their treachery and unkind words. Maybe you will be able to teach us as well. Come now and we will find you a place to rest and tomorrow we will start your training."

A small hand reached out and grabbed his and started leading him into the clearing. He could not see all of them, but he could see their eyes. The gathering of Woodsprites parted as Gerald was led into the clearing. Then the same tiny voice said, "Please you make a fire with your magic." Gerald was confused but thought they meant make a fire with his rock and blade. He bent down and scooped up some dried pine needles and dried vines from the clearing floor and piled them in the center of a circle he had drawn in the dirt with his knife. He sat about pulling out all grasses, weeds, and wood from the circle and then sat down next to his pile of dried grasses and needles and struck the knife blade with his rock from bird cave. Instantly a spark fell on the pile of dried grasses and a small fire started.

He made it larger and larger with the remains of the grasses from the fire circle and then turned to the closest Woodsprite and said, "We will need some good dead and dried wood to keep it going." As if by magic pieces of wood started flying in from all directions. He piled on twigs, then branches and finally some substantial logs. He had a roaring fire going now that lighted the entire clearing in its glow. Now he could plainly see Hundreds of Woodsprites standing watching him with their haunting yellow eyes. He could also see hundreds of tiny wooden mounds that looked like very small houses. They were dome like in shape and only about one-half a rod tall. He could see that all the entrances faced the same direction. They were all pointed in the direction of his fire. He turned to the Woodsprite closest to him and said, "Are you William the person I came to learn from? If you are, I have a present for you."

William nodded and said, "Yes I am William. I will be your teacher while you are with us."

Gerald reached into his leather pouch and brought out the old tattered Orioles baseball cap and held it out to him. William took the cap and placed it on his head and it immediately fell off. Gerald picked it up and adjusted the back strap and placed it back on his head and said, "This used to be the crown of the Lady of the Green." She gave it to me and now I give it to you. Leaders should always have something that can identify them as a leader. The crown on you looks very, very regal. I would know you as the leader of the Woodsprites anywhere. William spoke in his tiny voice and said, "Gerald Boranum you have given me the best gift I have ever received. You will forever be welcome in the home of the Woodsprites." He held up his hat for all to see and then placed it back on his head. When he did, a cheer went up that sounded like a bunch of children screaming. William puffed out his chest and strutted around the fire. He then pointed to a little house close to the fire and said, "That hut is yours while you are with us. Sleep now and we will start training in the morning light."

Gerald crawled inside the small wooden hut and found that he couldn't stand up but the floor was covered with pine needles. He spread his blanket and put his food pouch at one edge of the hut along with his water pouch and lay down in a curled up position and fell fast asleep.

As the sun was just popping over the trees to illuminate the clearing Gerald heard a tiny voice say, "Get up young king, it is time to start your training." Gerald crawled out of his hut rubbing the sleep from his eyes and was immediately jumped on by William who put his spindly little arms around his body pinning Gerald's arms at his side. Gerald rolled over to pin William to the ground. When Gerald rolled three more Woodsprites jumped on top of him. They now had him pinned to the ground with William underneath him.

William said, "The first rule of self-defense is to expect the unexpected. You must always be on your guard at all times. If this had been a real battle, you would have been dead by now." William told the rest of the group to release Gerald and they all stood up and brushed themselves off. The other group of three started to chuckle amongst themselves until William snapped, "I don't think this is funny or humorous. This young lad has come to us for training not degradation. I will not have him made fun of, do you all understand?" They all nodded their understanding

438

and went and sat by the remains of the smoldering fire.

William turned to Gerald and said, "Let me introduce you to these three warriors. They are the best of the Woodsprites in battle." As they approached the three they stood. William said, "The first of your training will be performed by Ragen." Ragen moved forward and bowed at the waist. William continued, "Ragen is a master with his hands." Ragen jumped across the fire remains and picked up a rather large log and hit it with the edge of his hand and the log split down the middle and fell to the ground.

William said, "Your next trainer will be Wallock. He is a master with his feet." Wallock stood and picked up one half of the split log and slammed his foot in to the middle of it and it broke in half.

William said, "Your final training will be taught by Mirth. She is a master in stealth and hiding. She can blend in to any background and not be seen until she is upon the enemy." Mirth jumped into the air and was gone. She just vanished right in front of his eyes. "Where did she go", asked Gerald?

"I am right here on top of your hut," said a tiny voice. Gerald turned and looked but didn't see her at first. But looking closer she was laying right on top of it blending in with the sticks that made up the hut. William continued, "Your final training will take place with me. Once you have learned from the best warriors you will fight me in order to graduate. Do you understand, young king?"

Gerald nodded his understanding and said, "When do we start?" William turned to Ragen and said, "Do you have his clothes prepared for him?" Ragen nodded and picked up a satchel of leather

440

and handed it to Gerald. Ragen said, "Put on these clothes and follow me."

Gerald opened the satchel and found a loose fitting leather smock with a white leather belt to tie around the waist to keep the smock shut. He also found a loose fitting pair of fine leather trousers that were very thin but very tough. Gerald slipped back into his hut and quickly undressed and put on the leather smock and trousers. When he emerged all of the other Woodsprites were gone except for Ragen. Ragen looked him up and down and said, "Take off your shoes you will need to toughen up your feet. Ragen started walking toward the tree line and looked back over his shoulder and said, "Well, come on young king. You have much to learn." Gerald pulled off his shoes and followed Ragen through the brush. The twigs and sticks dug into the bottom of his feet like knife tips but he didn't complain or whimper. Gerald followed Ragen to a cleared area near the tree line where a large circle had been drawn in the soil. Inside the circle were several poles supporting leather bags filled with straw, mud sand, and rocks. He also saw several small saplings bent double to the ground and held there with a leather rope. Once inside the circle Ragen grabbed Gerald's hands and looked at the palms the edges and the back of them. Ragen let go of his hands and said, "We will have to toughen these up quite a bit."

Ragen led him to the first leather bag filled with straw and said, "This is the first bag. You will hit this bag with the side of your hands and the palms of your hand. Then you will hit this bag with the back of your hands and with your closed fists. You will start now and not stop until I tell you too. You must hit the bag like you were going to hurt it. Start now with your palms."

Gerald started slapping the bag with one hand and then the other. Ragen shouted, "Hit the bag like you want to hurt it, not like you want to scold it."

Gerald started hitting it harder and harder. Though each slap stung his hands, he never said a thing. He just bit his lower lip and continued slapping the bag. Ragen found himself a comfortable place to sit and would tell Gerald when to change hand positions. Several times he had to chide Gerald into hitting the bag harder, which Gerald did. The soft bag training lasted for three days from dawn till dusk. Gerald was given water and food breaks only. Otherwise he was hitting the soft bag. The tops, sides, and palms of his hands were bruised and his knuckles were raw from hitting the bag. Every night Ragen would examine Gerald's hands and rub them with a lotion from the leaves of an Alloonne plant. By morning his knuckles would feel better even though his hands were black and blue. On the fourth day Ragen took Gerald to the circle and

443

stood him in front of the bag filled with sand. Ragen said, "Poke the bag with your finger to feel its strength. The first hit to an opponent will tell you his strength. Remember it."

Then just as Gerald stood ready to punch the sand bag Ragen reached down to the ground and picked up a log. The log was about a half-rod long and two hands in diameter. Ragen said, "Put up your arms to carry this log." Gerald extended his arms and Ragen placed the log across both arms then he said, "You hold this log until I tell you to drop it. Do not drop it unless I tell you to, do you understand?" Gerald nodded his head and stood there. Ragen went and sat in his usual place. After a while Gerald's arms began to ache and he wanted to drop the log, but something in his mind said not to. Eventually his arm muscles began to cramp and tears started to roll down his face but he still didn't drop the log. Eventually Gerald stood there all day holding the log and never dropped it once. At the end of the day he was physically spent. His arms ached, his back ached, and he was dead tired.

Ragen led him back to his hut and when they were in front of the hut Ragen said, "You are either very strong or very stubborn young king. Even I cannot hold the log for an entire day. You have broken my time by several arcs of the sun. Now I must try and regain the longest time by holding the log longer than you." He said this almost angrily then he said, "I am also very proud of you, you are a good student and will make a great warrior. Tomorrow we start on the bag of sand." He rubbed some liniment into the shoulders arms and back of Gerald and then said, "Get a good night's sleep for tomorrow we start your real training." Gerald just looked at him in wonderment but was too tired to ask him what he meant. It took all his effort to climb into his hut and he immediately fell asleep.

The next day he surprisingly felt better. His shoulders ached a little but he felt pretty good. As promised he started hitting the sand bag under the tutelage of Ragen. His hands had been given a day of rest, but they were taking a really severe beating with this heavier bag. Never the less, he kept at it all day long. This went on for three days. On the fourth day when Gerald went to the circle there stood Ragen with two logs. He told Gerald to lift his arms and only put one log across his arms. He hoisted the other over his arms and stood there beside Gerald. The day was a little warmer than usual and before long both of them were sweating profusely. Gerald knew that Ragen was going to try and hold his log longer than he. Gerald decided right there and then that he would not allow Ragen to best him at log holding.

They stood there all day not even taking the time for water or food. Just about sunset the Woodsprites started to gather around them to see who would drop the log first. But neither did. The sun went down and still they stood there. A small fire was started so that all could witness this contest between the warrior and his young apprentice. They had remained silent all day and then finally Ragen broke the silence and said, "There would be no dishonor if you were to stop now and drop your log. We would be both regaled as heroes. No one has ever held a log this long before. Gerald looked at him and said, "I will drop mine right after you drop yours." Ragen just stared at him with contempt and continued holding his log. Just about mid night Gerald turned to Ragen and he was weaving back and forth like he was going to faint. Gerald dropped his log and rushed to his side to help him. A large grin crossed Ragen's face and he laughed in his tiny little voice and said, "I knew I was stronger than you." Then he dropped his log and slapped Gerald on the back and said, "That fainting trick gets them every time, I have never had it fail me."

447

"You tricked me," said Gerald. Ragen looked at him and said, "Sometimes the strength of the mind is more powerful than an entire army. Use your head and your body my young king. They both serve you and only you can choose which to use when they are needed." " It's not fair," said Gerald. Ragen chuckled and said, "Another lesson you need to learn is that life is not fair, it is what you make of your life that is. Come now my young king and let's both get some rest because for tomorrow your real lessons start." " What have we been doing up till now, playing", asked Gerald quizzically? "No, my young king, we call this conditioning for what is to come," said Ragen. Ragen led Gerald back to his hut and just as Gerald was crawling in Ragen slapped him on the rump and said, "You are a good student and someday you will make a very good king."

The next morning Ragen shook Gerald's hut and said, "Come out and defend yourself

448

young king." Gerald emerged from his hut bleary eyed but alert and ready to learn. Ragen led him to the circle of training and said, "Today we learn the dance of defense. Every battle if watched from a distance is made up of attack and defense moves. The defense moves will keep you alive while you are waiting for an opening to use an attack move against your opponent. Attacks can come from any direction so defense moves let you move around to ward off attacks without them harming you. Defense moves will guard you against weapons and bodily assaults. Your entire body when in the defense mode can save you from attack from all sides. You must learn to feel and listen to everything around you and not just see. Each defense move is like part of a dance. When you put them all together you can defend against anything. I will teach you defense moves in small parts. When we are finished you will know all the dance moves.

Ragen moved Gerald's arms to a raised position with the elbows bent and said, "Legs slightly apart, knees partially bent. This is movement number one it will protect your head. You must remember this move because it is the start of all others." Ragen reached out to slap Gerald and his arm and hand were stopped by Gerald's. Ragen tried the other arm and again it was blocked. Now Ragen started to circle Gerald and tried again and again to slap him. Gerald blocked all the slaps. Ragen now pulled out a black hood and said, "Now place this over your head and try and stop me." Gerald put on the hood and said, "But I can't see you, how will I stop you?" "Use your ears and listen for me," said Ragen. Ragen reached out and slapped Gerald on the right side of his head. Then he moved and slapped him on the left side of his head. Now he started dancing around Gerald slapping him whenever he felt like it. Finally Gerald closed his eyes and started listening to where Ragen was and started to dodge and twist and put his hands up. Gerald found he could hear Ragen's arms move through the air and he could hear the scuffle of his feet on the ground. Slowly but surely Gerald began to block some of Ragen's slaps. In about one arc of the sun Ragen could no longer slap Gerald. Gerald was blocking all of Ragen's advances. Finally Ragen said, "Remove the hood, and now we go to move number two."

Ragen positioned Gerald for move number two and said, "Remember move two it will protect your body." Ragen punched Gerald in the stomach and said, "This will get worse before it gets better so protect yourself. Ragen threw another punch at Gerald's body and Gerald blocked the punch. Then Ragen slapped Gerald on his right cheek. Ragen laughed and said, "You haven't forgotten move one have you?" This session went on for more than another arc and then out came the hood again. Gerald caught on quicker this time and was soon blocking punches to his body and head by movements one and two. Finally Ragen said, "Let's stop for a few minutes and get some food and drink."

Gerald removed the hood and Ragen punched him in the left side and slapped his right cheek. Ragen said, "Never take your eyes off your opponent." Gerald said, "How many movements are there to this dance?" Ragen replied, "Twenty-five basic movements and twenty five more but the last twenty five are just derivations of the first ones. If you master the first twenty-five you will be a good match for William." The rest of the afternoon was spent teaching Gerald three more basic defensive movements. When it was time for the evening meal Gerald was tircd and sore all over his body from being slapped and punched. That night he dreamt of what he had learned today.

The next four days were spent teaching Gerald the rest of the defensive dance and by the end of the fifth day Gerald was holding his own against Ragen. Ragen had started punching harder and slapping with a lot more ferocity than in the beginning.

On the sixth day Ragen moved Gerald to the bag filled with rocks and the punch training started all over again. Gerald's hands had become conditioned to the abuse and did not hurt as much after a day or two of punching the rock bag.

On the seventh day Ragen took him to the training circle and said, "Now it is your time to hit me. I don't think you will be able to, but give it a try." Gerald assumed position one and started to circle Ragen. In Gerald's head he was planning his approach and attack along with what defensive moves he would need to counter Ragen's attack. As he was circling him he saw that as he moved to

453

his left Ragen moved a little slower than he did when moving to his right. Gerald feigned a punch to the right and slapped Ragen on the left cheek. Ragen was shocked and annoyed that he had been slapped. Gerald repeated the same move and slap with his hand against Ragen's cheek. Now Ragen was getting angry and started his attack on Gerald. Each time he punched or slapped Gerald blocked them and in retaliation he would hit or slap Ragen on his left side. Finally Ragen figured out what Gerald was doing and changed his stance to protect his left side. Doing that opened up Ragen's right side and Gerald started counter punching his right side. Almost enraged now Ragen said, "You have learned very well young king." Ragen had barely gotten the words out of his mouth when Gerald smacked Ragen on the end of his little nose and it went CRACK!!! Ragen pulled back and straightened his nose and said, "Why did you do that?" "Very simple," said Gerald, "You took your eyes off of

454

me and I know you know that rule." Ragen started to laugh with the trickle of blood coming out of his nose. He reached up and wiped it away with one hand and took a punch with the other. Gerald simply reached out and grabbed his hand and held it there. Ragen said, "We are finished and now I pass you on to Wallock. He will teach you the art of foot fighting. I can't believe your broke my nose! You can take the rest of the day off and Wallock will greet you in the morning." Gerald went to a nearby stream and took off his clothes and jumped in to cleanse himself after a hard days exercise. Just before his evening meal he wrote his mother and father a letter in his journal.

The next morning Wallock greeted him and said, "Let me see your feet." Gerald took off his shoes and showed Wallock his feet. Wallock grimaced and said, "We will have to toughen them up a little before you can fight with them. Leave your shoes in your hut and follow me." With that

Wallock took off at a run and soon disappeared into the forest. Gerald was close on his heels but Wallock was a much faster runner. Gerald was wondering where they were going but soon figured out that Wallock was toughening his feet. He had been running for about one arc when his feet started to hurt. Wallock had left the forest and was running down gravel paths and over rocks. Then he would run through trees where the undergrowth was thick and sharp. After about two arcs of running Wallock stopped because he was out of breath. Wallock turned to Gerald and said, "Let me see your feet again." Gerald picked up one foot and then the other and presented them to Wallock. Neither one was cut, but they sure were bruised. They hurt like mad, but Gerald was not going to complain. Wallock turned and started walking back to the encampment. Gerald followed him close behind. They reached the training circle about two arcs before sunset.

Wallock turned to Gerald and said, "Assume defensive position number one." Gerald obeyed and Wallock now took Gerald's feet and positioned them a little further apart and his right foot slightly in front of his left. Then Wallock said, "Do you fight with your right hand or left?" Gerald replied, "I fight with both, I feel comfortable either way." To which Wallock replied, then you can move either foot in front of the other depending on what you need to defend or fight at the time. Now I want you to kick the bag of pine needles with the top of your foot." Wallock demonstrated and then pointed to Gerald.

Gerald kicked the bag using the same motion that Wallock had just used. The bag made a big Thump noise when he hit it. Wallock looked at Gerald and said, "I want you to kick the bag two hundred times with your right foot and two hundred times with your left foot. Then we are done for the day. Gerald started kicking the bag

457

counting each stroke of his leg. His feet, calves, and legs were almost in a muscle spasm by the time he had finished the kicks with each foot. He limped back to his hut only to find Wallock leaning against it with a small leather pouch in his hand. He reached out and handed it to Gerald and said, "Rub this into your feet and legs tonight and you will be fine by morning." Gerald did as he was told and before long was fast asleep.

The next morning Wallock led him to the circle and said, "Lie down on your back and put your feet up in the air." Gerald complied and Wallock lifted a heavy log onto and across his feet. The log was very heavy. Wallock said, "Keep your legs straight and balance this log into the air and keep it there until I tell you to put it down. Then he turned around and left the circle and disappeared amongst the huts. Gerald focused his mind on the task at hand and kept the log balanced. When his legs grew weary he relaxed his knees a little and

458

then straightened them again. Just about mid-day
Wallock returned dragging even a bigger log
behind him. He told Gerald to drop the little log
and bend his knees. Gerald did as he was asked
and Wallock pushed the large log on top of
Gerald's feet and said, "Now push it in the air."
Gerald did as he was commanded and lifted the
log until his knees were straight. Wallock then
said, "Now do that two hundred times and then
you may quit for the day. Gerald started counting
and pushing with all his might and slowly the log
started moving up and down. When he got to two-
hundred he continued counting aloud he continued
counting until he got to three-hundred. He gave a
mighty shove and the log went crashing into the
bags of sand and rock. He got to his feet and
could barely stand. His legs felt like they were
pieces of grass in the wind. Slowly he started
walking toward his hut not looking at anyone or
saying anything to anyone. When he got to his hut
there stood Wallock with his miracle bag of

liniment. Wallock said, "Rub this on to your legs, and you will feel better by morning. By the way, why did you do three hundred leg lifts instead of the two hundred that I told you to do?" Gerald smiled at him and said, "I did what I do not think you can. I don't even think you can lift that log with those spindly legs." Wallock just smiled and said, "I will see you in the morning. Have a good night's sleep." The next morning in the training circle Wallock started showing Gerald the several different dance steps for foot fighting. Training continued on the sand bag with kicks and thrusts learned during the lessons of the day. When they were finished Wallock said, "Let me see your feet." Gerald produced his feet one at a time like he had done on the other occasions. Wallock just nodded his head and left for the evening. This type of training went on for the next six days. Each day a new number of dance steps would be taught and then end the day with the bag training. He was now kicking the rock bag with his feet and legs.

On the eight day Wallock said, "Today we fight." They squared off with Wallock taking the initiative right away trying to kick and hit Gerald has they moved about the circle. Wallock landed a few kicks but mostly glancing blows that did not hurt Gerald. Eventually Gerald noticed that Wallock would always go to his left when circling him but would fight from the right side with right leg kicks and thrusts. So Gerald started moving to his left forcing Wallock to move to his right. Once this happened Gerald kicked Wallock just above his left knee pushing it back until he heard a popping sound and Wallock fell to the ground in agony. Gerald rushed to his side and Wallock kicked him squarely between the legs and Gerald gasped and fell forward on the ground. Wallock looked at Gerald and said, "Never take your eyes off of your opponent." Then he threw back his head, stood up, and started laughing. He reached down to help Gerald off the ground and Gerald whirled around and swept his feet out from under

461

Wallock and he landed flat on his back so hard it knocked the wind out of him. Gerald looked at Wallock laying there gasping for air and said, "I will remember that from now on." They helped each other up and walked back to their huts. On the way back Wallock said, "I think you are ready for Mirth. She will teach you how to be invisible. She will teach you to walk through bells and make no sound. She will be your toughest trainer by far."

Chapter 31 - Mirth the Invisible

The next morning Gerald was awakened by someone pulling on his leg. Somehow during the night he had turned around in his hut and stretched his legs out through the doorway. His feet still ached from the training of Wallock and his hands were just beginning to feel normal again. He wondered to himself what would hurt on him when he was finished with Mirth. When he emerged from his hut Mirth was standing right in front of him. She was larger than Wallock or Ragen. She stood almost four hands taller than either of them. Her arms and legs were not nearly as bony as theirs and her hair was pulled back and fastened in the back. She had broad shoulders and, unlike the males, she wore a full set of green clothes. Her clothes were not made of leather but of a cloth that was thin but not see through.

She noticed him looking her up and down and said, "Yes young king I am a female warrior. There are only three female warriors in the entire Woodsprite gathering. We pride ourselves on being the best at invisible. We are able to sneak into any encampment and not be seen. So far only the females of our race have been able to master this art. It is unlikely that you will succeed. But William has expressed his desire for me to try and teach you these ancient arts and so I will. To begin with you will have to change your clothes. Here is a set of greens that should fit you. Put them on along with these slippers. Then come to the training circle and we will start."

Gerald slipped into his new clothes and slippers which surprisingly fit like a glove. They were so light and airy that he hardly knew he had anything on. He tugged at the fabric and it was very strong and tough but soft to the feel. He made his way to the training circle but didn't see Mirth anywhere. All of the bags, logs, and rocks had been removed and replaced with piles of sticks, trees, branches and a big bog of mud. He stood there looking around and wondering when Mirth would appear.

From out of nowhere came Mirth's voice and said, "Why are you standing there? You must use your eyes, ears, and nose to find me, now get with it." Gerald started moving around the circle

464

looking at the twigs, branches and the trees. He couldn't see anything. He moved to the pile of branches and closed his eyes and listened. He could hear nothing. He repeated the same for the pile of twigs and trees. When he reached the edge of the mud bog he closed his eyes and took in all the sounds of the forest and one by one he ignored them until only one sound remained. It was the sound of someone gently breathing in and out. He opened his eyes and stared down into the mud. There in the middle of the mud was Mirth laying face up. She had smeared mud on her face and was lying perfectly still. It was hard for him to see her chest move up and down because she had slowed her breath to a very shallow one. He pretended that he didn't see her and walked back to the pile of twigs and picked up a long large stick. Walking back to the mud he poked the stick at the lying figure and said. "You can come out now because I see you."

From behind him came her voice just as she pushed him into the mud bog. "Evidently you don't," she said. She continued, "What you saw was what I wanted you to see, a mud replica of me lying there. I have been up in this tree watching every move you made. Gerald now drenched with mud stood up and said, "I looked up in the trees and listened as well, and I didn't hear you breathing." Mirth replied, "Have you ever heard of holding your breath? I can hold mine for almost four tics of the sun. How long can you hold yours?" Gerald didn't know the answer to that question because he had never had to hold his breath for anything he could remember.

Gerald walked out of the mud bog and said, "Now my nice clean clothes are all muddy." Mirth shrieked with laughter and said, "Follow me dirty boy and let's get you cleaned up. Gerald followed her to a nearby stream and she jumped in and disappeared. Gerald looked up and down the

466

stream but could not see her. He thought she might drown and jumped in to save her. He floundered around for several tics of the sun but could not find her. He dove to the bottom of the stream and could not see her anywhere. He did this several times and then he surfaced and heard Mirth laughing from the shoreline. There she sat on a big rock just rocking back and forth with laughter.

Gerald walked out of the stream and noticed that his clothes were clean and they were almost dry. Water was just running out of the fabric and away from his slippers. "What kind of cloth is this", he said? Mirth replied, "It is made of Speringus web. It is virtually indestructible. Swords and arrows will not pierce it and water does not cling to it nor does dirt or mud. Because it is so fine a thread it reflects the sunlight or moonlight or firelight. When you are wearing it, your clothes will take on or reflect the color of your

467

surroundings and make you almost invisible. Keep it with you all the time and wear it when you need to. If you pull your hands up into the sleeves they will disappear as well. Your face and hair will be your give away points. But with a little application of some of these colors, she threw him a leather pouch filled with small vials of colored powders; you can become completely invisible to watchers. The colors rub off easily so be careful not to scratch or rub your face and hair once you have applied them or you will be seen. Now that you are dry let's continue your training back at the circle."

When they arrived back at the training circle someone had rigged up a labyrinth of strings with bells hanging from them throughout the circle. Mirth turned to Gerald and said, "When you can walk from one side of this circle to the other without ringing as much as one bell your training will be complete." Gerald watched her as she walked into the circle and started darting this way and that, doing summersaults, bending backward and crawling on her belly until she stood and walked out the other side of the circle. She turned to him and said, "Now it is your turn. You cannot touch any string as you pass through. If you do a bell will ring and you must start over. We will do this every day until you can make it through. Do you understand?"

Gerald nodded his agreement and walked toward the first row of strings. He had already forgotten the path she had taken so he tried to find his own path. He stepped over the first string and his head hit another string and the bell tinkled. "Start over," said Mirth. He tried again and again a bell chimed. "Start over," said Mirth. This same thing went on for almost four arcs of the sun. Finally Mirth said, "Stop and use your eyes. Pick out the best route through and then try again."

469

Gerald stood and stared at the layer upon layer of random strings stretched across the circle. Little by little he started seeing a path through the maze of webbing. He successfully crept, bent, dodged, and bent over backward until he was at the middle. His thigh brushed ever so slightly against one of the strings and the little bell chimed. "Start over," said Mirth, without so much as a complement for him getting as far as he did. Gerald tinkled and clanged his way back to the beginning and turned to face Mirth. She was still sitting on a tree stump on the far side of the circle. The sun was beginning to go down and shadows were being cast throughout the web making it difficult to see all of the strings. This time he only made it about a third of the way through before he heard the chime of a bell. Without saying a thing he turned around and made his way back to the beginning.

Mirth said, "OK, young king, I think that will be enough for today. Tomorrow we will work on you finding a path through the web. You are doing much better than I expected. I will see you in the morning."

Gerald walked back to his hut with his body aching all over from the bending and gyrations he put it through trying to avoid the strings in the web. After having something to eat he crawled into his hut and fell fast asleep.

He awoke early the next morning and went to the training circle and walked around the web and observed it from all sides. Finally he climbed one of the small trees and looked down on the top of the web. In his mind he began to see a way through the web. The more he looked the more he saw what his body would have to do to slink his way through the maze. At one arc after sunrise Mirth showed up and said, "Please focus your mind to find a way through. You can do it and then imagine in your mind what your body will have to do to negotiate its way through." Gerald stood poised on the starting side of the web when Mirth walked around the web and took his arm and led him to another starting point. She winked at him and said, "Start from here and go to the opposite side." Gerald was going to protest but new fare well that he would lose any argument he might give her about changing the starting location. So he just walked around the web again and back up into the tree focusing on the starting point and what lay between that and the end point. By midday Gerald had made multiple attempts to cross and had made it beyond the middle of the maze on three occasions without ringing any bell. By mid-afternoon he had made it two thirds of the way across the maze and was standing there contemplating his next move or series of moves. A slight breeze was kicking up and suddenly several bells started to tinkle from the wind. Mirth said, "Start over." Gerald replied, "That wasn't me, it was the wind." "Sure, sure," said Mirth"; Start over." " No, I won't," said Gerald. "I didn't ring the bells so I will start from here." "No, you will not," said Mirth. "You will start from where I tell you to start."

Gerald just shrugged his aching shoulders and weaseled his way back to the beginning. Within a matter of sun tics he was back to where he had last stopped before. Now he could see his way clearly through the rest of the web. Twisting, bending arching, and crawling he found his way out of the web. Mirth smiled and said, "Very good young king, very good. Now all you have to do is complete this web by firelight and you are finished. She handed him a small vial of liniment to rub on his shoulders and back, and legs. He limped back to his hut and rubbed himself down with the black salve she had given him and very soon fell fast asleep.

473

The next two days were spent teaching him how to blend in with trees, weeds, rocks, dirt, mud, and anything else Mirth could find. She taught him how to apply the color to his face and hair. They would take long walks through the forest trying to disappear from each other. Finally on the third day Mirth came to him and said, "Today I want you to rest for tonight you will cross the web by firelight." Gerald had noticed that the maze of strings had been re-arranged to make a different conglomeration of pathways and dead ends throughout the web of bells. He slept a little that day but mostly he wandered around the web and observed it from all sides. He stayed in the tree above the web for almost two arcs of the sun committing the web structure to his memory. By nightfall he thought he had memorized the web from all sides and had figured pathways through it from all angles. As night began to fall a fire was started inside the training circle but away from the maze. The firelight danced over the webbing

474

casting some of it in shadow and other parts of it in bright glows of red and yellow. The little bells reflected the flickering light of the fire.

Mirth walked into the circle and grabbed Gerald by the arm and led him to the web. She said, "Start here and go to the other side. I will be waiting there for you. You have been a good student and I have confidence that you can do this if you truly focus. Gerald shook his arms and legs and bent over and touched his toes and bent backward and slowly stood on his hands and then back to his feet. Without saying another word, he stepped into the web. As cunning and bending as a jungle cat, and the slithering of a snake Gerald bobbed and weaved his way through the maze. Bending backward and onto his hands twice and one handstand he slipped through the maze with ease. When he walked out the other side Mirth threw her arms around him and planted a big old kiss right on his lips. They were both a bit embarrassed by it and they started to laugh.

Mirth looked very solemn for a minute and biting her lower lip she said, "Now you must fight our leader, William. He is very cunning and very strong. He has been our leader for quite some time now. He is trained in the same techniques that you have been. Unlike you he has fought for the forest many times and has been victorious each time. If he bests you do not think you have lost. Please take it as a compliment that you have fought the strongest and most clever warrior among all Woodsprites. It is unlikely that you will win. Use all your skills you have been taught. You will need them."

She hugged and kissed him again and then she was gone. It was like she disappeared before his very eyes. Wow I wish she had taught me that move, he thought.

Gerald spent the rest of the evening deep in thought as to how he should fight William. Should he be aggressive, defensive, or elusive? Should he use all three of his new learned skills or would one of them be enough? The answer eluded him; he didn't even know when he was to fight William. If he just let William defeat him without so much as a good scrap then William might think his best warriors had not done their job, or would he think that Gerald was not strong enough to be king someday? All of these questions and no answers were floating around in his head. Then a thought came to him, why not use all the knowledge he had learned since being with the Lady of the Green to defeat William. Would defeating him be a good thing or would it make the rest of the Woodsprites lose confidence in him as a leader? No answers, just more questions popped into his head. With his noggin filled with questions he fell into a restless sleep.

Chapter 32 - The Fight with William the Woodsprite

The next morning he awakened to the beating of drums and the blaring of horns. He sat up in his hut and put on his Speringus clothes and slippers and crawled out of the doorway. There standing by a roaring fire was William. He was equally dressed wearing the Oriel cap that Gerald had given him upon his arrival. Gerald could feel the warmth of the fire as he approached William. These cool mornings before the season changed to cold were refreshing, but a nice warm fire got the body moving and the blood flowing in the morning.

As Gerald approached William said, "I am told that your training with us is finished. Each of my warriors has told me that you are a good student and a quick learner. I must say that your body has grown since you arrived. Your arms are larger as are your chest and legs. The training must agree with you. It is now time to show me how much you have learned. You must use all of your skills to try and best me in combat. He reached up and took off the hat he was wearing and handed it to a nearby warrior and turned to

Gerald and said, "Now defend yourself, because I am going to use all of my skills.

Gerald looked at him and said, "I always thought the mark of a great leader was to have faith and confidence in the people he is leading. What message are you going to send to your warriors if you do not believe what they tell you?" William looked confused and said, "What in the tree spirits name do you mean?" You just told me that your best warriors told you that they have trained me to the best of their ability and that I was a good and willing student. Now you challenge me to fight you and in doing so you're essentially telling them you did not believe what they told you. That doesn't strike me as the mark of a great leader. William looked at him questioningly and tilted his head to the side trying to understand this young man with such older thoughts. William opened his mouth to say something and Gerald threw a handful of brown and orange powder in

480

the air and disappeared. When the powder cleared William looked around and didn't see Gerald anywhere. William closed his eyes and listened. No breathing could be heard but he detected footsteps leading away from him. He turned to his right and saw Gerald heading for the training circle. William caught up to him just about the time he was at the web of strings and bells. Gerald jumped, twisted, flipped, and slithered his way through the web not touching any of the strings. Gerald turned around on the other side and looked at William and said, "If you really want to fight me, come through the web." William looked at the strings and gingerly stepped into them. He was very good and twisted his way into the middle then he bent backward and flipped over another string then he lost his balance and fell backward into the web and all of the bells started to ring. Gerald smiled and said, "Start over."

William was now getting angry and ran at Gerald through the rest of the webbing. William lunged at Gerald and using a defensive move, Gerald blocked his lunge and moved aside letting William fall to the ground. William sprang from the ground with surprising agility and launched himself at Gerald. Gerald moved aside again and said, "We can do this all day long if you want to, but I see no need to fight you. I can see you are very good and why the Woodsprites chose you to be their leader. I know you can fight and fight to the death if the situation calls for it. This situation does not. I don't want to fight you. I want to learn from you. I want to become the great leader of my people like you are with yours. Gerald was now trying to stroke William's ego and it seemed to be working. William dropped his arms from the fighting stance and straightened his body to a standing position. William smiled and said, "I believe my warriors have taught you well." "Oh, they did," said Gerald. "One thing they taught me

482

above all others was, never take your eyes off of your opponent." With that Gerald leaped into the air and landed behind William and grasped him around both arms and his chest. Holding him tight against him and pulling him up with his feet off the ground he whispered in his ear, "What I have learned here will stay with me forever. If I am ever to become a great warrior I will tell everyone that I owe it all to the Woodsprites.

Gerald released him and put him back on the ground. William turned to him and put a hand on his shoulder and said, "It is time you returned to the Lady of the Green. There is nothing more we can teach you. I will be watching you as you grow to the great king I think you will become. Go in peace with the forest. You will always be welcome in our camp and in the forest. If you ever have need of us all you need do is ask."

There was a great feast that night and the next morning Gerald mounted his flying stick and headed for Greenhaven.

Chapter 33 - The Teachings of Mergrom

When Gerald arrived at Greenhaven there was a crowd of people gathered to greet him as he landed. The Lady of the Green and Mergrom were standing next to Soil and Sprout and a group of onlookers. When he landed The Lady went to him and hugged him tightly. She released him and took a step backward and said, "You have been gone a very long time and you have grown and developed in your absence. Your body has filled out and you somehow look wiser. You will have to tell me and Mergrom all about it over our evening meal. In the meantime I will give you time to catch up with Sprout and Soil while Mergrom and I finish our talks." She turned and faced Mergrom and the two of them walked off toward her tree house.

Sprout and Soil had hundreds of questions and wanted to know if he had defeated William in a fight. Gerald relived all of his training experiences for them and showed them a couple of dance moves but never really answered the question about fighting with William. Once all the tales had been told Gerald excused himself and went to his room and took a very long shower and redressed for dinner. He decided to wear his Speringus clothing that had been given to him by Mirth. He finished dressing and went to the quarters of the Lady of the Green.

He respectfully knocked at her door and she bade him to enter. She and Mergrom were seated on the floor on cushions with a tray of food between them. She motioned for him to sit on the empty cushion and join them. He sat down and she said, "Don't you look splendid in your Speringus clothes. You will have to pass them along to your children as they become of age. They should fit you for two to three seasons more, and then you will outgrow them. For now though they fit you like a glove. Mergrom and I are talking about your continued training. I think it is time that

486

you go with him and he starts your training in magic and sorcery. He and I may not always see eye to eye on everything, but he is my friend and a valuable ally. What he will teach you is old magic.

Old magic has been handed down from generation to generation. Mergrom is the vessel in which all of this knowledge resides.

We think you need some time with your parents before your next training begins. It has been a long time since you visited with them and it will do you and them good to spend some family time together. I am sure they will have many questions to ask and you have many stories to tell.

Mergrom has some preparing to do before your arrival at his residence so he will come for you in Belledrade when he is ready."

The remainder of the evening was spent eating, drinking tree water and talking about all that he had learned from the Woodsprites. As the evening wore on Gerald could see that they were treating him as a young adult rather than a child. He was gratified that they could see that he was maturing and felt good about being included in some of their adult conversations. Gerald showed them the powders that Mirth had given him to help him become invisible. He asked Mergrom if he knew where he could replenish his supply when what he had was used up. Mergrom replied, "My dear young king, when we are finished with your plant training you will know where to go to find anything you need. But for now, if you need to refill your powder vials, just ask me and I will see to it."

Gerald told the story of his graduation fight with William and they both shook their heads in astonishment. The Lady and Mergrom could now see how this young man was not just growing in body but in stature and maturity as well.

The Lady of the Green finished the evening by saying, "Gerald you have become like a son to me during your stay with us. I know you will become the greatest king Belleadaire has ever had. You have become a servant of the forest and the land. You now know all of the benefits that the forest can provide and I know you will protect it. You will always be welcome in my home and in my heart. If you ever need my assistance in the future all you need do is call on me and I will be at your side. All of my powers are at your disposal when you need them."

Gerald thanked her profusely and hugged her like a son and bade them both a good night. Though he was sad to be leaving Greenhaven he was excited about seeing his mother and father again. He went to his room and packed his journals, books, clothing, and all the trinkets and baubles he had collected over the seasons. That night when he slept he dreamed of flying, of swimming, of exploring caves and of all things learning to shoot a bow and arrow. When he awoke the next morning he made his way through the village saying his good-byes to Sprout, Soil and all the others he had become friends with during his stay in Greenhaven.

When he returned to his quarters the Lady of the Green was waiting sitting on his bed with a sad look in her eyes. Tears welled up in Gerald's eyes and he ran to her and embraced her and started sobbing. He held her for a tic or two and then releasing her. Wiping the tears from his eyes he said, "I know what I am about to say would offend Alexandra but would you mind if I called you mother as well?" Tears ran down the Lady's cheeks as she nodded her approval and was too choked up to say anything. Gerald kissed her gently on both cheeks and wiped away the tears. He gave her one last hug then threw his bags over his flying stick and left the tree house.

490

He flew straight north for about six arcs of the sun before he saw the parapets of Belledrade. He didn't realize how homesick he was until he saw his father's castle.

Circling Belledrade castle several times he gently eased himself onto one of the upper tower landings and looked out over the city. It was good to be home he thought. I wonder where everyone is at this time of day. It was just about evening mealtime so he entered the tower and made his way down to his room and opened the door. There stood his mother and father. As he opened the door they yelled, "Surprise," and Alexandra ran to him and threw her arms around his shoulders and hugged him tightly. When she released him she had tears running down her cheeks. Gerald leaned forward and kissed them gently away. She held him at arm's length and turned to King Gerald and said, "Our little boy is now a young man. Look at him, Papa. He is all grown up. Look how big he has become."

King Gerald walked forward and hugged his son and said, "We will have to start taking you on hunts and have the knights start to train you in the ways of battle." Alexandra broke in and said, "He will have time for that at another time. For now it is just good to have him home. Now come. We have a special meal already prepared and we want to hear all about your adventures and training with the Woodsprites and the Lady of the Green." They descended the stairs together and when they entered the dining hall all of the King's knights were standing at attention along both sides of the room. When they entered a resounding cheer filled the hall. Gerald blushed a little at all the attention he was getting and could only think of bowing and nodding as he was led to a table set in the center of the room.

Standing by the table was a young boy about the same age as Gerald. As they approached the table the boy bowed at the waist. King Gerald looked at his son and said, "This young lad is Phillip Grimley. He will be staying with us for as long as he wishes. He has decided he wants to become a knight. His training is going to start within the next few days. Why don't you and he get to know each other during that time? I am sure he wants to hear the stories you have about your training. Phillip is from the Waterlands. His father and I were very good friends." Prince Gerald nodded to Phillip and sat down at the table. Once he was seated as the guest of honor all the knights sat down along with Phillip. Gerald turned to Phillip and said, "I have never seen or heard of Waterland, where is it and what does it look like?" Phillip started to lose his fear and said, "Waterland is north of Reedland and is mostly comprised of a group of small islands. The largest island is attached to the shore of the mainland by a long

493

stone bridge. The other nine islands are spread in almost a circle from both sides of the main island. My grandfather and my father built bridges between all ten of the islands so each of them could trade with the next. We are mostly fishermen and boat builders and have enjoyed many years of peace and prosperity. About one cycle ago a fleet of vessels appeared on the horizon and started sailing toward our islands. As they drew closer we could see they flew the flags of the dreaded Water Woggs. They are kin to the Woggles of the mainland except these Woggs live on and under the water. They have built a small city under the Great Sea that only they can dive down to. There they have lived for many cycles and usually do not come to shore or the mainland. My father decided to meet with them to ascertain their intentions and why they wanted to enter Waterland. As their boats drew closer my father sailed his boat out to meet theirs. All seemed to be going well, when out of the water raised a giant

494

sea monster with hundreds of Water Woggs riding on its back. The monster attacked my father's boat and it was quickly overrun by the Water Woggs. Unlike their land locked kinsmen, Water Woggs have breathing slits on both sides of their neck just below their ears. These slits allow them to breathe underwater as the marine life does and it also allows them to breathe on land. Their skin is very slimy and green and their yellow bulging eyes are kind of spooky. They have no eyelids so they always look like they are awake. Even dead they just stare at you. My father put up a tremendous battle and killed many Water Woggs. Between him and the four knights he took with him they killed over seventy Wogg warriors. But in the end there were just too many of them and my father and his last remaining knight were dragged into the sea. We never recovered his body or any of the knights. The Woggs left their dead and took ours. As quickly as they arrived they turned their boats around after the battle and sailed back out to sea and disappeared from view. My grandfather sent several small boats out to retrieve my father's barge and bring his body back for burial. We were surprised to find only dead Woggs aboard. My grandfather then sent word to all the islands to fortify their coastlines with guards and signal fires. They are to light the fires at the first sign of a Wogg attack and the rest of the islands will send help and their knights to ward off any attack. My grandfather fearing another attack contacted your father and told him the story of how the Woggs took my father's life. Your father and mother graciously asked me to stay with them for as long as I want to. When I grow up, I will have all the skills of a knight, and I will hunt down the killers of my father and bring them to justice or destroy them. It will be their decision."

Tears started to trickle down his cheeks as they all sat stunned by the account of his father's death. Gerald spoke up and said, "Do you know how to fly? I can teach you if you want to learn."

Phillip wiped away his tears with his sleeve and said, "Oh, could you? I have always wanted to fly on one of those flying sticks but my father thought it too dangerous and would not permit it. I don't own a flying stick but I would really like to learn!"

Gerald smiled and looked at his father and said, "Well, I think we have a few extra ones lying around the castle that would fit you very nicely. What do you say father, do you think we could find one for him?" King Gerald nodded his head and winked at his son and said, "Why yes, I think there is a spare stick or two we could scare up for him. Do you know anyone who can teach him the fundamentals of flying?" Gerald was a little taken back until he saw the wink his dad gave him. Then he said, "Well I should be able to teach him the fundamentals, but it will be up to him to learn the finer points. Maybe we can take a flight and he can show me Waterland from the air."

King Gerald spoke up and said, "Let's concentrate on getting him off the ground and safely back before we plan any trips." Gerald nodded his approval.

Phillip was ecstatic and said, "When can we start, when can I have my first lesson?"

Gerald said, "Let's have some dinner first and then I will find you a good flying stick. Tomorrow morning would be a good time for your first lesson. Why don't we meet in the garden at about two arcs after sunup? That will give us plenty of time and space to get you airborne." Phillip beamed from ear to ear because secretly he had always wanted to fly a stick.

One by one all of the king's knights, dressed in their finest armor, filed by Gerald's place at the table and welcomed him back from his training with the Lady of the Green. They all told him that he looked more filled out than when he left. Some of them told him that it was about time he started his knight training. Gerald thanked them for their compliments and told them graciously that he would do his knight training after his lessons with Mergrom were completed. Gerald regaled them all evening with tales of his time in the forest and especially his time with the Woodsprites. Some of his tales might have been stretched a bit to his advantage but not much. He was beginning to become a very good storyteller. There was much laughter and they all talked well into the night. When it was time to turn in for the night Phillip reminded Gerald about their flying lessons in the morning to which Gerald replied, "Get a good night's sleep Phillip for tomorrow you need to be fresh and alert, for tomorrow you will fly like a bird!"

Chapter 34 - Phillip Grimley Learns to Fly

When Gerald arrived at the garden the next morning Phillip was already there and waiting for him. Gerald had risen early and found the flying stick he was looking for. One of the king's personal flying sticks. It was longer than Gerald remembered it, but it had almost twice the amount of reeds attached to the stick that most flying sticks had. He presented the stick to Phillip and you would have thought Gerald had given him a pot of gold. Phillip thanked him again and again. He promised to keep it safe and in his presence at all times.

He went on and on until Gerald finally said, "Phillip, you are most welcome and that stick is now yours and it will accept only these commands." He handed Phillip a list of written commands that his father had written down that very morning. When Gerald told his father that he wanted to give Phillip one of his flying sticks it was the king that had suggested writing the commands down for Phillip to study. Phillip committed the commands to memory and was really waiting to get on the stick itself. Gerald patiently showed Phillip how to hold the stick, point it, and ride it and the proper way to lean left and right, up and down to direct the stick where Phillip wanted to go. Now it was time for the first ride. Phillip mounted the stick and gave the proper Boomba command and he raised gently into the air about one rod off the ground. He wobbled back and forth and forward and back until Gerald showed him how to plant his feet against the reeds for stability. Once Phillip pushed his feet into the top of the reeds he stabilized himself and was ready to fly. Without warning he shouted Boomba-fo and took off with a squeal." Pulling up on the tip of the stick made him shoot up into the air and over the castle wall before Gerald could even mount his stick and become airborne.

Within a matter of tics Gerald caught sight of Phillip flying like a leaf in a strong wind. He was cutting circles, lines, diagonal and even spirals in the sky. He was a very quick study. When Gerald finally did catch up with him he flew up to Phillip's side and said, "For today, we will circle the castle and close by. Tomorrow we will go on a short trip to the Silver Mountains just north of here. Phillip yelled with laughter and did a loop-de-loop in the sky before turning and heading back to the castle. The rest of the day was spent on landings and takeoffs from different parts of the castle and all around Belledrade. They would fly to a rooftop and land then take off then land on a road and then take off. They practiced on almost anything they could find to land and fly away from. Phillip and Gerald were having such a good time the day went by fast. Phillip was a very good student and in no time at all was flying, landing and taking off of any object they could find. They flew side by side and Gerald let Phillip try and push his flying

502

sticks to the limit and then they would fly out over the small farms around Belledrade and swoop down out of the air to startle flocks of sheep and cattle that were grazing in the fields. Phillip took to the flying stick like a natural. Before long he could soar, then stop his stick in midair and rest before flying off again, and perform some aerial maneuver that he would think up in his head. As the sun was setting in the west Gerald flew up beside Phillip and said, "Let's turn back to Belledrade and I will race you back to the castle." Without hesitation Phillip turned and rocketed back toward the castle. Gerald was taken by surprise at the speed Phillip was traveling and soon lost sight of Phillip as he flew into a low hanging cloud.

Gerald lay down on his stick and commanded it to fly faster. He shot through the sky like a comet. Soon he saw the outskirts of Belledrade loom up on the horizon but did not see Phillip anywhere. As he circled the castle he saw a contingent of guards pointing into the air. Gerald thought they were pointing at him until he rolled over and looked above him. Falling from the sky was Phillip without his flying stick. Gerald turned his stick around and flew directly at Phillip. Phillip was screaming and flailing his arms like a windmill in a stiff breeze. He looked like he was trying to fly like a bird but was falling like a rock. Phillip shot past him and Gerald turned his stick toward the ground and dived after him. Closing the distance between him and Phillip only took a few tics. Pulling up behind him he reached out and grabbed Phillip by the neck of his shirt and commanded his stick to slow. The combined weight of the two on Gerald's stick kept them falling. Though not as fast as free-fall but they were still plummeting toward the castle roof. Gerald commanded his stick to fly up and they slowed even more but still they were rapidly approaching the rooftop. When they were about two rods from the roof Gerald pulled up on his stick with all his might and they slowed just enough to both tumble onto the parapet floor with a thud. Gerald landed on top of Phillip and they both started rolling across the floor. When they both came to rest they were leaning up against the castles outer wall. The guards came running over to them expecting to find two boys injured. Instead they found two skinned up laughing boys still feeling the rush of adrenalin coursing through their bodies.

Lifting them both to a standing position the guards could see they were not seriously injured so their concern immediately turned to scorn then relief. The Captain of the Guard grabbed them both by the shirt collars and shook them gently and said, "What kind of prank is this you're playing? Do you know what would have happened to you if you had not stopped in time? That was a foolhardy move on both of your parts. You, Prince Gerald, are supposed to be teaching him how to fly safely, not fall from the sky like a

wounded bird! What were you thinking?" Phillip
shook himself loose from the Captain and said,
"This is not Gerald's fault. I am the one to blame
here. I lost my grip on the flying stick and if it
hadn't been for Gerald I would be squashed all
over the castle roof by now." The captain told
them that they should go below and have the
healer look at them and see to their scrapes and
bruises then they would see the King and Queen
to put some restrictions on their flying routines.
Gerald looked at Phillip again and they both
started uncontrollably laughing again. Then
Gerald said, "Where is your stick?"

Phillip cupped his hands around his mouth
and in a commanding booming voice yelled the
command for his stick to land. Within a few tics
they saw his broom racing toward the castle
parapet. It swooped down from the sky and gently
came to rest landing in Phillip's hand. They both
put their sticks over their shoulders and walked

toward the turret door and down to see the healer with the Captain of the Guard close behind. After checking with the healer the Captain took them to the dining hall where the king and queen were waiting on them to start their dinner. The Captain ushered them to the table and explained what had happened and that they had both been checked by the healer and they were both fine.

King Gerald wrinkled his forehead and said to the boys, "I think you both have had enough excitement for today and maybe even tomorrow." Alexandra stood and embraced both of them and kissed each one gently on the forehead. She then said, "Maybe we should have Mergrom teach Phillip how to use the flying stick. It might be safer for both of them."

Gerald took a step forward and said, "I will continue to teach Phillip. He is a very good student and I am sure he will not make the same mistake again. Learning to fly and flying will

507

always have its perils; it will become easier and safer the more times he does it. Today was his first day and I am sure, like me, his muscles ache and his hands are sore from holding on tightly to the handle of his flying stick. I can't tell you how many times I fell off the stick my first day. Luckily for me I didn't fly high but many times Sprout had to pick me off of one roof or another or lift me out of some of their vegetable gardens. It wasn't until about the third or fourth day that my arms and hands stopped aching and I finally got the grip I needed to stay on my stick. So, if you don't mind Mother, I will continue his training and we promise to be safer and less foolhardy tomorrow."

Alexandra squinted at Gerald and then a smile came over her face and she said, "Tomorrow I will fly with you and maybe you can teach me some of the finer points of flying. Mergrom told me that you fly like you have been on a stick all of your life. If he thinks you are that

508

good then who am I to stand in your way? But I will need you to teach me as well so that I can see for myself how good you are and how Phillip is progressing." Gerald bowed slightly and knew better than to question his mother's motives.

They all set down and started their evening meal when the King said, "Well, Phillip, tell us what you learned today and what you saw from way up in the sky." Phillip started telling them all about the wonderful things he saw. He said, "It's like being a bird. You can see so far away and the experience is so exhilarating. They all listened to Phillip prattle on about his flying experiences and what he had learned and done that day well into the evening. When they were all finished eating and listening to the stories of the day Alexandra told them they had better get a good night's sleep for tomorrow was going to be a long and tiring day for all of them.

When they awoke the next morning a gentle rain was falling. They all gathered in the main dining hall for the morning meal. Alexandra was dressed in leathers along with a hooded leather cape. She noticed the boys were not in leathers and suggested that they change before flying. Gerald looked at her and said, "I thought we would spend the day with a little archery practice since it was raining." Alexandra smiled at him and said, "You are not going to let a little rain stop you from flying are you? Besides, when we fly, we can fly away from the rain or above it if we want to chance the storm clouds." She winked at the king and then she said, "Get changed boys and I will meet you atop the castle wall by number three turret."

The King knew how accomplished a flyer the Queen was and knew she was going to do some teaching of her own this day. He winked back at her and said, "Now you boys take it easy on your mother today. I know it's been a while since she has flown and she may be a little out of practice." The boys ran back to their rooms, changed into flying leathers and capes, and were soon climbing the castle turret steps to meet the Queen. Alexandra, by experience and time in the sky, would be considered a master flyer. Flying in a gentle rain would not be a problem. They would fly away from the storm front and soon be in dry sunshiny weather.

When the boys appeared at the turret doorway Alexandra was already astride her flying stick hovering about two rods off the floor. She had her hood up and pulled tightly around her face and the cape was securely fastened so that you could barely see her hands grasping the stick.

When the boys appeared she said, "Come on gentlemen we are wasting the daylight hours. Get a move on!" With that she flew off into the rain like an arrow from a bow. She made one circle over them and flew off to the west. Phillip was second up in the air chasing after her. Gerald made sure his hood was tight then he took off and soon caught up to both of them. They all flew in a straight line until Alexandra saw a break in the clouds and she headed her stick skyward and up through the hole in the clouds. The boys soon followed suit and they were in full sun above the rain and flying to the west. The Queen turned to Phillip and said, "Show me your turns and ups and downs." Phillip complied and did right-hand and left-hand circles around both of them while they were still flying west. Then he flew up almost out of sight and then came swooping down again and almost ran into them. "OK, OK," said the queen. "That was very good," she continued. Then she turned to Gerald and said, "Now you show me what you can do." Gerald nodded and did his circles and loops and then he turned himself upside down and flew just above his mother so that she was looking up at him and he, down at her. Alexandra started laughing and did the same thing. Taking their lead, Phillip flipped upside down but instead of locking his feet under the stick, he was hanging from the stick by his hands. Gerald flew over to him and pushed him back up so he could climb on his stick and fly naturally. Once astride his stick he wrapped his feet securely around the stick and flipped upside down so that all of them were flying that way. Looking down at the ground they all realized they had outrun the rain clouds so all at once they headed for the ground.

Eyeing the ground, Alexandra saw exactly what she was looking for. Below them nestled in a meadow was a small lake surrounded by green fields of grass and wildflowers. She pointed toward the lake and they all flew down to have a look. They gently landed on the shore of the lake. The air smelled fresh and clean, after the rain. The aroma from all the surrounding flowers filled the meadow with a fragrance that was almost intoxicating. Alexandra dismounted from her stick, turned to the boys, and said, "Now we are going to play a game called Do as I Do. If you play the game well, you won't get wet. If you don't, well, I hope you both know how to swim." She jumped on her stick and shot out over the lake and stayed very close to the surface. She crisscrossed the lake several times and then on a return pass she bent down so her hand was just above the water. Instantly she stuck her hand in the water and came out holding a fish. She came back to the shore and stopped, dropped the fish on the ground and looked at Phillip and said, "Well, do as I do."

Phillip got the idea instantly and shot out over the lake. Following a similar path as the queen he circled the lake and then back and forth until he spotted what he was looking for. Shooting back across the lake skimming the water he reached down and snatched another fish from the lake. Holding onto it and his flying stick was causing him to veer up and down and becoming somewhat unsteady. Gerald and Alexandra feared he would fall into the lake, but he didn't. He finally made it back to shore and dropped his fish beside Alexandra's. Then he turned to Gerald and said, "Do as I do."

Gerald mounted his stick and instead of flying across the lake he flew up in the air about five rods above the lake and stopped his broom and hovered there while looking down at the lake. Phillip and Alexandra looked at him wondering what he was doing. Finally and gently Gerald's flying stick started descending slowly toward the surface of the lake. As it descended it shifted left then right and slowly ever so gently down, down, down. When Gerald's feet almost touched the water he shot one of his hands down and grabbed a rather large fish. The fish flopped and turned in his hand until it finally took both of his hands to hold onto it. Directing his flying stick with his knees he edged the stick back to shore and dropped it alongside the others.

Alexandra said, "Well done boys. Now let's prepare these fish and have some lunch. Phillip, you gather some wood and start a small fire. She reached into the small leather pouch she was wearing over her shoulder and withdrew a small but very sharp knife and soon had made short work of cleaning the fish. Gerald found willow sticks that he cut and cleaned to mount the fish on. Poking the sticks into the fish and sticking one end in the ground close to the fire he positioned the fish so that they would cook and be smoked at the same time. While the fish were cooking Alexandra wandered the field picking some wild berries to go with the fish. Returning she laid her find down on the ground close to the fire and said. We will have these with our fish along with water from the lake. Gerald looked at the berries and said, "While those look delicious we can't eat them or we will get very sick. Those are called JUJU berries and are what the forest people call fake food. While they look inviting and even taste quite good they cause terrible stomach pain and vomiting." Gerald took the berries and flung them into the lake. "Sorry mom, I learned all about them from the Lady of the Green."

Alexandra looked at him and said, "Thank you for that lesson in berry finding. I guess the fish will have to be eaten without and fruit or vegetables."

"Not necessarily," said Gerald. He walked over to the edge of the lake and began pulling out some reeds growing there. Taking them to the water's edge and rinsing off the roots he cut the top of the vine off just leaving the root section and a small portion that had grown just below the water. "These are called mumble tails. They are very fibrous and almost have a sweet taste when

517

eaten raw. They almost taste like a potato when boiled. I think with the fish raw would be better. He sliced off a piece and handed it to his mother and Phillip. They both popped the piece into their mouths and began chewing. Almost at once both of them spat out the mumble tail root. Gerald laughed and said, "Don't chew, you suck the juices out of the root and spit out the rest. The root tastes terrible when you bite into it but the juices are very sweet. Here, try again," and he handed them both another piece of the root. This time they both just sucked on the root stem and a sweet taste of honey filled their mouths. They both smiled and then spit the roots into the fire. When the fish were cooked they ate beside the lake and talked of many things.

Once they were fed and the fire extinguished, Alexandra stood and said, "Do as I do." She jumped to her stick but instead of sitting on it she stood on the stick and balanced herself like she was walking along the top of a fence rail. Slowly her broom moved out over the lake. Carefully balancing herself with her arms she continued across to the opposite side where she jumped off and motioned for them to come. Gerald had tried this trick before but had never mastered it with as much grace as he had just seen from his mother. Gerald stood on his stick as it rose into the air. Arms outstretched for balance. The broom started moving forward out over the lake. He was quite unsteady and stopped his stick about mid-pond. Moving up beside him was Phillip. He was just as unsteady as Gerald. Then Phillip said, "Take my hand and we will steady each other." Gerald reached out and said, "Wow that really works." They both commanded their sticks to move forward and soon they were standing next to Alexandra on the far shore. Gerald eyed her mother cautiously and said, "What other tricks do you have up your sleeve that you want to teach us?" She winked at him and

519

said to Phillip, "That was a stroke of genius to balance yourselves together to fly standing. And to answer your question Gerald, I may know several more flying tricks than you. I have been flying a long time with your father and he is really good. Now I believe it is time for a tag the leader game. I will fly off and you two try and catch me. You must fly close enough to touch me and then you will be the leader and we must catch you. Do you both understand how the game is played?" They both nodded their heads appropriately.

Alexandra took off her cape and wrapped it around her flying stick and tied it there with some leather straps. The boys did the same. She smiled and mounted her stick and shouted, "Catch me if you can!" She shot toward the sky in a cloud of dust and was very high up before either of the boys could give chase, but chase they did. Phillip had the advantage because he had one of the king's old flying sticks with more reeds. He could fly faster than Gerald or Alexandra. Soon he was flying like a seasoned professional and gaining on Alexandra. Gerald was slowly catching up with both of them by using his brain to figure angles and the shortest distance between two points to try and make up for his lack of speed. Phillip pulled up beside Alexandra and reached out and slapped her arm and said, "Now catch me if you can!" He shot off to the right at breakneck speed and headed directly for the forest. With Phillip leading the pack they started dodging in and out of trees and then down to the forest floor and then back up again. This was very dangerous at the speeds they were going and Alexandra knew that any miscalculation could spell disaster and multiple injuries if they were not careful. She started slowing down to see if Phillip would do the same and as though he was reading her mind, he did as well. Gerald was not as cautious as his mother wanted him to be and swooped by her from above and dove down at Phillip tagged him, saying, "Now catch me if you can?"

Gerald pulled up hard on his stick and shot straight up out of the forest and into a cloud bank. As soon as he entered the cloud he made a sharp right turn, then a left then kept it straight for a count of ten. When he reached ten he pointed his stick straight down and shot out of the cloud and then stopped midair and hovered. Neither Phillip nor Alexandra was in sight. He sat on his stick and rested to catch his breath. The extra padding of his leather cloak wrapped around his stick felt good. He would have to remember to do that all the time.

In a little while Alexandra and Phillip emerged from the cloud and spotted Gerald calmly sitting on his stick. They both headed toward him at breakneck speed. What they didn't know was that he had positioned himself directly over the small lake they had rested at earlier in the day.

Patiently he waited and waited and closer and closer they came. Still he just sat there. When they were just about upon him his stick fell out of the sky like a heavy rock plummeting toward the ground. Gerald hugged his stick with all his might and could see the lake coming closer and closer. He peeked over his shoulder and saw his two pursers close behind. He laid flat on his stick and his speed increased. In his mind he knew he had to time his last maneuver perfectly. He could hear the screams of excitement behind him and now he could see the surface of the lake very close. With all his might he commanded his stick to stop and he pulled up on the tip of the stick with every ounce of strength he had. His stick stopped just above the surface of the lake but the other two shot by him, splash, splash. They both hit the water sending torrents of it high into the air. Gerald started laughing. When they both surfaced he was still laughing so hard he almost fell off of his flying stick.

Alexandra was the first to speak and said, "Where in the devil did you ever learn that trick? Who taught you how to fly with such precision?" Gerald couldn't stop laughing. For you see Alexandra had dislodged a lily pad and a big old frog which was now sitting on top of her head on the lily pad. All he could do was to point at her and laugh. Phillip was doing the same. She felt the top of her head and shrieked as the frog jumped back into the lake.

Gerald helped retrieve their flying sticks and soon all three of them were on the shore around a roaring fire trying to dry out. Gerald had found the wood and started it. As they sat there he told them the story of Sprout, the boy who taught him to fly. He told him of the adventures they had flying and of the bird cave.

When they were sufficiently dry, Alexandra said, "I think it is time to head back to Belledrade and have an evening meal with your father. He

524

will be most interested in that last maneuver you did on your stick. He may want you to teach him how you do it.

Once the fire was put out and everything collected they put on their capes and hoods and flew back to Belledrade.

\

Chapter 35 - Living with Mergrom

The days passed quickly at home with his mother and father and his new brother Phillip. It seemed like he had only arrived when one morning coming down for breakfast he saw Mergrom sitting at the table with his mother, father, and Phillip. Phillip had been crying because his eyes were red and there were remnants of water streaks on his cheeks. When he sat down he said, "What's wrong? Why is everyone so sad?" King Gerald put a hand on his sons shoulder and said, "Mergrom has come to take you to live with him for a while to teach you the magic of the land, water, and air. This will be your second time away from us and we all have gotten use to you being home and now we must say good-bye again. Phillip will start his knight training today and will live with the knights until you return from your training with Mergrom."

Gerald knew this day would come but secretly he had hoped it would be a long time from now.

Mergrom looked very wizardry in his moon and star robe. His long white beard and hair also helped with the image of a wise and powerful wizard. They talked during the breakfast meal and Mergrom was telling the King and Queen what training regimen he had laid out for Gerald and when they could expect to see him again. After breakfast the boys went to their rooms to pack their clothes and belongings for their training and went back to the main hall where Mergrom and the King and Queen were waiting.

Mergrom put his arm around the young king's shoulders and said, "Now, now, my boy, don't be so sad. Our adventure is about to begin and when we are done you will be a man and be the wisest of all the Kings that Belleadaire has ever had. You will be able to come home anytime you wish. I will not keep you against your wishes.

Let us be off to my home, my realm, my mother earth." Mergrom tapped his staff onto the stone floor three times and there was a gust of wind and everything started to blur. When things cleared again they were standing in front of a cottage next to a large lake. Gerald looked around him an all he saw were Woggs.

Mergrom turned to him and said, "Welcome to Woggrace young king. These are my people and this is my home when I am here. This is where we will start your training. There are many ancient manuscripts that you will need to read and understand before we start any practical sorcery. We also need to teach you how to protect yourself. I think the bow or sword would be your weapon of choice but we will leave that up to you to determine. In the meantime let me show you to your room and introduce you to Merelene. She is the sister of the former high priestess of the Woggles.

The door to the house opened and there stood a beautiful bronze goddess. She had long black hair, smooth creamy skin, and big brown eyes that looked like they stare right into your soul. Gerald turned to Mergrom and said, "Why, she isn't a Wogg. Look how different she is and how beautiful she is." Mergrom smiled and said, "This is how all the Woggles used to look. Merelene was away on a trip when The Lady of the Green cast her spell upon the woggles. All that were present in the green rain and fog changed. All that were not present are as they use to be. There are several Woggles that did not change that night. They are a constant reminder to the rest that if they are good and follow the commands of the Lady of the Green then they may be turned back into woggles again by the new Lady. Merelene and the other unchanged ones are helping me teach the Woggs how to live talk and eat with their new bodies. We have had to learn a new language to speak to the Woggs and it has been a real challenge. Merelene will show you to your room and you can get some rest before we start your training in the morning. Anything you need, all you need do is ask her and she will get it for you." Merelene took Gerald by the hand and led him into the home of Mergrom.

Once inside she led him to a room with his name on the door. Merelene turned to Gerald and said, "This is your home now. None can enter without your permission. I am here to serve you and Mergrom. So whatever you desire just ask me and I shall get it for you. Mergrom has asked me to oversee your first training lesson tomorrow morning. Please get a good night's sleep and be prepared to fly early in the morning. Wear leathers over your Speringus clothing.

Tomorrow we go to find you a horse that will be with you for the rest of your days. We must fly up into the Silver Mountain's where the great herds of wild horses graze. From them you will pick your mount and I will teach you how to ride. We must teach your new companion how to carry you and you will have to teach him how you want to be carried. So rest well, my Prince, because tomorrow will be long and somewhat painful." She opened the door for him and ushered him through and then promptly turned and disappeared in a cloud of smoke. Gerald watched her disappear and said to himself, "I have got to learn how to do that disappearing act." He looked around his room and it was perfect. He found new clothes, flying leathers and a long bow and a quiver of arrows. He was tired and cleaned up in a bowl of water that had been left on his dresser found a night shirt and stretched out on a mattress filled with goose down and fell fast asleep.

Early the next morning he was awakened by a gentle knocking at his door. Merelene said, "It is time to get up and get dressed young prince. Food will be served in fifteen tics. We fly in thirty."

531

Gerald jumped up, put on his Speringus garments, his new set of blue leathers along with a pointed cap with a blue feather on one side. His leather moccasins rounded out his dress and he turned and went out into the main room.

Merelene was waiting there in an identical set of leathers and cap. She was beautiful, Gerald thought to himself. She looked a lot better in her leathers than he did in his. She motioned for him to sit and they ate a hearty meal finished off with a dark warm liquid that Merelene called tea. It was very tasty, especially with milk and sugar added. Gerald was about to ask her to teach him the magic of disappearing when Merelene stood and said, "Get your flying stick and I will teach you the disappearing magic later." He looked at her and said, "How did you know I was going to ask you about that?" She looked and him and said, "I am surprised that Mergrom didn't tell you that I can read thoughts." She stood and grabbed her own flying stick and said, "I will meet you outside in two tics." Gerald retrieved his flying stick and walked outside to see Merelene hovering just above the ground sitting on her flying stick.

When she saw him she flew off toward the north. Gerald jumped on his stick and was soon flying beside her as they headed toward the silver mountains. The air was crisp and cool as they flew north and Merelene wasn't particularly talkative, during their trip, so Gerald started daydreaming about what type of horse he wanted to pick. Should he pick it on color, size or let Merelene pick it for him? She seemed to know more about them than he did. Maybe he would let her choose for him. No sooner had that thought crossed his mind than Merelene turned toward him and said, "You need to pick the one that picks you. I will not be riding your horse so it would not be right for me to choose for you." Gerald turned his head with a snap and said, "Along with your

533

disappearing trick you will also have to teach me to read other people's thoughts." She just smiled back at him and starred him in the eyes and said, "That is one trick I cannot teach. It must be born to you and is as much a curse as it is a blessing. It is something that haunts you at times and at other times is very satisfying. What I can teach you is how to read peoples body language. With this knowledge you can tell whether a person is telling you the truth, or may be trustworthy. Or the person might be someone you should be weary of.

After your horse has picked you as its master we can start with other training that I can help with." They flew on in silence for quite some time until they could see the tops of the Silver Mountains in the far distance. In another arc or two Merelene suddenly pointed down and below them was a meadow filled with horses. She pointed her stick toward the ground and headed straight for the herd. As they flew closer Gerald could see a herd of wild horses that numbered in the hundreds. There was every color imaginable! There were rich browns, chestnut, blacks, whites spotted and mottled. On a bluff high above the herd stood a magnificent white stallion that stood there regal in stance as he overlooked his herd below. Gerald put his sights on this magnificent creature and edged his flyer closer. As he descended toward the white creature it looked up at him and reared up on its hind legs as though to greet him.

Gerald landed his stick not two rods away from him. He put his stick over his shoulder and slowly approached the white horse. The white horse stood its ground and didn't move a muscle as Gerald came closer. When he was within a body length from him a slight breeze blew across the bluff and caught the horses mane and tail and blew the hair in waves across his back. Gerald reached out a hand to touch the horse when it

535

said, "Young master, I would not touch me before we have been introduced. That would be rude." Gerald stopped in his tracks and stood there looking at this white towering steed. Without hesitating Gerald said, "My name is Gerald Boranum, prince of Belleadaire. What may I call you?" The horse pawed at the ground with his front right leg and bent down on one knee and said, "My herd calls me White Tail, young king, but you may address me as you wish." Then he continued, "What brings you and the Woggle to this mountain meadow on such a fine day?"

Gerald stood there for a moment and then said, "The Woggle is my friend Merelene and she has brought me here to pick a mount of my choosing that will live with me and serve as my ground transportation for wherever I desire to go. Please rise, White Tail. I am but a prince of Belleadaire. My father is the king and he deserves your respect. I have not earned yours so you need not bow to me." Merelene was standing about ten rods away from them listening to the grunts, whinny's and sounds passing between the two of them. She didn't realize they were talking to each other. She did not know the way of talking or listening to the animals.

White Tail said, "Have you made your choice yet, young king?" Gerald looked at him and said, "How old are you White Tail?" White Tail looked at Gerald and said, "I am eight cycles old. This is my first season as herd master. My father has his own herd higher up in the mountain meadows. His herd is twice as big as mine. You may want to choose from his herd because he has some of the finest runners that I have ever seen. I will take you to him and introduce you if you would like me too." "I don't think that will be necessary," said Gerald. Then he continued, "White Tail would you consider becoming my mount and companion when I am not flying?" White Tail just stood there for a moment eying Gerald and then a smile started at his lips and grew until his entire face looked upon the young king with kindness and respect. Then he said, "Have you ever ridden a horse before?"

Gerald stammered with his reply until he said, "Well, none as handsome and regal as you White Tail." "Well then, maybe we should try each other and see if I like you and you like me," he said. Then White Tail did something that Gerald had never seen before. He knelt down on all four legs until he could be mounted easily by Gerald. Then his head turned to Gerald and he said, "Well, don't just stand there, climb aboard and let's take a ride and see how you fit."

Gerald put down his stick and grabbed a handful of mane and swung himself up on his back. Once aboard, White Tail stood up and trotted off toward the herd. Since there was no saddle Gerald pressed his legs tight against the great horse's sides and gently applied pressure to his knees when he wanted to go one way or the other. Immediately White Tail understood his knee commands and away they ran. Down into the grazing herd they ran and then through them and onto the plain below. Gerald held tightly to the mane and lowered his head so his body was leaning forward on the back of White Tail. Faster and faster they ran. Merelene jumped on her flying stick and sped after them. It seemed to Gerald that riding astride this most handsome of horses was effortless. It was as though they were reading each other's thoughts. When Gerald wanted to go left White tail turned left. When it came to jumping White Tail cleared any obstacle he came upon. With one giant leap he would clearly leap high above and then gently come down with barely a jolt. Gerald bent back his head and yelled at the top of his voice, "Yahoooo!!!!" White Tail turned around and they soon were speeding back up the mountain path toward the bluff. When they arrived,

Gerald slid down from his back and said, "I believe you are the greatest horse that has ever lived, White Tail."

White Tail turned to the young prince and said, "You are the best rider that has ever been on my back, young king. I would be most honored to become your mount and companion during our lifetimes. But in order to do so, you must give me a name that only you can bestow."

Gerald thought for a minute and then said, "Since you fly across the ground like the breeze across a plain I think I would like to call you White Wind. What do you think of it?"

White Wind turned to him and said, "I think I like it." He then reared up on his hind legs and shouted to the herd below. "From this day forward

I shall be known as White Wind, carrier of the future king of Belleadaire."

Gerald blushed a little and then Merelene came flying up and landed behind him. "What is all the commotion about," she said.

Gerald turned to White Wind and said, "Merelene, I would like to introduce you to White Wind. He has chosen me to be his rider."

White Wind bowed down again in respect to Merelene and then in horse talk said, "I am very pleased to meet you Merelene. Any friend of Prince Gerald is a friend of mine."

Gerald turned to Merelene and said, "He is very pleased to make your acquaintance."

Merelene replied, "When did you learn to talk with the animals of the land?" Gerald smiled and said, "Actually it was they who taught me to listen. Once I listened to what they had to say, I could converse with them. I can teach you if you would like. Listening to the animals is so enjoyable because they have so much to say."

"So you understand them and they you? Is that correct?" said Merelene.

Gerald turned to White Wind and said, "I think we are returning to Woggrace and I would like to get to know you better. Can you leave with me now and put someone else in charge of your herd?"

Without a word White Wind flew across the pasture and stopped in front of a large black stallion and conversed with him for a while and then came back to Gerald.

"We can leave anytime you would like, young king. I have turned over my duties to Midnight and he will maintain the herd." Gerald leaped up on his back and turned to Merelene and said, "White Wind and I will be returning to

Woggrace on the ground. We need time to get to know each other and what better way than a long trip through the country."

Merelene looked perplexed and said, "I cannot leave you here with this horse and fly back to Woggrace. You are in my charge and I am responsible for you."

Gerald looked down at her from astride White Wind and said, "I absolve you of all responsibility for me. White Wind and I will be in Woggrace in three days. If we do not appear then you can come looking for us. Besides, I know Mergrom will keep his eye on me during my travels. If I need him all I need do is tap the ground three times with my flying stick and he will come to my aid. So go on back to Woggrace and I will see you in three days."

With that said he nudged White Wind forward and down through the pasture they went.

543

They left Merelene standing on the bluff. As she watched them ride away she just shook her head and mounted her flying stick and flew off in the direction of Woggrace.

Exactly three days later Gerald and White Wind rode into Woggrace as promised. Once White Wind was stabled and fed Gerald went to find Mergrom or Merelene. When he threw the door open to Mergrom's house he expected to see Merelene or Mergrom waiting for him. Instead the house was empty and looked as though it hadn't had anyone here for days. Gerald went to his room and looked around and everything was as he had left it four days ago. He went to the table and there was a note from Merelene.

The note said:

COME TO PORTINGTON. A NEW SEA
CREATURE IS THREATENING TO DESTROY
THE CITY. MERGROM AND I ARE THERE TO
HELP.

Merelene

Gerald grabbed his flying stick and ran out the door and leapt for the sky. Before long he was flying at break neck speeds northeast toward the shipbuilding city of Portington. It was the only seaport that Gerald knew about. Even though Belleadaire had a long coastline most of the coastline was guarded by high cliffs and shallow bays. Portington had the only deep-water seaport that could dock large cargo ships. It also made it ideal for shipbuilding and repairing. His course took him over the castle of Rushmore which was his mother's ancestral home. It glistened in the sun light as he flew over it. The white stone it was made of reflected the sun's rays every day of whatever season it was. He kept flying northeast until he could see the blue of the ocean loom up on the horizon. He followed the coastline north until he saw the city Portington stretch out before him. Then he wondered how will I find Mergrom or Merelene?

It didn't take him long to figure out where they were. Large explosions and a raging fire was looming on the horizon in the direction of the waterfront. As he flew toward the waterfront, he could see fireballs being tossed and exploding. He saw large spouts of water rise from the sea and being thrown at the shoreline. People were running in all directions from the dock area. Waves were crashing against the docks and fire was being thrown back at the sea from the docks. As he flew lower he could just make out two figures in the middle of the maelstrom. There stood Mergrom with his staff raised high above his head creating his fireballs and throwing them at something in the harbor. Merelene was at his side with her arms raised in the air like she was pushing something out to sea. As he flew closer he could see that Merelene was creating giant

546

waves and sending them toward whatever was in the harbor.

Just as he was about to land behind them a huge roar erupted from the center of the harbor and a gigantic sea creature emerged from below the water. It looked like half shellfish and half man. It stood on two legs like a man but its body was encrusted in large protective reddish green shell plating. Instead of arms it had two articulated appendages that had claw structures at the ends of them. Its eyes were extended from its head on long movable stems. These were protected by a very large shell like forehead that extended well out over the eye stems. The top of its head was a solid shell that extended down its back till it reached a boney tail that was thrashing every ship in the harbor. When it tried to advance toward the shore, Merelene would create a wave and wash it back. Mergrom's fireballs were being batted away by the clawed arms or bouncing off the shell armor. Neither the creature or Mergrom and Merelene were making much headway. Roar after roar erupted from this creature as it tried to make its way toward the shore.

Gerald landed next to a building behind the two and immediately picked up a bow and quiver of arrows. Though he was not as proficient with them as he wanted to be, he still considered himself a pretty good shot. As he ran to their side, Mergrom shouted, "Stay back Gerald. This is beyond any magic you have learned and I promised your parents to keep you safe." Gerald nodded and moved behind the two of them. Looking up at the creature he could see that any arrow would just bounce off the shell and fall harmlessly back to the harbor.

Eying the creature carefully it seemed to be protecting its head from the fireballs. Whenever a fireball would come near he would throw his arm or claws in front of his eyes to

protect them. Immediately Gerald thought that the
eyes must be the most vulnerable spot on him.
He bowed his first arrow and aimed it at its head.
He waited until the arms had fallen from the
fireball and then he unleashed his first arrow.
Swoosh it went through the air and just before it
hit, the creature lowered its head and thunk. The
arrow just bounced off the boney skull and fell into
the harbor. He needed to get closer. He grabbed
his flying stick and shot into the air.

Wave after wave and ball after ball was
slowly moving the creature out into the harbor.
Mergrom and Merelene increased their onslaught
of water and fire. As the creature was backing
away Gerald flew around behind him and stayed
there protecting himself from the fireballs. As
soon as the last fireball hit the creatures arm,
Gerald made his move. He shot from behind the
creature's head and as he passed the edge of the
protective forehead he unleashed two arrows in

quick succession, swoosh, swoosh. The first arrow hit the right eye in the center and disappeared. The second arrow hit the left stem just below the eyeball but buried itself deep into the eye stem. A scream from the monster reverberated off the dock buildings. The monster rubbed wildly at its eyes trying to understand what happened. Swinging its clawed hands to and fro and rubbing its head below the brow Gerald could see that his arrows had done serious damage to the creature's sight. Suddenly one of the creature's arms flew out and struck Gerald and knocked him off this stick and he fell into the harbor. Mergrom and Merelene saw what happened and began their onslaught again. This time the creature couldn't see the fireball coming and so the first of four balls hit him directly in the eye area. The creature screamed again in pain. Merelene created a huge wave and washed the creature over backward. Mergrom took advantage of the fallen beast by loosing a lightning bolt from his staff that hit the creature directly between the eye stems, just before his head went under water, tearing a tremendous hole in the soft flesh between the stems. The creature gurgled and slipped below the water. Instantly the harbor started turning red with the blood issuing from the beast.

Mergrom turned to Merelene and said, "Do you see Gerald anywhere?" "No, I don't," said Merelene. What neither of them had born witness to was how Gerald was saved from certain death by his flying stick. When Gerald was knocked off his stick he shouted, "Boomba-do." His stick had obeyed his command and as Gerald fell toward the water his stick fell with him. They reached the water at about the same time and Gerald reached out and grabbed it just before slamming into the water. He instantly commanded it to level out and he flew under the nearest wharf. He thought he was safe there until the creature fell and created a wave that washed him and his stick against the rock seawall. There he wedged himself between the bottom of the pier and the seawall.

Mergrom and Merelene were running up and down the pier shouting his name and looking into the water to see if they could find his body. Once the water receded Gerald shot out from under the pier and shouted back, "Here I am." Then he flew up and landed on the wharf.

Mergrom and Merelene ran to him and threw their arms around him. Then Mergrom backed away and said, "That was the most foolhardy thing I have ever seen. It was reckless, it was stupid, and it was also the only thing that saved our skins. Don't you ever do it again! What would I tell your mother and father if you had been injured?" Merelene hugged him again and then kissed him on the cheek.

Gerald looked at them both and said, "Well it seemed to me that you two needed just a little more help to subdue that water beast. Though I have a few scrapes and bruises and I am thoroughly wet I am not injured. Therefore you don't have to tell them anything."

Merelene said, "Where did you learn to shoot like that from a moving flying stick?" "That was the first time," said Gerald. Gerald looked back at the harbor which had turned completely red by now and said, "What was that creature, Mergrom?"

Mergrom shook his head and said, "I have never encountered anything like that before. It is probably one of the new creatures coming from the south that was trying to find a home in the north. The southern region has undergone a complete transformation over the past seasons and many new creatures have come from that area. Creatures that are not native to this land

553

seem to be coming from everywhere. I know the Lady of the Green and myself are very concerned about what is happening in the southern region and now with the strange and menacing creatures spilling over into the northern realm I need to let her know about them."

Mergrom embraced Gerald and whispered into his ear, "Thank you for being brave and helping us defeat this monster, but please, next time don't scare an old man to within a tic of his life! If there is a next time, please pay attention to what I say and follow my commands."

They all walked arm in arm up the pier as people were starting to come out of their houses and back into the streets to see what happened or where the monster was.

There would be a party in the town tonight and the three of them would be the guests of honor.

The entire city of Portington turned out to with a hero's welcome for the three slayers of the sea monster. Much wine and food was consumed by all and Mergrom, Merelene, and Gerald were each given keys to the city by the Governor Executive of Portington. The party lasted well into the night and Gerald had never seen Mergrom consume as much wine as he did that night. Even though Mergrom wasn't feeling very well, early the following morning all three flew back to Woggrace.

Chapter 36 - New Creatures and Magic Training

On their trip back to Woggrace, Mergrom
explained to them both the number of new races
of people or animals that had appeared over the
last hundred cycles. The number was enormous.
Mergrom explained that he had never seen such
an explosion of new beings coming into existence.
Even in the ancient scrolls there was no mention
of any such happening. That is why the Lady of
the Green had taken it upon herself to find out
what was happening and why all these new
creatures were suddenly marching north to find
new homes and places to live. Most of the
creatures were welcome and somewhat friendly,

others were not, and then there were the monsters. Several monsters or beasts had been killed or isolated by the Lady of the Green or Mergrom in order for the rest of Belleadaire to survive. He was going to contact the Lady of the Green as soon as they returned to see if she had any new information about these beasts.

By the time they arrived at Woggrace, Mergrom was feeling much better so he bid his farewell to Merelene and Gerald and flew off toward Green Haven to meet with the Lady. Before he left he instructed Merelene to give Gerald scrolls 149 and 150 to read. Once read, she was to teach him the fire magic and the invisible magic. He said he would be back in a day or so to check in on them and the training.

His parting comment to Gerald was, "Try not to burn the place down before I return. The fire spell is a little tricky to master, so be careful." Gerald started to reply but Mergrom was already out through the door and gone. He turned around to look for Merelene and she had also disappeared. Gerald just sat down at the table and rested his head in his hands. He jumped out of his chair when Merelene whispered, "Do you want to learn the invisible magic or do you just want to sit there and mope?" Gerald whirled around and looked in all parts of the room and even at the ceiling. Then he said, "I know you are in this room and I will find you." "I doubt that," said Merelene. Gerald scanned the room again and saw a shimmer in the light to the darker side of the room. It was as though he were seeing heat waves from the ground on a hot, dry day in the second season of the weather cycle. He pretended not to stare at the shimmer. He carefully walked around the room trying not to be obvious as he approached the shimmer. He slowly walked to the fireplace and picked up a long piece of kindling and then walked back to the area that was shimmering. Slowly he reached out with the stick and poked at the shimmer. The stick disappeared through the shimmer then it was jerked out of his hand and disappeared behind the shimmer. Immediately he heard Merelene laughing almost uncontrollably. Gerald approached the shimmer and walked right through it. Now he was nose to nose with a laughing Merelene. He jumped back and she wasn't there. She was gone, but the shimmering cloud was still there. Once Merelene could control her laughter she too walked through the cloud and was standing in front of Gerald. "How do you do that," he asked? That is one of the magic spells contained in the scrolls you are supposed to read. She held out her left hand which contained two scrolls and handed them to him. In her right hand was a small mound of powder. She held her hand up to her mouth and gently blew across the mound of powder. Poof, she disappeared again behind the simmering cloud. He waited for a few tics and

559

as the shimmer dissipated Merelene was also gone.

He looked around the room again and didn't see her or the shimmering cloud. He looked at the scrolls in his hand and sat down at the table and untied the ribbon around scroll 149, rolled it open on the table and started to read. The title of the page read, "*INVISIBLE MAGIC*" - From Cavoria.

As he read down the page he discovered that the shimmering cloud was a mineral found in the caves of Cavoria. The mineral in its raw form was in crystals and transparent. Once extracted from the mine or cave it was heated to its melting point in large closed top pots over a bellowing fire. Once the mineral had completely melted into a molten state the top was removed and the contents dumped onto sand gathered from the deserts of Arradia. The molten mineral now started to melt the sand and as both of them cooled to a solid again it became a transparent sheet with specks of sand buried in the surface of one side of the sheet. The sheet was then taken to a gristmill for grinding. Not your ordinary gristmill for grinding flour from wheat or corn, but one with special grinding stones that crushed the sheet finer and finer until it became a dust. Once it became a dust, it was loaded back into the melting pot and again converted to a molten state. This time as it was poured out of the pot it was dumped into vats of water that rapidly cooled the molten mass. As the droplets formed in the water they cracked into tiny shards as they fell to the bottom of the vats. Once the mineral had been dumped into the water vat the water was drained away and the material was again returned to the grinding stones of the gristmill to be pulverized into a very white powder. This powder when blown or thrown into the air would act as a reflective and translucent barrier which made things appear invisible on either side of the barrier. The powder was so light and fine, that the powder could stay in the air for a long time. If the person expending the powder continually replenished the cloud with new powder the barrier could be in place for as long as the cloud maker wished.

Gerald read about this mineral with fascination until he finished the entire writing on both sides of the scroll. He sat back in his chair and wondered how he could get some of this fantastic powder. As he was deep in thought wondering where Cavoria and Arradia were located, a hand was placed on this shoulder. He jumped out of the chair and landed nearly a body length away from the chair. There stood Merelene laughing again as she startled him with her touch. "Oh, did I frighten you", she said? "You certainly did," replied Gerald. "How did you do that? I didn't see the shimmer this time," said Gerald.

Merelene replied by saying, "This time I chose not to let the rays of the fireplace bounce off of your side of the cloud. Outside it is harder to see because the sunlight is diffused by the clouds in the sky. You practically are invisible to anyone around you or at least to people in front of the cloud."

"Where can I get some of that powder?" Gerald asked. Merelene held up a small bag in her hand and said, "This is all we have left. If we want more then we must journey to Cavoria and ask Queen Marabella to supply us with it. She is a friend of Mergrom's and will gladly give us some. The mineral is not found very often but when it is, it is all converted to invisible dust. Queen Marabella keeps all the dust in her vaults in the palace in Draken. Draken is the capital city of kingdom of Cavoria."

Gerald said, "How long will it take us to get there? If we leave now can we be there before nightfall?" "No," said Merelene. "Draken is at least a two day flight by stick and even longer by horse. I think you will need to master the fire spell before we travel to Draken. As soon as you master the fire, we can leave and refresh our supply of invisible powder." She blew across her hand again and disappeared. Gerald lurched forward and through the cloud, but she was gone again.

He sat down again at the table and unrolled the scroll numbered 150. The name at the top of this scroll read, "*FIRE FROM THE CORE*" - Volcania.

This was a very long scroll and was several pages with writing on both sides of each page. Gerald read through the scroll once and then started again. The first time through it didn't make sense to him, so he thought it only right to read it again and again until it was clear what the scroll was to teach him.

The day was winding down and he became hungry and was tired from all of the flying. Gerald stood up from the table and poked around the kitchen until he found some fruit, cheese, and bread. He also located some cow's milk that was still fairly cool. He poured himself a big glass and ate his meal in silence as he reread scroll 150. After his meal he became sleepy and rolled up both scrolls and took them to his room with all the intention of studying 150 again. Once inside his room his bed was calling his name. Without undressing he lay down on his bed and fell fast asleep. He awoke the next morning to the sounds of birds singing outside his window. Rubbing the sleep from his eyes, he splashed some water on his face and quickly dried and went to the kitchen. There was a note on the table from Merelene that read;

There is hot tea in the kettle on the fire. There are hardboiled eggs in a bowl by the washbasin. Please get some breakfast and then start your studies again on scroll 150. I will be back late this afternoon and we can try out your spell techniques. Please do not burn the house down or hurt yourself in the meantime.

Merelene

That was the entire note, so after Gerald ate some breakfast he settled down and opened scroll 150 again and started reading. The gist of the scroll was this.

To make fire you must first be part of the energy that surrounds you. You must become part of every living thing and every non-living thing. You must expand your mind to think in the smallest of terms and yet your mind must also think in the largest of terms. Once your mind becomes part of your surroundings, you will see what elements you need to make fire. You will be able to manipulate these elements to conjure the flame.

Gerald sat there confused for a few tics then closed his eyes and let his mind start to devour everything around him. He saw wood and then he saw the tree that grew the wood and then he saw the sapling that grew the tree, then the seed, then the molecules that made up the seed then the atoms that made the molecules. When he finished with wood, the he went to water, then air then the soil, then the animals and beings that roamed the planet's surface. On and on he went until he had covered everything he could think of from its smallest to its largest. He could see now that everything was made of atoms and all atoms had been combined to form certain things, elements, beings. If you aligned the atoms in a certain order they would become fire.

His back and bottom began to hurt and he opened his eyes and looked around the room. Candles were burning and there was fresh food on the table. Gerald stood and now realized why his back and bottom hurt. He had been sitting in the chair all day and had not moved. He had been totally engrossed in thought and was oblivious to everything around him.

Sitting by the front door reading a book was Merelene. When Gerald stood Merelene came to him and asked him if he was all right.

Gerald replied, "Other than my legs and back I feel fine. I have never seen the world as I have perceived it today. I know what makes fire and I believe I can if I need to." He shut his eyes and began sorting through all of his thoughts until he opened his eyes and place his finger on a cup sitting on the table. The cup began to glow on the inside and then the inside of the cup started to whirl in a small circle. Tiny specks of red began to appear swirling in the void inside the cup. Faster and faster the inside begun to spin. More red dots appeared and then the whirling mass burst into flame that shot out of the cup in a vortex about two hands long. The swirling mass threw off heat and a brilliant white light that flooded the room with its brightness. Gerald continued to stare at the cup and did not remove his finger. Suddenly the cup burst into a thousand pieces but Gerald stood there with his finger touching the edge of the flame.

Merelene couldn't believe her eyes. No one had ever made fire on their first attempt. Gerald had not only made fire, he was controlling it. He was manipulating matter and energy to make a flame that only he could extinguish.

Little by little Gerald made the flame smaller and smaller until it was no bigger than his hand and it was now floating in the air. He reached out and slid his hand under the flame and held it there for a moment and then extended his other hand above the flame and slowly brought them together until they touched. The flame was gone.

His face was drenched with perspiration and he looked exhausted. Gerald slumped back down in the chair and turned to Merelene and said, "You can tell Mergrom that I made fire and didn't burn the house to the ground. I now understand more than I ever have before."

From the doorway came a very satisfied voice that said, "I am very glad you didn't burn the house down and what pleases me more is that you have proven that your mind is very strong and can do anything you set it to. Once more it proves to me that you and Merelene can work together to develop other skills of a wizard."

Gerald turned to Mergrom and said, "I do not want to be a wizard. I want to be a boy then grow into a man then into a king. So far, my boyhood is fleeting away and soon I will be a young man. You are the wizard. I will be king someday. That is all I have ever wanted." Gerald tried to stand and walk to Mergrom. When he stood, the room started to spin and spin. Gerald physically started to turn in circles and then everything went black.

Gerald awakened the next morning with Mergrom and Merelene sitting beside his bed staring at him. As his eyes opened they focused on Mergrom with a questioning look. Mergrom just smiled from ear to ear and shook his head in an affirmative manner. He brushed Gerald's hair back on his head and said, "You are right, young king. I do not need to make you into a wizard. All I need to do is teach you how to think and use your magnificent brain. You have proven to me that you could be a very powerful wizard if you wanted it. But I know in your heart you want to be king. Your devotion to your subjects will be unparalleled in the history books. Your magic training has come to a close. I suggest that you explore the forest and your kingdom and get to meet your future subjects.

The southern region is in a permanent upheaval and looks like it will be so for some time to come. There are new races of peoples and beings' coming from the southern region and the entire landscape has been changed to accommodate these new beings. The Lady of the Green has returned from the south and told me that she may never go back. Her heart is saddened by what she has seen there. She has removed her protection from the southern region and will not venture there again. I think you should mount White Wind and explore your kingdom. Your time with me is finished and you can now learn on your own. All you ever need to do if you want me to come to you is take your flying stick and hit the soil with it three times and call my name. I will always be by your side and you will become the finest King that this planet has ever seen."

Mergrom and Merelene left the room and left Gerald alone with his thoughts. Gerald got out of bed, dressed himself and started packing his belongings for his long ride home to Belledrade. He would wander through the deep forest and contemplate his life and what he still needed to learn before the day came that he would have to assume the role as the King of Belleadaire.

EPILOGUE

Gerald left Woggrace late in the afternoon and set out for Belledrade. White Wind took his time wandering and weaving his way through the deep forest. He relished the alone time. He could witness first hand all that he had learned and heard since his training had begun with the Lady of the Green. As he rode he unconsciously recalled all the names of the trees, flowers, birds, and animals he saw as he rambled through the forest. A rush of knowledge shot through his head about each specimen he observed. Deep within the forest the sun filled light of day had turned to an almost twilight hue. His keen eyes still sought out the smallest of details as he continued to ride.

He saw a six-winged butterfly that was as large as both of his hands together. It flew with him for the longest time as though it was just as amazed to see him as he was to see it. But at last it fluttered away and disappeared among the foliage of the woodland.

As evening started to fall over the forest, the details below the forest canopy became blurred and deep in shadow. Gerald decided that it would be best if he stopped for the night and made camp.

After tying White Wind to a small tree Gerald gathered dead tree branches and piled them in a circle of stones and sat down and stared at them. He shut his eyes and let his mind start to see them not as solid but as their component atoms and molecules. Eventually his mind started to move the atoms and molecules faster and faster until they created heat and finally a small flame appeared in the pile of dried wood. Gerald drew his mind back and sat there admiring the small campfire he had created. Warming himself he settled back and began to eat some fruit and nuts he had brought with him. He laid back and looked up at the trees which almost covered the entire sky above him. Staring intently at the canopy he could see here and there the faint glow of a distant star shining brightly in the heavens but losing its glow as it made its way to the forest floor.

He smiled and said to himself I wonder if there are more places like this in the heavens.

The New King is next!

Made in the USA
Lexington, KY
18 August 2019